THE

BRIGHTEST

STAR

Paul Price

Edited by Helena Sharman, Lucid Language Ltd.

Printed in Victoria, BC, Canada

Note for Librarians: a cataloguing record for this book that includes Dewey Decimal Classification and US Library of Congress numbers is available from the Library and Archives of Canada. The complete cataloguing record can be obtained from their online database at: www.collectionscanada.ca/amicus/index-e.html
ISBN 1-4120-2939-2

TRAFFORD

This book was published *on-demand* in cooperation with Trafford Publishing. On-demand publishing is a unique process and service of making a book available for retail sale to the public taking advantage of on-demand manufacturing and Internet marketing. On-demand publishing includes promotions, retail sales, manufacturing, order fulfilment, accounting and collecting royalties on behalf of the author.

Offices in Canada, USA, UK, Ireland, and Spain
book sales for North America and international:
Trafford Publishing, 6E–2333 Government St.
Victoria, BC V8T 4P4 CANADA
phone 250 383 6864   toll-free 1 888 232 4444
fax 250 383 6804   email to orders@trafford.com
book sales in Europe:
Trafford Publishing (UK) Ltd., Enterprise House, Wistaston Road Business Centre
Crewe, Cheshire CW2 7RP UNITED KINGDOM
phone 01270 251 396   local rate 0845 230 9601
facsimile 01270 254 983   orders.uk@trafford.com
order online at:
www.trafford.com/robots/04-0767.html

10   9   8   7   6   5   4   3

Dedication

To the memory of Grandad.
Never was there a better man
who walked this earth. Missed by
all who knew him.

Author's Acknowledgements

Here are just some of the many people, without whose kindness and caring, life for me and my family might not have been what it is today.

Dr. A Lupoli
Dr. G Milner
Dr. M Doshi
Frances Mann
Jackie Childs
Emma Hastings
Sally Wilcock
Sue Dyer (Without whose encouragement I would never have written this book.)

Love and thanks for so much to Carole, Dan, Luke and Poppy.

Contents

Three Generations

Chapter 1

"Grandad, Grandad! Mum says to hurry up – she's just putting the dinner out."

"Ok, ok, Molly," the old man replied, looking out of the small window of the snug bar of the village pub.

"We don't want to upset your Mum, now do we?"

He stood up with a painful look on his face, downed the last drop of beer from his glass and headed for the door.

"I'm coming, little one," he said as he moved slowly towards the door. "See you later," he shouted over his shoulder to the group of old men he had been sitting with. He always received a riotous reply of, "Not if we see you first!"

As he came out of the small but cosy pub, the small girl ran up to him smiling broadly. "Pork and all the trimmings for dinner today, Grandad, and Mum says if we get back before she dishes up she has a jam roly poly for afters. So come on, hurry up! You know it's my favourite!"

As they started to walk away from the pub, a familiar voice rang out.

"You won't get far without this", it said, waving an old walking stick above his head.

"Thanks, John," he shouted. "Don't know what's up with me today."

"I'll get it, Grandad," said the little girl, and off she ran back towards the pub.

"Be careful you don't fall," but by the time he had said it she was already on the way back.

"Here you are, Grandad. Now come on, hurry up or there'll be no pudding for us!"

As the old man and the girl walked slowly through the village, the girl chattered away at such a speed about a great many different subjects. The old man was totally bewildered, but amused.

"Slow down," he said, "one thing at a time, please!"

"Were you really born in the village, Grandad?"

"Yes, little one. In the same house that we now live in. In fact, I was born in the same bedroom that you and your Mum share now."

"When we were all little we didn't have an inside toilet or bath. We had an outside toilet and washhouse, and no hot water. When it was bath night my Mum used to fill the old boiler and light a fire under it, and every so often she would stoke the fire until the water was boiling. Then Dad would get an old metal bath from the barn and put it in front of the fire in the kitchen and fill it with water. Mum would shout for the youngest first and then she would work her way through all of us, scrubbing from top to toe with carbolic soap, using the same scrubbing brush she used for the floors and the washing. When we were all done, Dad would partly empty the water out of the bath and top it up with more hot water. Mum would shoo us kids out of the kitchen and she and Dad would both then get in the bath. It was many years before we found out what all the laughing, squealing and splashing was about, and before you ask, little one, your Mum will tell you when you get older!"

"Oh Grandad, you're such an old fuddy duddy! Everyone knows what's happening when mums and dads want to be on their own. Anyway, these days Grandad, with separate bathrooms grown ups can just lock the doors and splash and squeal all they want."

At that comment, the old man decided that it was time for him to divert the conversation.

"Do you see that field over there, little one? When I was your age, my dad used to take me there after he finished work and we would play and play until Mum shouted for us to come in for bedtime. When my brother got older, we would all go to the field and take an old ball with us to kick around. You see, we didn't have any of the toys you have today to play with – no radio or television. The only music we ever heard was either at school or church on Sundays."

"Grandad, why haven't I ever met your brother? I've heard you talking about him with Mum, but when you see me you always start talking about other things. It's the same when you talk about Dad – only Mum gets upset and starts crying. I know she misses him very much and I often wonder why God needed another star when he already has so many in the sky."

"Oh little one, you've got so much to learn and so much life in front of you. I tell you what, if you can run to the War memorial before I count to twenty, I'll buy you an ice cream after dinner."

Off she ran, laughing and shouting.

"Come on, Grandad! I can't hear you counting and I'm at the bottom of the hill already!"

"Six, seven, eight, nine," shouted Grandad. "Is that better?"

"Oh Grandad, you've cheated!"

"Ten, eleven, twelve. Come on, little one, hurry up! I might even beat you myself. Thirteen, fourteen, fifteen."

"I'm nearly there, Grandad!"

"Sixteen, seventeen, eighteen," he shouted.

"I'm there, I'm there," she replied. "Now it's your turn to do a bit of running, Grandad. You're already part way up the hill. Come on, just run the last little bit, pleeee-ase!"

"What are you trying to do to me? If you wear me out, I won't be fit to take you to the shop for your reward. Anyway, I'm nearly there now."

He made it to the memorial and sat down on the bench that the local people had provided when the council had put up the monument in the early 1920s. Since then it had always been looked after and kept spotlessly clean by the villagers. A small flower garden had been made by the side of the memorial, so there were always flowers all the year round.

"Molly, did you know that on Armistice Day all of the villagers gather around the memorial to remember their dead fathers, sons, brothers, uncles and friends who gave their lives so that those of us who are left can have a better life? At first, some of our old comrades would come to remember and afterwards we old soldiers would retire to the pub and talk about the old times, but as the years have gone by less and less of them have made it to the service."

"Grandad, are you alright? You look a funny colour," questioned Molly.

"No, I'm fine. Just a little out of breath. I'm not as young and fit as I used to be."

"Is that why they put this bench here for you to sit on? Why isn't your name on the stone? You fought in the

War didn't you? I thought that everyone who was in the War had their name on the stone?"

"It doesn't work like that, little one. There were a lot of young men who went off to the War but many never came back to their homes and loved ones."

"What do you mean, Grandad, when you say that they never came home? Did they stay in the countries where the War was?"

"Well, not exactly. You remember when your Daddy didn't come home?"

"Yes, I know what you mean, Grandad. They went to God to be his stars."

"Yes, that's right. Anyway, it was decided to have these memorials with the names of all of God's new stars from the War put up in every city, town and village across the country so that we would never forget their sacrifices for their country and everyone who now lives here."

After a few minutes silence, Molly asked, "Did you know anyone whose name is on the stone, Grandad?"

Slowly the old man lifted his walking stick and even though he couldn't see the names properly without his glasses, he knew exactly where they all were.

"This one," he said, "was my brother, Philip." He moved the stick down and over the stone. "This is Harry and just slightly below is John." He moved his stick back over and down, and said, "Mustn't forget Peter. I know a few more, but not as well as those I mentioned. We were the inseparables. Had been from a very early age. We were the best of friends and where one went, the others were not far behind. Do you remember that field I showed you where I played with my Dad? Well, that's where we all met. It became a regular meeting place with a few others from the village, too. We were always making up father and son football teams and during the summer months when we were out of school, we would play until late into the evening. Then, as we got older, we started to make our own fun and got into all sorts of mischief. Ah, they were the good old days. We used to have many adventures together. I remember when…"

"Molly! Molly! Is that you by the memorial? I thought I told you to go and fetch Grandad and to hurry back?"

"Sorry, Mum. Granddad is sitting down here having a rest. He says he's not feeling too well."

"Oh, I'm alright," butted in the old man, and with a wave of his walking stick he said, "Come on Molly! Let's see who can get home first!"

As they got closer to the cottage, they could see Sarah standing by the gate tidying up the rose bushes on either side of the path. When she heard them coming she looked up and a broad beaming smile crept across her face.

"There you are," she said, "I thought you'd got lost."

"Sorry, love. You know what I'm like these days. I forgot my old stick and Molly had to go back for it."

"Then," Molly jumped in, "Grandad and me had a bet that I couldn't reach the stone monument by the time he counted to twenty, and guess what – he owes me an ice cream now! Can we walk down to the shop after dinner? Anyway," she continued, "when Grandad finally got to the stone he sat down because he wasn't feeling very well."

Sarah looked over to her father and the smile quickly turned to a look of concern.

"What's wrong, Dad? Same thing?"

The old man quickly glanced at Molly and then shifted his gaze to his daughter.

"It's nothing to worry about. I think I might have over done it coming up the hill. I'm not as young as I used to be, you know."

Sarah smiled at her father.

"Ok," she said, "we'll go down in the car for our ice creams after lunch, but not until all the dishes have been done and tidied away. Is that a bargain?"

Molly looked at Grandad and they both said that it sounded like a good deal to them.

"But Mum, even though we're a bit late, do we still get the jam roly poly as well?"

Sarah laughed out loud.

"You certainly drive a hard bargain! What do you think, Dad?"

"Well, I don't see why not, after all she's just like you were at that age. Hollow legs, I think they called it!"

"Come on then," she coaxed them, "by the time you two have cleaned up, the dinner will be on the table."

As they all made their way up the path, the old man's thoughts were recalling the doctor's words a few weeks earlier.

"Well, Bill, I can't find any obvious signs of a problem, but after the symptoms you've described to me, I don't think we can be too careful. I'll get in touch with the hospital and get them to send you an appointment for some more detailed tests and then we can see what's keeping you going. You never know, we might be able to sell it. Anyway, it'll probably take two to three months to come through, so if you get any further problems just pop in and I'll have another look. I'll see you in the pub tonight as usual?"

"You try and keep me away," Bill had replied. "Should be a good game. The visitors have got some good players, so we'll need some straight, sharp arrows to see them off!"

"Come on, Grandad. Stop daydreaming. I've had my wash, it's your turn now. I've run some clean water. I'm going to see if Mum wants any help."

Sarah was in the kitchen, busily putting out the dinner.

"Are you two ready yet? Don't let it get cold."

She hoped they wouldn't notice the tremble in her voice. It just seemed so soon since her husband David had died so suddenly with no warning whatsoever, and the ordeal of the aftermath – the funeral, all the insurers and the solicitors to deal with – David had always dealt with all the money matters and everything else like that. Although his Mum and Dad had helped out as much as they could, the majority still fell to Sarah to sort out. Molly was so distraught; they just used to lie in bed together crying all the time. Then her father had come over on the train. It hadn't taken him long to see what was happening.

"Right, you two are coming home with me. You can stay for as long as you want, so get packing. I don't want to be late back, there's a match on at the pub tonight and I don't want to miss it."

That was nearly two years ago now and they were still there. Sarah had sold the house and settled all the bills and associated problems in London and had made Dad's home their family home.

"And we both seem to have settled down with Dad really well," thought Sarah to herself. "Molly's settled into the local school and made a few good friends. I've managed to renew one or two old friendships, too."

These were girls who had married locally, so sometimes it felt to Sarah like she had never left home. Her Dad had been so caring and thoughtful since they moved back there. She was sure that they wouldn't have got through it all without him, and he and Molly are like two peas in a pod. They go everywhere together. In fact, she seemed to have been like a breath of fresh air to her grandfather. He was getting on in years and Sarah knew that he wouldn't be with them forever, but she prayed to God that he would stay with them for a good little while yet.

"Mum, Mum are you alright? You look like you're in a trance. Is there anything I can do to help?"

"No, darling," replied Sarah. "Just sit yourself down. It's coming now. Dad, it's on the table. Hurry up, will you?"

"Coming, coming," shouted Grandad, and a few seconds later he appeared in the doorway. "I thought that as this is such a lovely day, it would be nice to open a bottle of wine," but before he could finish, Sarah butted in.

"I thought you were saving that for a special occasion?"

"Well, to me, today is a special occasion. After all we've been through and we're all healthy and happy and together, and if that's not special then I don't know what is! Molly, get me and your Mum a glass and bring that small glass as well. I don't think your Mum will mind you having a tiny drop?"

"Just this once, then," Sarah said. "As long as it doesn't become a habit."

"Oh Mum", Molly said, "you never say that when I drink lots of milk!"

Pop went the cork and the wine flowed over the top of the bottle like expensive champagne.

"Quick Molly, pass me a glass or I'll spill most of it."

"Here Grandad, pour it into this", as she quickly passed him one of the glasses.

"Whoa, there it goes. Now, pass me the other glasses, please."

Sitting down, he then filled a glass for Sarah and just a tiny drop for Molly.

"Is that all, Grandad? I'll hardly get a taste with such a measly spot."

Glancing at Sarah, he picked up her glass and with a slight nod of the head said, "Ok, ok just a little more but not too much, we don't want you going to sleep after dinner now, do we? Anyway, that's my privilege. It comes with age."

"You mean it's a way of getting out of the dishes," butted in Sarah.

"Let's eat," said Grandad, hastily "I'm starving and this looks sumptuous!"

"Dad", Sarah said, looking over the table deep into the old man's eyes, "before Mum passed on, she always used to say a prayer before we had our meal. Now, I know you're not particularly religious and neither are we," she glanced over to Molly, "but do you think that we could say something on this, as you said earlier, 'special day'?"

The old man looked back into his daughter's eyes and for a split second thought he was looking into the eyes of his wife.

"Why not," he said, "only you must do the deed, just like your Mother would have done."

As all three of them shut their eyes, bowed their heads slightly and linked hands across the table, Sarah spoke softly.

"I know it's been a while since anyone from this family has spoken to you, Lord, but as you probably already know, we've been going through a hard time just lately. We know it's probably not a good excuse in your eyes but we hope you will try to understand. Anyway, we would appreciate it if you would give us your blessing and also bless the food we eat, our health which is so precious to us and keep our loved ones safe, including those already in your keeping. We'll all try a little harder to keep in touch more often. Thank you, Lord. Amen."

Sarah looked over to Molly, who still had her eyes shut.

"Mummy", she said, "do you think Lord Jesus would ask Dad if he could shine a little brighter at night as there are so many stars in the sky, I can't tell which one is Daddy?"

"I'm sure he will, darling, now say 'Amen'."

Grandad also said Amen at the same time and they all let go of each others hands.

"Your Mum would have loved those words. You know what she was like about religion. Now, let's eat."

The conversation over dinner was nothing out of the ordinary, with the exception of quite a lengthy debate about the size of the ice cream Molly was going to have later.

"Who's for pudding?" said Sarah, collecting the dirty dishes and disappearing into the kitchen.

"Yes, please," squealed Molly. "Lots and lots and lots, Mummy."

"What about you, Dad?" shouted Sarah.

"Oh, I don't know if I've got any room left after that splendid meal. I only just managed to finish. Maybe just a small portion then. If there's any left, we can have it later on in the week, can't we?"

Sarah came back carrying three bowls with steam rising from them.

"Be careful. They're piping hot," she said. "If you want any more, you can get it yourselves," she laughed.

A short time later all the bowls were empty.

"Come on, Mum," said Molly, "I'll help you with the dishes."

"Oh yes?" questioned Sarah. "What's all this about? It has nothing to do with the ice cream shop, has it?"

Molly smiled coyly at her Mum. "Just trying to be helpful."

"Here, I'll help too," said Grandad.

"No you won't," chastised Sarah. "You can take your paper and go and have a rest in the garden. It's such a lovely day, nice and sunny and just a gentle breeze."

"Just like the days – no weeks, when I was a lad."

"I've put a deckchair out with a couple of pillows in your special spot – and a blanket for if you feel a bit chilly later on."

"Oh don't fuss, woman! It's far too hot for blankets. In fact, I may take my shirt off later. Now that would be a sight to see!"

Yes," said Sarah, "you'd frighten off all the birds better than any scarecrow!"

Grandad chuckled to himself as he headed across the garden to where the deckchair was waiting. Putting the blanket on the grass beside the chair, he slipped gently down into the seat and adjusted the pillows.

"Ah, that's better," he said to himself. "Damn this bloody chest pain! After all these years, why has it suddenly started to come back now?"

He caught a movement out of the corner of his eye and smiled to himself. He spun around as fast as he could, nearly tipping over the chair.

"Got you!" he said. "Thought you could sneak up unnoticed on an old soldier, did you?"

Molly jumped up. "Don't shoot, don't shoot, Grandad! It's only me. Mum sent me over with the paper you forgot. She says you'll forget to put your boots on one of these days."

"Come here, you little rascal," as he grabbed for her, but she was too quick and darted away, shouting, "Mum says I've got to leave you alone so you can rest, but I'll be back later", and off she skipped to the cottage.

The old man settled himself back into the chair and started to read the newspaper. He flicked through a number of pages but there was nothing that caught his eye, so he dropped it onto the grass, mumbling to himself. "Load of old rubbish these days. Nothing interesting to get your teeth into. I don't know why I buy them. Still, they make good firelighters", and again he chuckled to himself. As he began to unwind and relax and he was getting more and more comfortable in the chair, he felt himself starting to drift off. Suddenly, with a slight jolt he became fully awake again.

"This won't do," he said to himself. "Elizabeth would not stand for it. She was full of energy and life. She never stopped from the minute she got up until it was time for bed. Mind, she needed it when she married me and came to live here with my Mum and Dad as well. They were hard days between the Wars. Mum never really got over what happened and when she died so young, we all knew it was more to do with a broken heart than ill health. My father was never the same after that either really. He and Mum had known each other all of their lives; grew up together. Even their parents knew they would get married when they got older, so it was no shock when they got engaged on Mum's eighteenth birthday and married a few months later and came to live in the cottage."

Flying the nest

Chapter 2

It was about five months after Mum died that they found Dad's body near the weir on the river. It was a Sunday and the weather was just on the change from winter to spring. The river was a little higher than usual, but not too much. Dad said he was just going for a walk before dinner. We had no inclination as to what was in his mind. In fact, to the best of our knowledge, there certainly had not been any change, either good or bad, when he walked out of the back door with his hat and stick. He'd said that he would see us sooner or later, smiled and walked across the fields.

Elizabeth and I both watched him until he had gone out of sight. She had commented that that was the first time she had seen him smile since Mum had passed on.

I remember saying, "Let's hope that he's turned the corner and is coming back to us."

Elizabeth looked up at me and smiled, "If it's God's will, whatever happens is always for the best."

A group of children found his body and sent for the local constable, and with the help of some of my Dad's friends, they carried him to the church. Shortly afterwards, there was a knock on our door. I turned to face Elizabeth and we both knew what was going to happen next.

They took Dad's body away and carried out their examinations, which concluded that he had slipped into the river whilst walking along the bank, and as the river was higher than normal, the current had dragged him into the weir, where he drowned. So that was what was written on his death certificate – 'Death by misadventure (accidental drowning.)' The funeral was carried out three days later, which the whole of the village attended.

I think it was about three or four months after Dad's funeral that we were sitting on a blanket in the garden, which was to become a very special place to us both.

We had neither of us spoken much about Dad's death. As we both relaxed more, I rested my head on her lap and looking up at the sun and the sky, I said, "Do you think they have found each other, you know, up there in heaven? Do you think they let Dad in after he.. ," I paused.

"After he what?" said Elizabeth.

"After he slipped and fell in the river and drowned."

"That wasn't his fault, and yes, I think that he has found your Mum. People like that will always be together, whether it's on this earth or up in heaven. God will always look after his children."

I looked into her eyes and said, "Looks like you can't get rid of me that easily then."

She smiled back and said, "Who says I want to just yet?"

We kissed tenderly and made our way back into the cottage and from that day forward the nature of my father's death was never mentioned again.

"Grandad, Grandad! Mum says do you want a cup of tea?"

"Yes, please. Two sugars – I'm on a diet!"

"You always have two spoons and you're not getting any smaller yet."

A few minutes later, Sarah came over with a large mug of piping hot tea.

"Here you are, Dad. Mind it's not too hot. How are you feeling now? You didn't look too good over dinner."

"It's just this pain in my chest. It doesn't seem to be getting any better."

"I know you've seen the doctor," Sarah said, "and he's ruled out any problems with your heart, but did he give you any idea what might be causing it? He knows about your war wounds in your chest, doesn't he?"

"He can't miss it when I take my shirt off, can he? He said he wouldn't be any the wiser until I've had some tests and x-rays."

"They certainly take their time sending you your appointment", Sarah said.

The old man could sense the concern in her voice.

"Don't worry, love. I've got a good few years left in me yet! Look, could you take Molly in the car to the shop? I'm feeling a little tired at the moment. Probably over did it earlier. I'll just rest here a while."

"Ok, Dad. We'll bring you an ice cream back."

As Sarah went back into the cottage, the old man sat up and drank his tea, staring across the rolling fields to the hills in the distance. He knew every inch of the area. This was his countryside and he knew all the hiding places, all the courting couples' seats – he had walked everywhere as both man and boy.

Just then a voice shouted, "We're off to the shop, Grandad. See you later."

He didn't turn round, but instead just waved his hand in the air and at the same time shouted, "Bye, see you later."

He drained the last drop from his mug and then settled back into his chair for a few minutes. As he drifted, he heard the opening and closing of the car doors and the engine starting and pulling off the gravel drive onto the road heading for the village. After a few seconds, the noise from the car was gone and it became peaceful once again. As he lay back in his chair, the old man could feel himself drifting off to sleep once again. His thoughts and memories were intermingled in his head. One minute he was a young boy, the next he was a young man and then an old man. The memories of that place which had caused him and his family so much hurt, so much pain and suffering; far too much for one man and his family to suffer. Memories which he had blotted out were now starting to creep back into his thoughts. He was beginning to experience some of the horrors from long ago when he forced himself to come out of the deep sleep that he had drifted into. He looked up at the sky and muttered, "The Somme."

Sarah and Molly pulled up in the car outside the village shop.

"What are you going to have, Mum? I want a large scoop of strawberry ice cream with a chocolate flake, all covered in strawberry sauce."

"Goodness me!" exclaimed her Mum. "Have you still got room for that after all that pudding you had after dinner?"

"Oh yes, please, Mum! Grandad would have bought me one."

"I know. He spoils you rotten! Now, I'll just have a scoop of vanilla. That will do me."

"What about Grandad? What shall we take him back?"

Sarah thought for a moment and then said, "Look, as it's such a lovely day, I thought we could park the car over by the school and then we could go for a walk through the meadow. And besides, it will give Grandad a little longer for his doze."

"Ok," Molly said. "You give me the money and I'll get the ice creams and bring them over to you at the school."

As Sarah waited for Molly by the school, she couldn't help but think back to her childhood. In those days, time seemed to go slower. There were no worries. Dad used to pick me up from school as often as he could, and as we were walking home he would tell me all about his adventures and what he had done when he was a boy.

"Come on, Mum," Molly shouted, "it's melting and running all down my hand."

Sarah grabbed a handful of paper hankies, got out of the car and took her ice cream from Molly.

"Here you are. Wipe your hands with these. I'll just lock the car and we can set off. Ok?"

As they were walking away from the car, Molly asked about Grandad's ice cream once more.

"Oh, we'll get him one on the way back and ask the shopkeeper to put it in a plastic container. Now, come on, let's see how many birds we can see, then you can tell Grandad when we get back."

The old man was just settling back into his seat after going to the cottage to use the toilet.

"Who says getting older is good?" he muttered to himself. "You spend half your time asleep because you're tired by all the trips you take to the toilet." Then he chuckled as he thought of the days when he and his brother and the lads were out together and they'd have a pee anywhere and it didn't matter who was looking. Once he started to remember his youth, he could feel the tears welling up in his eyes, so he reached into his pocket for something to wipe them with.

"Nothing in there," he said to himself, rummaging through his pockets. "What did I do when I was young?" So he proceeded to wipe his eyes and nose on his shirt-sleeve. "Not much changed there, then!" he smiled to himself.

After lying in his chair for ten or fifteen minutes, he started to wonder where the girls had got to. Then, after a moment's thought, he decided that they had probably gone for a spin in the car, so shutting his eyes he was determined to get forty winks before they came back.

It wasn't too long before he was in a deep sleep, but to look at him it would only seem that his body was at rest; his mind was still very active. Once again, memory after memory flashed through his mind until suddenly, over the fence there was a chorus of voices shouting to him.

"Bill, Bill! Are you and Phil coming out for a game? There's already five lads on the field, and with us and the two of you we can have a match."

"Hang on! I'll find Phil and ask Dad if it's ok."

Five minutes later, we were all running over the fields heading for another grudge football match with some lads from another village. Our team consisted of me, my brother Phil, Harry (who always played goalie), John (who could run like the wind but was a better cricketer than footballer) and, finally, there was Peter. What can you say about Peter? Well, he was the youngest, but his Mum always sent him to school with the best lunch box and there was always a little extra for us, his best pals. You see, Peter's mum and dad had come into a little money when an elderly relative had passed away, which made them fairly well off. His dad had been able to pack up his farm-labouring job and had bought a small plot of land and was starting to grow flowers and vegetables. The rest of us thought it was probably more of a hobby than to make money, but he was good to us and paid us well for helping on the land. John's father worked for a local land owner who lived in a big house at the far end of the village. His main job was Head Gardener, but he was also very good at general repairs and maintenance, so in the winter months when most of the land workers were laid off, he was kept on, working on the house and outbuildings. Harry's father and our Dad worked together. They had been pals for years, almost from first school when his parents had moved into the village, with the exception of the time when they fell out over my Dad who pinched his girlfriend, whom he later married. After a few words were said and several blows exchanged, it was not long before they were pals again. This one and only falling out had become a regular topic of conversation at Christmas when our families all came together, and to the sound of riotous laughter, my Father would always say it would have to be an exceptional woman who could make old friends stay at loggerheads for long. To which my Mum could always be seen smiling to herself and would say to all who were listening that the least she said about the matter the better!

Our two fathers had started up a small forestry business, and with a horse and cart, and saws and axes, they travelled all around the area working for whoever required their services. Sometimes they came home at night, other times not. It was a very hard job and the pay was poor, but with Mum's vegetable garden and some chickens, we were better off than most.

For us lads, life seemed to consist of school and jobs at home for our mums in the winter months, like collecting firewood and clearing snow – and sometimes getting paid! Then, come the spring, a whole new world opened up to us. There was football, cricket, swimming in the river, pennies to be earned, ice creams to be eaten, trips into the local town and only occasionally did we get the chance to go to a passing circus or fair. Then there was Harvest Festival where everyone would help with the gathering of the crops and then arrange a big celebration in the village. There were also well-dressings and Bonfire Night and many, many other occasions too numerous to mention, both in our village and in many of the surrounding villages. What a life, you'd think and you'd be right. For five young lads it was utter bliss, the years soon rolled by.

Although I can't be certain, thinking back things began to look ominous around the time when we lads started to look at the local girls in a slightly different manner – not just as goal posts and on the odd occasion playing in goal and fetching the cricket balls for us! Instead, we began to see them as things of beauty and as very appealing. It's funny though, before this sudden transformation they were willing to do almost anything to belong to a gang, but now they appeared to be transformed into some superior being who still did not acknowledge our existence – funny that!

Although life in our village went on as normal and us boys carried on with our usual distractions, there was now the additional past time of spotting girls and trying to follow them without being seen – which was sometimes virtually impossible with five of us charging around. I think we all noticed a change in the atmosphere surrounding the grown ups, too. On most Saturday nights, our fathers, and sometimes our mothers as well, would meet up in the village pub and as a treat we would get a glass of something or other whilst we sat outside. In the past when we had looked through the window, some of the men would be playing cards, dominoes, skittles or darts and the women would all be sitting around the same table gossiping away. Sometimes there was a roar of laughter and raised voices about how the games were being played, but all in good fun. However, lately most of this had stopped. The women now sat in the corner whispering and the men sat around talking of countries and places we had never heard of. They talked of armies of revolution; they'd talk of assassination, too – using all of the kinds of words that we were never taught at school. They talked of our King and his cousins who were powerful leaders in distant countries. Voices were lowered and the men huddled closer together as if they knew someone was listening. This would carry on for several minutes as we were all standing under the window, and then, as if by some kind of inexplicable occurrence, we all heard the same one word at exactly the same time. We were all suddenly introduced to the meaning of the word 'war'.

After this night, life carried on in the village pretty much as before. For us, with the exception of Phil, the onset of our working life kept us very busy from dawn to dusk. Unfortunately, we didn't achieve a very high standard of education, so we all knew that we would be making our livings working with our hands, and probably on the land with our fathers. However, because Phil was younger than us he still had more time at school before he could join us, which we all took great pleasure in reminding him at every opportunity.

As the autumn turned into winter, the news concerning the War, that was allowed to be released, seemed to point to good gains for us with not many casualties. However, on the side of the enemy, casualties were higher and we were also taking more prisoners. There were quite a number of appeals for volunteers to join up and form a new army, which, when fully trained and equipped, could be shipped to the front to finish the job.

After Christmas, several young men from our village, along with others from surrounding villages, made their way into town where a temporary recruiting centre had been set up. They were all given medicals and signed up there and then. About a couple of weeks later, they were given travel warrants to the training camp. On the night before they went, all the local men gathered in the village pub where a great deal of beer was drunk, lots of advice on how to beat the enemy was given, songs were sung, tears were shed, backs were slapped and hands were shaken. As we all slipped home in the darkness, all our thoughts were with the first, but not the last, volunteers to go to war in distant, unheard of lands. They were fighting for what, we didn't know. Nobody had explained it to us really, just that it was for King and country. As we walked up the hill to the cottage, Dad said, "At least you won't have to go. The papers say it will all be over soon and anyway, you're not old enough this year."

"But Dad, me and the lads have been talking and we all want to go. It sounds like a great adventure which we certainly don't want to miss."

"What about your mother? She'll be heartbroken if anything happens to you."

"And Phil said he wants to go as well."

Dad laughed, "He's far too young, as you well know."

"But Dad, we've heard that they don't worry too much about age as long as you look old enough and pass the medical. Phil looks older than all of us and he's taller than me anyway."

As we crunched up the gravel path to the cottage, Dad turned to me and by the light from the cottage window, I saw an expression I had never seen on my Dad's face before; a mixture of fear and anger and pride all in one.

Then he said, "Whatever you do, you and Phil must not tell your mother. There's no point in her worrying over something that will not happen."

Winter once again turned to spring and slipped steadily on into summer. Our work was going well and the local council wanted more and more from the land. We were all working flat out to produce food for our brave soldiers. The army had taken over the Manor and turned it into a hospital, which meant that all the surrounding roads and lanes were getting busier and busier with ambulances. It also seemed that general military traffic was getting heavier, and on some nights and at weekends, quite a number of army personnel could be seen in the village and visiting the pub. They were friendly enough and would stop for a chat but they never said much about the fighting overseas. They would shout to me and the lads and ask us when we were going to join up. They said that the army would give us a good life, good food, good money, free fags and a chance to see the world. We told them that we weren't old enough yet, but we did ask that when they got there that they didn't win the War all by themselves and would save some for us for the next year!

It was about mid August when the sign was put up in the window of the local shop asking for anyone with or without nursing skills who could spare some time helping out at the hospital that had been established in the Manor. In our village, there were several women who had had nursing training who volunteered immediately, and then my mother and quite a few other women from around the area also went up to see if they could be of any help. It turned out that they were badly understaffed and therefore managed to find jobs easily for all who volunteered. In our spare time, me and the lads would go and collect and chop wood for their fires and the boiler, as coal was in short supply. We could always talk to the staff, but they wouldn't let us go on the wards. Occasionally, we would hear a patient cry out and would be told he was probably dreaming, but to be honest, I think we were more afraid as to what sight we might have seen had we visited the patients, so maybe it was for our own good that we were denied access. Even Mum and the other ladies wouldn't talk about their work but I know that sometimes my Mum would come home with tears in her eyes and Dad would take her in his arms and comfort her while she wept on his shoulder. They would then go to their room where Mum would share whatever horrors she had had the misfortune to have witnessed that day.

As the days turned to weeks, my mother slowly managed to control her feelings, but the horrors she was being subjected to were taking their toll. The atmosphere in the village was getting worse by the day and the news from the front was not good. We had lost several engagements and casualties were high. The talk of an early end to the War had long stopped and our troops were now digging in on a long front, as were the enemy. There were also urgent calls for more volunteers and it was being suggested that wives and girlfriends should try to persuade their loved ones to sign up as it was brave and courageous to do so. We often wondered why there was no mention of coming back unhurt. To us, that was a mystery.

Towards the end of September, the news that we had been dreading started to filter through. Within our area, five of the volunteers had returned from the front with serious injuries. In fact, two of them were hospitalised at the Manor House. A further four were missing in action – probably taken prisoner, but the worst news was that six had been killed in action, one of whom was from our village. This news was absolutely devastating. There was a connection with nearly all of the people in the area with these lads. They had all been born in the surrounding villages and most of them had gone to the school in our village. There were several funerals at our church that followed. People came from all over. Naturally, they were very sad occasions. Flags were draped over the coffins as they were carried into the church, and after the services it was dreadful to see some of the mothers breaking their hearts over the graves. This was something that will never be forgotten by all who were there.

It was a long time before news of the missing lads came through but they did manage to confirm that one was in Germany in a POW camp and the other three had been officially posted as missing presumed dead in action, but their parents still hung on to the possibility that they might come home after the War was over. But they didn't.

Normality reigned for most of us, except that we were expected to work longer hours to try to produce more of everything. It was as if something was affecting the entire population of the village and the surrounding area. No explanation could be found, but the atmosphere was so strange. Hardly anyone would talk about the War anymore, and if they did, you could see the hidden emotion in their eyes. Quite a number of people had friends or relatives serving in France and you could only imagine what it was like waiting for news to filter back from the front. The news in the papers didn't really say much and told you even less than people were managing to find out through their own contacts. Still, one thing for sure was that it was all so exciting to us lads. At every opportunity we would meet up and talk about the War. We couldn't get enough of every little detail that any of us had managed to pick up. It was analysed and poured over for hours. I think we fancied ourselves as generals commanding the various armies. We all knew we could do better and couldn't wait to get over there to show them how it should be done.

We'd all made a pact when we'd come back from the first funeral that as soon as we were old enough, we would all join up together, except Phil who would have to wait a few more months. Although, at the rate that he was growing he would look older than us by Christmas. At every opportunity, the rest of us used to make fun of him because he wouldn't be old enough to join up with us. At mealtimes, Mum used to say that he had hollow legs because he always ate twice as much as the rest of us. Dad said he had worms, but Phil just shrugged his shoulders, glared over the table at me and kept on eating.

Soon it was getting close to Christmas. Both Harry and Peter had just turned eighteen; John was next and then me after Christmas. We had decided that we would stay at home until mid February, just before my birthday, and then we would go into town and find out where we could join up. Every time we talked about our plan, Phil would turn moody and wander off to sulk, but at home his intake of food kept going up and up. No one had as yet brought up the question of what to say to our parents and it was not discussed until Christmas Eve. This was a particularly special time for us to be all together as the landlord let us into the pub as long as we sat in the corner and kept quiet. Part way through the evening, John asked, "Has anyone told their family yet – you know, about signing up?"

There were a few moments silence, then, one after the other we all shook our heads, indicating that we hadn't.

"Well," said Peter, "if I tell mine, they'll go mad and try and stop me."

We all looked at each other across the table and agreed. After a pause, they all looked towards me, as if for advice. So, after many ideas, I said, "Look, whatever we do, it's not going to be right for them and us, so I think that we should say nowt, go and sign up and then see what happens. I don't think they could get us out once we've signed up and from what we know you normally go away after about two weeks. What do you all think about that?"

Within seconds, it was all agreed and the subject was never mentioned again. Thinking back, if any one of us had known then what the future held for us, we would perhaps have been grateful if our parents had been given the opportunity to stop us going. However, it was not to be.

January soon disappeared and before we knew it the time we had all agreed on was almost upon us. None of us could describe what we were feeling as we made our arrangements to go into town, but at the same time not let on to anyone else what was going on.

"I don't know why it takes two of you to go into town just to get a pair of boots. What will your Dad say when you don't turn up for work. He was up and gone before daylight."

"Don't worry, Mum. He knows all about it and Phil told his boss as well, so stop fussing and hurry up with breakfast or we'll miss the bus!"

As we were running down the path, Mum shouted, "When will you be back?"

Phil looked at me and we both shouted that we'd be back sometime before dark.

"Don't worry, Mum. We'll get something to eat at dinner time. Bye."

We both jumped the low gate as Mum shouted to us to be careful and mind that we didn't fall on the ice.

It was a typical February day – very cold and crisp with the remains of snow that had fallen about two weeks previously. Most of the roads were clear, but like the paths, were very slippery in places. As we slid and tumbled our way down the road, both of us roaring with laughter, we heard someone calling us from the direction of the village. We both stopped for a minute to try and see who it was. It was Phil who saw Harry first. He was at the bus stop, jumping and waving and shouting but we couldn't quite hear what he was saying. Then I spotted the bus moving through the trees towards the village. I pushed Phil and gasped, "Bus coming, come on or we'll miss it."

Winging it down the road, we just got there as it was about to pull away. We paid our fare and went to the back of the bus where Harry was sitting with a big grin on his face.

"Thanks for waiting," I said.

"I shouted you – it's not my fault that the bus was early," he said.

Phil knocked his hat off and we started to rough him up until the driver shouted down the bus to pack it in, otherwise we would be walking the rest of the way to town. At that, we all sat back down, grinning at each other.

It takes about one and a half hours to get to town on the bus, and there's only one return journey per day. By the time we got to town, John and Peter had joined up with us. The bus stopped in the town square and as everyone was getting off, the bus driver told us that the bus would be returning at 5 o'clock.

"Don't be late or I'll go without you, then it'll be a long, cold walk back to your Mum's."

"At least we've got mums and dads," said Harry, cheekily.

"Young buggers! You should all be in the army now at your ages, fighting for King and country instead of giving me a hard time. Now bugger off, or I won't let you on tonight."

The rest of us piled off the bus and we all stood there waving at him as he pulled out of the square.

"Right, where do we sign up then?" John said. We all looked at each other with the same blank expression and shrugged our shoulders, and stood there looking around the square.

"What about going and asking at the police station," offered Peter. "They're bound to know where it is."

So, off we trudged.

It took about fifteen minutes to get there and when we finally arrived, we all filed into the front office. We stood at the counter and as no one was around, we all started shuffling our feet and coughing politely. After a few minutes, still nobody had appeared, so Phil started thumping his chest very loudly. With that, a stern-faced policeman in full uniform walked briskly to the desk.

"Now lad," he said, "are you sure it's the police you need? With such a bad, chesty cough like that perhaps you should go and see a doctor."

Phil's face went white and he took several steps back from the counter.

"Sorry sir," he stammered, "We...we just wanted ..."

Peter stepped up, "He's trying to say that we want to join the army and would like to know where the recruiting office is, please sir."

"Ah, come to take the King's shilling, have we lads? Well, you'll not get it here. You need to go to the Town Hall. Know where that is?"

We all shook our heads.

"Well, it's at the back of the square – it's got a sign up so you can't miss it."

He looked at his watch.

"You should make it before they shut for the afternoon – you see, they only open mornings whilst the weather is bad."

"Thank you, sir," we all said in unison, and with that we all turned and headed towards the door.

"Hey you," the policeman said pointing towards Phil, "if your cough is no better when you see the MO, they won't let you join up, you know."

We all turned and looked at him and Phil thanked him for the tip. The policeman then broke into a broad grin right across his face.

"Well done lads and good luck to all of you. Stick together and make sure you all come back. I've got a son out there. Joined up last year. We've had a couple of letters from him and he says he's ok and it's not too bad out there. Take plenty of socks with you. Now go and get off or they'll be shut."

As we ran through the streets towards the Town Hall, Phil came up alongside me. "Bill," he said, "I know what you lot have been saying, but I'm coming with you."

These few words stopped me in my tracks. The others gathered around with puzzled expressions.

"What's going on then?"

Phil looked at each one of us in turn, then at me and said quite clearly, "I'm joining up as well. I don't want to be left behind."

"But you're far too young. You've only just turned seventeen. What will your Mum and Dad say? You'll never get in – you don't look old enough."

"I'm taller than all of you and heavier than Harry and you Bill, and you're not going to stop me."

The four friends looked at each other earnestly. Peter said, "What if we tell them your proper age – they won't let you in then."

"I know," Phil said, "but I'll just move around the towns until I find a recruiting officer who will sign me up. Whatever you lot say, I will go to War. I want to go with you, but if not I'll go on my own."

There was utter silence among us, until Peter said, "Is this why you've been eating like a horse since we decided to join up?"

We all laughed heartily, relieved that this had eased the tension.

"Look," said John, "let's let the army decide if he passes all the tests and can fool them about his age. Then, if not, and he's out, it'll be nothing to do with any of us. What do you say?"

"Seems fair to me," Peter said.

"And me," Harry agreed.

"What about you, Bill?" They all looked at me, but I couldn't take my eyes off my younger brother. I knew he was bigger than me and would probably pass all the tests, but I still couldn't forget that he was so young – barely turned seventeen years old. I had a terrible feeling that this War was not a place for anyone of any age, never mind a seventeen year old lad. I was brought back to reality by Phil's voice.

"Well, it's up to you now. I'm your brother. What's your answer?"

I looked at him again and in the last few minutes he seemed to have grown from my younger, immature bother to a determined young man who knew exactly what he wanted.

"Well," I said, "I'll agree, but on one condition. You can tell Mum and Dad it's nothing to do with me and that you did it without telling me."

The others all let out a huge cheer and jumped up and down in the street, slapping each other's backs.

"The time! The time!" Phil shouted. "They'll be closed if we don't hurry," so off we ran, just like a group of pals heading to a village fair or barn dance, laughing and fooling around, whilst in reality we were heading into something that was going to change all our lives forever.

Within a few minutes, we had found what we were looking for. Breathlessly, we stood staring at the poster on the wall and the sign over the door. Looking at each other, Peter said, "This looks like the place lads, and it's open."

"No turning back now," said John.

"Come on then. Let's get it started," I said, moving forward and grasping the door handle slightly nervously.

None of us had any idea what was going to happen, but when it did, it was all over very quickly. We saw an army doctor for a full medical, which consisted of listening to our heart and lungs, a quick look in our mouths and eyes and answering two or three questions. He then told us to take down our trousers and underclothes and putting his hand between our legs, he asked us to cough.

"Fine, you'll do," he said. "Next."

I still don't know to this day what he did that for. Still, we had many a good laugh in the weeks ahead at some of the suggestions as to what he was looking for. Then the next stage consisted of the form filling. We all thought it would take an age, but all they required were as follows: Name, age, address, next of kin (which was more informally explained to us country folks as the name of your mother and father). As, one at a time, we completed the process, we sat patiently awaiting the conclusion. Eventually the doctors both sat down together, obviously talking about us in lowered voices. Occasionally they would look up at one of us and then after a brief pause start talking again. After about five minutes, they stopped their discussion and looking at us, they asked if we had any questions before they carried on. None of us really knew what to say or had the courage to say it, but I suddenly burst out, "Sir, could we all serve together as we've never been apart for years?"

"I think we can arrange that," said one of the doctors. "Now listen very carefully. Over to you, Sergeant."

"Right, lads. You've all passed your medicals with flying colours. You'll receive your orders and travel warrants telling you where to report to in the post within two weeks. Now, we just need your marks or signatures on these forms and you will then be in the King's army and will make your relatives proud of you. So, line up here and sign next to your written name. As we did as he told us to, he came up to each of us in turn and shook our hand saying, "We're all proud of you and we know you'll do your best for your King and country. Good luck."

And that was it. We were all sworn in and back outside on the street a little bewildered, and it only took one and a half hours.

"Well, that's it lads," I said.

"Not quite," replied Peter, "the hardest bit is yet to come."

"What's that, then?" butted in Phil, "The basic training?"

"No, something much harder than that."

We all thought for a few seconds, then Harry said, "I think I know, and I think you're right, Peter."

"Oh, come on," begged Phil. "Tell us what it is then."

Peter looked at us all individually and in turn. He then said quietly, "How are we going to tell our parents that we've signed up to go and fight in France?"

We all started to walk back towards the town centre, but nothing was said for quite a while. I think, like me, we were all trying to come to terms in our minds with what the repercussions were going to be with our families, and how exactly we were going to tell them. Of course, when we would tell them was going to be an issue too, because we knew our orders would be coming through within the next two weeks.

"Anyone hungry?" interrupted Peter. "I'm starving."

"Me, too," joined in Phil. We all laughed at him saying that he didn't have to stuff himself anymore because they'd already signed him up in the army now"

"Leave me alone! I'm still hungry and could drink a nice mug of tea as well."

"How long until the bus?" I asked Peter. He was the only one of us who had a watch. After taking a quick glance at it, he informed us that we had about two hours, if the bus was running to time.

"Where shall we go then?" said Phil. "I don't know anywhere, does anybody else?"

We all either shook our heads or shrugged our shoulders. Just then, we saw the policeman who we had spoken to earlier. He was walking away from us on the other side of the road.

"I know," I said, "We know he likes you, Phil. So just walk over to him and ask him where we can go."

"No fear," whined Phil, "I'd rather go and face the whole German army on my own than him,"

"Go on!" we all goaded him. "Time's running out."

"Ok," Phil replied, "but you lot can pay for my tea!"

We all agreed and off he went. He stopped the policeman and they started talking. You could see that he was giving Phil directions as his arms were waving up and down furiously. After a few more minutes, he shook Phil's hand and they went their separate ways. Phil made his way back to us and the policeman looked over to the rest of us and tipped his helmet in our direction. We all returned his compliment and then gathered around Phil.

"Don't push, don't push!" he ordered. "Just follow me, I know where to go," and off he went at a sprightly pace, followed closely behind by the rest of us.

It took about fifteen minutes to get to our destination. We all stood in front of a large building, which turned out to be part of the market where there were stalls all across the front and down both sides.

"Well," said Phil, "where is it then?" looking around him. "According to the directions that I received from ...."

"Oh come on, stop mucking about. We're all starving – where is it?"

"Ok – through the double doors, straight to the back and it's on the left or right – or right, no left…"

Phil started to get annoyed as we made our way through rows and rows of stalls selling everything you could think of.

The Market hall was so crowded that we had to force our way through. As we came to the back, Phil pushed his way to the front, turned to the left and stopped outside a small shop. Written on the window was 'Sandwiches, Tea, Home made cakes' and then on a small board was 'Vegetable Soup' and 'Home made bread available lunch time only.'

"Is this it?" I said to Phil.

"Well, the policeman said he comes here when he's on his rounds and he reckons they serve the best food in town, so don't blame me if it's no good!"

"I don't care what it's like, I'm starving so let's go in."

A bell rang when the door opened and a lady who was standing behind the counter looked over to us.

"Afternoon lads. Five of you, is there? Well, sit where you want and I'll be over to take your orders."

It wasn't a very big room, with only about ten to twelve seats in all. A couple of the tables were already taken so we went over to the wall and pushed two tables together and pulled the seats around. Although it wasn't very big, it was very clean and tidy; the decoration and curtains were showing their age, but they were also clean and well mended. We were just talking amongst ourselves when the lady moved from behind the counter and headed over to our table.

"Glad to see that you've made yourselves at home! Now, what can I get you? We haven't got much, but let's see if we can fix you up."

Looking around the table, her eyes stopped at Phil.

"Now, you look hungry – what would you like?"

We all started to snigger at Phil, who in turn, glared back at us.

"Something I said?"

"No, no," he almost whispered. "Have you got any sandwiches?"

"Yes, what do you want?"

Thinking briefly, Phil replied that he fancied either meat or cheese and some cake with a cup of tea.

"Don't want much, do you?" mocked the lady. "What about the rest of you?"

We all looked at her and replied that we would also have the same.

"Right, I'll see what I can do, then. Can't promise, but I'll have a look," and off she went, disappearing into the back of the shop where we could just make out the faint sound of voices.

We sat in silence as we waited in anticipation as to what might be forthcoming from the kitchen. Within five minutes, a young girl came from the back carrying a large metal tray containing a metal teapot, five mugs, milk, sugar and spoons. She struggled between the other tables to reach ours, so as I was the nearest, I stood up and reached over for the tray, saying, "Let me help you with that – it looks heavy."

"I can manage," she replied tartly, and with that she brushed me to one side and started to unload the tray onto our table. "Mum says if you want any more, just ask, but don't use too much sugar as we're running short. I'll go back and bring your food, if it's ready."

Off she went, skirt flying as if I had offended her with my offer of help. Looking back at the table, the lads had already started pouring out the tea.

"Fancy your chances with her?" grinned Harry.

"Who, me?" I stammered bashfully, "I was only trying to help, that's all."

Those few words then started a barrage of micky-taking and teasing which only stopped abruptly when the young girl appeared again. This time, she arrived with two large plates filled with sandwiches, with her mother following closely behind with some smaller plates and on another large plate, slices of sponge cake. This time, I thought better of offering my help and just sat there while they laid the food out in front of us. However, I did manage a few sideways glances at the girl. I'm sure she caught me looking at her one of the times, and on her way back to the kitchen, she looked back. Our eyes locked and she smiled at me.

"That's it, lads. That's the best I can do under the circumstances. I hope you enjoy it. What are you celebrating, anyway? Someone's birthday?"

"No," I replied quickly. "As a matter of fact, we've all just joined the army and start our training in two weeks. Then it's off to France. We'll show them how it's done, won't we boys?"

The woman stood there, just looking at us for a few minutes, her face going slowly ashen in colour. "But you're not old enough, any of you. Do your parents know yet? What do they say?"

We all glanced sideways at each other and as usual it was left to me to reply. I looked up at the women, whose eyes were beginning to fill with tears.

"We're all old enough, or we will be by the time we have finished our training." I thought briefly and then carried on. "Our parents all knew that as soon as we were old enough, we were joining up, and as our ages are all slightly different, the older ones have waited so that we could all go together."

I thought that a little bending of the truth wouldn't matter, and as we didn't know her, or she us, and the chances of us meeting up again in the future were very remote, not quite telling her the truth wouldn't matter too much.

She heard what I had told her, but it was obvious that she didn't believe me because as she looked around our table, she said "Such young faces, you have. No experience of life. I will pray for you to all come back safely. Now eat up, I have things to do out back."

As she turned and walked away, we noticed her reach into her apron pocket, take out a handkerchief and start wiping her eyes as she disappeared into the kitchen.

We could all make out a gentle sobbing sound followed by some quiet whispering of soothing words. It was quite obvious that our presence that afternoon had caused some unhappy memories to return.

"Well, I'm not waiting any longer," said Phil, "I'm starving."

So, we all tucked into the sandwiches.

There was a good mixture of both meat and cheese and when these were polished off, we all started on the cake. It was delicious and we all commented on how much it tasted like our own mothers' baking. When all the tea was gone, I said that I would pay at the counter, so we all chipped in our money and I got up and went to the front of the shop looking for the woman or her young daughter. Meanwhile, Peter looked at his watch and said with alarm in his voice, "Come on – we'll miss the bus if we don't hurry!"

"Look," I said "you go on and when I've finished here, I'll catch you up."

"Right," said Peter, "No time to argue. Come on lads, let's get going."

They all sprang to their feet and headed for the door. As it opened, the door-bell rang and it rang again when it closed. Still no sign of the woman.

"Excuse me," I said, raising my voice slightly, "Could I pay please? If I don't go soon I'll miss the bus."

Still nothing, so I thought I would leave the money on the counter, but I didn't know how much we owed, so I shouted, "Excuse me please, can I pay the bill?"

I waited for response, but still nothing.

"Well, that's it," I said out loud. "I can't do any more."

As I started for the door, I thought I would go down the passage and knock on the kitchen door, then if she's not there, I'll have to run or I'll miss the bus. As I looked across the small room and went down the side of the counter and entered the passageway, I thought I could hear someone sobbing, and as I approached a door I gently put my ear close to the door, which confirmed my previous thought.

"What do I do now? Knock and go in, or just walk out?"

My mind was turning over the options when the decision was made for me. The door suddenly opened and I found myself looking down at the young girl.

"Oh, it's you!" she said, "I thought I heard someone coming towards the door."

"I'm so sorry to disturb you, only I've been trying to get your attention to pay our bill. The others have gone on and I have to catch them up or I'll miss the bus."

"Come in, please," she said. "It's good of you to take the trouble. There are many others who would not have bothered. I'll just ask my Mum how much you owe".

And with that she went to her extremely distressed mother, and putting her arms around her, she moved closer to her and gently spoke a few words, then waited a short while as there was no reply. She spoke again but all the response she could get was more tears.

"I'm so sorry about this. It's just, well, after she spoke to you and your friends about the War, it brought back things from the past that would have been best left there. You see, I had an older brother who joined up right at the start of the War. He was only 17 1/2 years old. Both Mum and Dad didn't want him to go but he ran away and the next we heard of him was a letter from France. Three weeks later, we had another letter but this time it was from the Army telling us how brave and courageous he had been and how well he had done his duty. But they were also sorry to inform us that whilst engaged in fighting with the enemy, he was seriously wounded and died later on the battle-field. It was such a terrible shock. We couldn't mourn him properly. We never saw his body or had the chance to bury him. Mum managed to be strong for me, but Dad could not come to terms with it and he started drinking. He lost his job and started to row about money. When he lost his temper and could not get any money for drink, he would turn on Mum and start beating her. Mum put up with it for so long, and she knew no reason why, but when he started beating me, she decided to leave him. So we packed our belongings and moved away. We stayed with Mum's sister for a while, then we moved here. We rent the place and live upstairs. It's not very nice, but it's better than other rooms we've seen."

I didn't know what to say. What could I say? I was lost for words. I started to mumble how sorry I was and if we had known, we would not have mentioned the War.

"Look, it's not your fault. None of you knew us or about our problems, so there's nothing to be sorry about. In fact, it's us who should be saying sorry to you. Mum said you were celebrating joining the Army."

" Don't worry about that," I said. "Look, I have to go. I think I might have missed the bus by now, but if I run I might make it."

"There's a short cut if you go out the back," she offered, quickly explaining the way. I followed her to the back door and as she was unbolting it, I put all the money from the lads and me on a table, saying, "I hope this will be enough for the food. If it's not, I'll bring you the rest when we get back." At that, the lady looked up and for a moment stopped crying and said, "You make sure you come back safe and sound. God be with all of you."

The door was then opened and I sprang past the girl.

"Good luck," she shouted, "What's your name?"

"Bill," I shouted, "What's yours?" As I was getting further and further away from her, I couldn't quite make out her name, so I stopped and turned around and shouted, "I can't hear, shout louder."

Then it became clear, her name was Elizabeth. I waved to her several times and she waved back to me and then off I ran again, weaving in and out of piles of rubbish thrown into the entry. I aimed several kicks at big rats as they crossed my path, but only succeeded in tripping myself up. As I dashed into the square, the bus was just pulling away, so I put on a spurt and started waving and shouting. As the bus was only moving slowly, I managed to run alongside it and hit the glass with my hand. Luckily for me, Phil's face came to the window and then the rest of them soon followed. They were all laughing and jumping up and down.

"Stop the bus! Stop the bus!" I shouted frantically, but it was obvious they had no intention of helping me. So, with one final burst I managed to draw up level with the door. To my horror, it was the same driver as this morning.

"That's it," I thought, "he won't stop for me, not after all the fun we had with him on the way here. Still, you never know." So I thumped the door several times to get his attention until he looked sideways and stared at me full on. A broad grin appeared on his face and to my amazement he stopped and opened a door.

"Come on," he said, "I waited a few minutes for you but your friends said to carry on as you were with a young girl."

"Thanks," I shouted down the bus. "Remind me to do something for you one day."

I turned to the driver to to say thanks for stopping. I'd have been in real trouble with Mum and Dad, especially if I'd have had to stay out all night. I reached into my pocket for the bus fare but before I could take it out the driver said, "You can have this one on me. Your friends told me what you came into town for."

He reached over and shook my hand.

"You're all very brave and I hope you'll get back safe and sound. Good luck to you and your friends."

With that, I moved to the back of the bus to say thanks to the others who were still laughing and thought it was great fun. They then asked me why it took so long to pay the bill, along with many other questions, which I refused to answer. Instead, I just sat on my own thinking about the most extraordinary day I had just experienced. Probably the best one of my life so far, actually. I must write down that we may owe money to the sandwich lady when we come back. If I don't, I'll probably forget. Also, I mustn't forget her daughter's name - Elizabeth.

I was drawn out of my thoughts by Peter. He was saying, "Look lads, are we getting together at the weekend as usual?"

We all nodded our approval and within a few minutes the bus had stopped a number of times and there were only three of us left on. Our stop came and as we got off the driver wished us good luck once more and then off he drove into the distance. We stood by the stop for a few minutes, talking about nothing in particular, then split up to go home. Phil and I said nothing as we went up the hill to the cottage. I could see Mum looking out of the window but when she saw me wave at her she moved discreetly away - after all, it wouldn't be right if her two grown sons thought she worried about them. I said to Phil as we walked up the path, "Now, don't forget. Don't say anything until we've thought about what to tell them. Okay?"

Phil nodded as he unlatched the door and went in. Dad was sitting by the fire, sharpening his axe and didn't bother to look up. Mum shouted from the kitchen, "Is that you two? I saw the bus go through the village. I bet you're starving. Did you have a good day?"

"Yes, yes Mum," we both replied.

"Well, Bill, come in here and let's have a look at your new boots. Where did you get them from? How much were they? Come on then, let's have a look."

We both froze. I looked sideways at Phil's blank expression on his face.

"He's not going to be any good at keeping quiet," I thought to myself. After a long pause, I answered. This prompted Dad to stop what he was doing and to look up at us.

"Come on, lad. Answer your Mother, don't keep her waiting."

"Sorry, Dad. Sorry, Mum, but I couldn't get any. We went to all the shops that sell them and they didn't have anything suitable, or in my size."

"Are you sure?" Mum said. "Did you go to the market?"

"Yes, Mum."

"Well, that was a waste of time then."

To my surprise, Phil stepped in saying none of the shops had much at all and when we asked when they might get some more in, they didn't know. All they would say was that it was the Army's fault as they were having all the leather and such stuff to make boots for the servicemen, and at that the moment there's not much left over for anything else. I shot Phil a quick glance and winked at him. I would never have thought of anything like that.

"Ah well," she said, "I suppose it's for a good cause. Now, go and get washed. I'm putting the food out. Go on."

As we moved past, Dad reached up grasping my arm and stopped us both.

"You wouldn't have been trying some of them boots on now, would you?"

"What you mean, Dad?" I said. "You have to be in the Army before they give you boots and uniform, don't you?"

"Just asking, just asking," he replied. "Now go and get washed as Mum told you. By the way, you'll both be working on Sunday to make up for today."

"Yes, Dad," we chorused.

The next few days, working with my father was not the same. In fact, it was never the same again but particularly in the days before our orders arrived. There was an air of closeness and affection between us as had never been shown before. He started to treat me as more of a grown-up than previously, often asking me what I thought about the job instead of just telling me what to do. It was as if he sensed something was not quite right and he was trying to give me years of feelings, emotions and knowledge in just a few days. It was almost as if he knew what was going to happen and it was his way of trying to blot it out from his mind.

Even Phil said he had noticed something strange in Dad's behaviour as we walked through the fields on Saturday night to meet the lads. When we walked into the village, we could see the others waiting for us outside the inn. We often came here as the landlord was not too bothered about who he served, as long as there was no trouble. It was a dimly lit room with only the light from the raging wood fire to see by. Harry went to get the drinks whilst the rest of us found some seats tucked away in the corner. When we all had drinks in our hands, Harry sat down and it was a long while before anyone spoke, we just sat staring into the fire and sipping our drinks.

It was Peter who spoke first.

"Well, has anyone said anything yet?"

Each one of us in turn shook our heads. "No," we mumbled.

"I just don't know what to say," John despaired, "I know it'll break my Mum's heart. I had been thinking of just going and not say anything, then writing to her from the training camp."

"You can't do that!" I exclaimed. I still had the vision of the lady at the tea shop, sobbing her heart out, fresh in my mind.

"None of us should even think about doing that. No, we must all pick our own time and do it properly. That's the only way."

No more was mentioned on the subject, and for the rest of the evening, we just sat around the table, quietly drinking with each of us thinking, but not sharing our thoughts.

"Come on, time to go," I eventually said. "I think we'd best not meet up again until it's time to go, unless our parents want to see us all together, that is."

This was accepted and we all set off in our separate directions.

As we approached our cottage, Phil, who hadn't spoken until now, said, "I can't do it. I can't tell Mum or Dad. Will you do it? I think it will come out better if you tell them. Please. Please don't leave it to me, I just know I can't do it."

I looked sideways and in the dim light coming from the cottage, as we walked up the path, I could just make out the tense and emotionally drawn face of my younger brother, my best friend. How could I say otherwise?

"Leave it to me, Phil. I'll sort it out. No point in both of us getting all upset, now. Come on, in we go."

The next four or five days just flew past and I knew that I was running out of time. Our orders would be arriving any day now, and I had got to do it sooner or later, or it would be too late. I took the opportunity whilst we were taking a break on Saturday from cutting logs for the hospital. Dad had just got his pipe going as we all sat around a small fire.

"Dad, there's something I need to tell you."

"I wondered when you would get round to it. Phil let it slip you'd met a girl when you went into town the other week."

"No, it's not that. I've joined the Army."

He never moved or said anything. He just sat there, drawing on his pipe. It was as if time had stopped for a few moments, then he said , "And when did all this happen, then?"

"When we went into town, we all joined up at the same time."

"You mean Peter, John and Harry went with you, too?" He turned sideways and as he looked at me, I could see the tears welling up in his eyes.

"Not all of you?" he pleaded. "Please don't say all of you."

I waited a moment before saying that we had all joined up together so that we could go together and not be separated.

"There's something else, too, Dad."

"No," he said. "There can't be any more." Then the realisation began to show on his face.

"Oh no, no, not Philip. No, please don't say Philip has joined up too? He's not old enough. None of you are really old enough, but Philip - he's only just turned seventeen. He hasn't long had his birthday. Not Philip, as well?"

"I'm sorry, Dad, but we couldn't stop him. He said if he couldn't come with us, he would join up somewhere else. At least this way, we can look after him when we get there."

Dad's head dropped forward and into his hands. His pipe fell from his mouth to the ground and he started to sob gently. This outpouring of emotion was the last thing I had expected from my father, and it had taken me totally by surprise. I had expected a big argument with a few hasty words, but not this. I had never seen my father, or come to that, any grown man display such emotions and I was at a loss as to what to do or say.

After a few minutes, the sobbing started to subside and he turned to me and said, "Do the pair of you realise what this will do to your Mum? You're her whole world. All she thinks about day and night. All her hopes and dreams are about you two. She'll be so distraught, so inconsolable. I just don't know what we'll do. We've talked about it in the past and she said she was praying the War would be over before you would be old enough to join up. I could tell you were both itching to get out there. Because you're nearly old enough, I tried to talk to her again a few weeks ago but all she would say was 'my boys won't go' and that was all. I tried to tell her you might want to go but she wouldn't listen. With all the sights she sees up at the hospital, she's so frightened it could happen to either of you. She just won't think about it and now this - you're both going. But surely, Phil's too young? It must be a mistake. We could go and see someone about it."

"Dad," I interrupted, "Phil wouldn't thank you for trying to stop him. He would only go and join up somewhere else. At least this way, we will all be together."

"Have any of the others told their parents yet?"

"I don't think so, but we all agreed that we wouldn't just go without a word."

Dad bent over and picked up his pipe, knocking it on the side of the log we were sitting on. Then, taking a burning twig from the fire, he relit it and continued puffing away for a few minutes.

"I don't suppose there is any way or anything I can say that would make you change your minds?"

"No, Dad, this is all we've talked about since the War started. We know we might get injured, or worse still we might not come back. We all know the risks but we're determined to fight for our King and our country, and nothing is going to stop us."

"I can see how determined you are to go through with it, so I won't be standing in your way, but I will be talking with your brother. Now, what about your Mum? When are you going to tell her?"

I thought hard for a few minutes, and then said, "I was hoping you'd tell her for us."

"I thought you were going to say that. When do you think you'll be going?"

"We should get our orders this week, then we think we will report within a couple of days to a training camp."

"So soon?" he said, "I'll tell her tomorrow then, so at least she has a few days to come to terms with it, although God knows what I'm going to say to her. Just tell me one thing, would I be right in thinking your visit to town was more to do with army boots than girls?"

"I think you could say a bit of both would be closer to the mark, Dad."

With that, he stood up.

"Kick that fire out, then we'll finish off here and go home."

I stood up and put the fire out, and as I moved to pass him he put his arms around me and pulled me to him.

"I just want you to know that as well as being afraid of you going, I am also very, very proud that you are my son.

This is a brave thing you and the others are doing. God protect you all and bring you home safely. Now, not a word to anyone about what happened here today. Some people wouldn't understand and I don't want them thinking I am going soft, now do I?"

With that, he released me from his vice-like grip.

"Thanks, Dad," I said. "For everything."

It took about three hours to finish the job and then we made our way home. I could see that Dad was having a hard time in his head. Far too many things to take in all at once, so I didn't speak to him for fear of interrupting his thoughts, as I knew all about the biggest one that he was wrestling with.

Going up the path he said, "I'll take Phil down to the inn for a drink tonight."

Then turning to me, "Only Phil though, not you."

When we got in supper was ready and Mum was pacing up and down.

"You're late," she said, "It's nearly bedtime."

"Away with you, Mother! The job was a bit bigger than I thought that's all, and as for bedtime, I'm going for a drink first. You know I always go on Saturdays. Are you coming too, Mother?"

"Not tonight. I have some sewing to do for the hospital. What about you, Phil?"

Turning from the fire to face Dad, he replied, "I don't mind if you'll stand me a drink."

Dad laughed,

"Don't I always? What about you, Bill? You coming or have I overworked you?"

"That will be the day!" I said. "Thanks for the offer but I am saving my money for better things."

"I bet it's that girl we met in town," Phil remarked. "Planning to see her again, are you?"

Mum butted in, "Now leave him alone. He can spend his money on whatever he wants. Come on now, eat your supper before I clear the table or you'll all go hungry."

Supper finished and the table cleared, Dad went upstairs to change, and then he and Phil went off for a drink. I sat in front of the fire gazing deep into the burning embers. I could hear in the background various noises coming from the kitchen as Mum tidied everything away. Then she came and sat at the other side of the fire, having brought her sewing basket and a pile of what looked like old rags.

"What are you doing now?" I asked. "Patching more clothes?"

Nodding her head, she looked up, "Yes, I think I am the only one who can sew up there. I always seem to get the biggest pile. Still, I don't mind. Some of those poor lads have got nothing and no one to care for them. I don't know what will happen to them when they're discharged. It's such a shame. Anyway, why aren't you going out? It's not like you to stay in on a Saturday night? Has it got anything to do with this girl you met?"

"Oh Mum, don't go listening to Phil. You know he just likes to joke. No, I'm just a bit tired, so I thought I'd have an early night."

"Why's that then? Is your father overworking you? I'll speak to him when he gets back, if you want?"

"No, it's not that, Mum. I think I might be coming down with something, so I thought if I went to bed early I might shake it off."

"Do you want me to mix you something up then?"

"Not yet, Mum. I'll just sit here by the fire for a bit, then go up."

"It's up to you," Mum said. "If you're no better in the morning, you can have something then."

After about an hour, I wished Mum good night and went to bed with so much on my mind I knew I wouldn't sleep, at least not until I had spoken to Phil. One thing though stuck out from the rest and I ripped at piece of paper from an old school reading book and scribbled MARKET, OWE MONEY, ELIZABETH. Folding the paper up, I tucked it between the floorboards on my side of the bed. I wouldn't forget where I'd put it, as that had always been my secret hiding place. Lying back in bed, I blew out the candle and waited for them to come home. It seemed like a lifetime until I heard their footsteps coming towards the cottage. The squeaky gate opened and closed and they walked up the gravel path towards the door. I listened intensely to see if I could hear voices. Normally, after having a drink, there would be incessant talking, joking, laughter and general larking about but tonight it seemed was different. There were no voices to be heard, just footsteps. Instead of opening the door and going in, they stopped a little way away from the entrance. I could just make out hushed voices exchanging a few hurried words, which I couldn't understand. Then they moved forward and came quietly into the cottage.

For a few minutes, all I could hear was the three of them engaged in general conversation downstairs. Then, I heard heavy footsteps coming up the stairs, so I shut my eyes and buried my head in the pillow. As the footsteps approached the door, I wondered who would come in. I was greatly relieved when the door opened and a voice said, quietly, "Bill, Bill, it's only me. Are you awake?"

I sat up quickly. "Yes, of course I am. Do you think I could sleep when I knew what was going on?"

"Oh, thanks for warning me about what was going to happen."

"I had no time, did I? Anyway, what happened? What did he say?"

"Well, to be honest, I was surprised. I thought he would go mad but he was really very softly spoken. He said he wished that I'd spoken to him about it first. Then he asked if I'd thought about how it would affect Mum. He understood why I wanted to go with you and the lads, and said how proud he was of all of us, and was I sure that this was exactly what I wanted to do and had I thought about it properly. Of course, I said I had and it's what I want to do more than anything. He asked me if I'd think again, for Mum's sake. Then we sat in silence for about thirty minutes, and eventually I turned to him and said that I was going with you and the lads, and that was final. We're going to fight the enemy and do our best and then we're all coming back home. We've all promised to look after each other and come back together. I said I couldn't let you down now."

Phil paused and then started again.

"Dad kept looking into his empty glass, then he got up, picked up both of our glasses, and looked at me and said that he agreed that I couldn't let you down and off he went to fetch another drink. After that, he hardly spoke until we came back, then just before we came in he said not to mention a word to Mum as he's going to tell her. What about you? What did he say to you?"

"Well, pretty much about the same really but he was very upset about you going because of your age. Anyway, that's all over now and he knows we'll be going very soon, so he'll have to tell Mum over the next day or so."

Suddenly, Phil asked, "I wonder if the others have told their parents yet? I hope so because they're leaving it a little late otherwise."

Phil undressed and climbed into bed, saying "Do you think it will be all right with Mum?"

I thought for a while, "I don't know. I really don't know. Now, come on, let's go to sleep and see just what happens."

After a very restless night, I became aware that as daylight started to pour into the room, Dad was standing at the end of the bed.

"Is anything wrong? Is it Mum?," I said springing upright, hurriedly.

"No, no," he said. "I used to do this when you were both little. I would stand here for hours, looking over you. I just thought this could be my last chance to look over you and protect you. It just seemed so fitting on the Lord's day. You see, when you come back you won't be my boys, you'll be men and I can't watch over men now, can I?"

Again, he was very close to tears.

"Don't worry, Dad. We'll all be back soon. Just you see, and we always will be your boys. Both of us will be very upset with you if you stop protecting and looking over us."

At that, his face started to change and the outline of a smile began to form.

"Not when you're a grown man and married, I won't. Anyway, I'm going to church this morning with your Mum for the early service, so you can either get your own breakfast or wait until we get back. We need some logs chopping for the fire and the tools need cleaning and sharpening, so there's plenty to do while you're waiting."

"I'm ready to go. Hurry up or we'll be late," shouted Mum.

I smiled at Dad and nodded, "I'm coming," he shouted. "I'll catch you up."

"No you won't. I'll wait. This is the first time in years you're coming to church with me and I want to enjoy every step."

Dad laughed out loud.

"Wasn't the last time Phil's christening?"

"Probably," she replied. "Still, I want to make the most of it."

He turned to walk away.

"Thanks, Dad," I said.

He hesitated for a moment, and then carried on down the stairs and out of the front door. I was straining to hear the last of their footsteps as they made their way down the road to church, with Mum so happy to have her beloved husband on her arm and Dad knowing of the huge burden of sadness and bad news that he was going to have to break to her. Would things ever be the same again? I think not. Things were definitely going to change but in such a way that I could never think possible.

We got up, washed, dressed and decided that Mum's breakfast was worth waiting for, so we got on with the jobs Dad wanted doing. Phil was sawing and chopping wood over by the old barn when I heard the door open. It was probably two or three hours since Mum and Dad had gone out. I was outside the kitchen sharpening an axe when I glanced up. Mum was looking out of the window at Phil, then she moved her gaze to me. I looked back down to what I was doing. Just that fleeting glimpse from her eyes and I could tell she knew, and it was so obvious she'd been crying. She suddenly looked fraught and full of pain and anguish. Never before had I seen such a transformation occur in such a short space of time, but I think the worst of it was the thought that it was her own sons that had brought this pain, sorrow and anguish, and all the other mixed emotions that come with such news. I don't think I will ever forgive myself for what Mum was going through and all that she would experience in the coming weeks and months ahead.

After about an hour, Dad came out.

"Come on, you two, there's food on the table."

As Phil came over, he looked at me and we both looked at Dad but there was no sign of what to expect. Mum was just going upstairs as we both entered the kitchen and sat down.

"She's not feeling too well at the moment, so eat your food before it gets cold," Dad said, "then you can finish your jobs. Have you got a game on this afternoon? Are the lads coming over?"

"We've got nothing arranged," I said, "but we might take a walk over to Peter's."

"Good idea," said Dad in a low voice. "It will give your Mum some time on her own to come to terms with it. Now eat up and be off with you."

We finished eating and cleared away.

Once outside, Dad said in a low voice "Don't worry about the jobs, clear off and don't come back until supper time."

The evening was closing in and it was nearly dark when we eventually came home. I very carefully opened the gate and once we were in the garden we made sure there was no noise when it closed. Phil ran in front to look through the window, then came over very quietly, saying, "I can't see either of them. They must be in the kitchen."

"Come on then," I said, pushing Phil towards the door.

"No, not me," he said. "You go first, you're the eldest."

This went on for a few minutes, each trying to push the other through the door. Neither of us had noticed but as we were jostling near the door, it had opened and Mum was standing there watching us in amazement.

"What's the matter with you two? I'm not going to bite your heads off! Now come on in and shut that door. You're letting out all the heat. Come on, don't just stand there, hurry up."

At that, we both pushed our way through the door and pushed it shut behind us.

Mum said, "I remember when you were little you used to carry on like that when you'd done something naughty. You'd argue as well about who was going to tell me. So, what have you done and who's going to tell me now?"

From within the kitchen, Dad said somberly, "Now Mother, you know what's going on and there's not much more to be said. Let them come through and have their supper. Then maybe we can all talk a little later on."

At that, Mum turned and went into the kitchen.

"Your Dad managed to get a little rabbit meat and I've baked an apple pie for afters, so hurry up or it will go cold and spoil."

We quickly hung up our coats and sat down at the table. Without turning from what she was doing, Mum said, "I hope you washed your hands. Just because you're going in the Army doesn't mean you stop being clean."

All three of us got up again from the table and went to the sink. As we sat down again, Mum said, "Thank you. Now, here you are and don't waste any."

We all ate with heavy hearts. Mum had excelled herself and under different circumstances she would certainly have been praised. Indeed, although I am not religious, it felt more like the last supper. When all was cleared away, we settled down by the fire, all tensely waiting for the first words, and wondering who was going to utter them. Finally, it was Mum who broke the silence.

"Well you two, your Dad has told me really all there is to tell. I know that you won't change your minds, you are your father's sons and just as stubborn. What I will say to you both though is this. I cried tears of joy when you were born; I cried tears of happiness when you were christened; I have thanked God every day of your lives. Today, I have cried tears of sorrow. When you go to War, I shall pray to God to keep you safe. I want you both to promise me you will come home. It matters not what condition your body or mind is in, as long as you are alive. You see, I don't want the next tears that I shed to be because of the news that you have been killed. Now, that's all I'm going to say to you both."

It took a few minutes for her words to sink in, but almost as one we both got up and sat on the floor on either side of her, laying our heads in her lap where she cradled us like two newborn infants.

"We will come back," I whispered. "We will, I promise."

For what seemed like an age, we just stayed where we were, with Mum occasionally stroking our hair, and she strongly resisting the ever-present urge to let the tears flow. But she was made of stronger stuff, which put her in good stead for the time ahead.

It was Dad who eventually broke the silence.

"Who wants a cuppa then?"

Mum declined and announced that she was going up to bed early, and not that long after, once we'd downed the last dregs of our tea, we decided that we would also go up earlier than usual as well.

As we undressed in our room, Phil said to me, "How do you feel about Mum and what she said?"

"Very guilty," I replied.

Phil continued, "I'm so sorry for what I've done to the both of them, and I'm really sad for all the hurt that Mum's going to go through, but saying all that, I think I've made the right decision about going. I want to make them both proud of me, but most of all I want to come home in one piece when it's all finished. What about you?"

"I haven't really thought about it that deeply but I think what you say is about right."

The next couple of days came and went with nothing out of the ordinary really happening, with the exception of Mum who seemed to be spending nearly all her spare time mending our clothes and darning socks. Still, it kept her mind off what lay ahead. Harry came up to see us on the Tuesday night. He didn't stay long, only to say that he'd told his parents. Also, he'd seen John who had also spoken to his family. Neither had seen Peter though, so they didn't know anything more. I told Harry briefly what our Mum and Dad had said.

"Sounds pretty much the same for me and John. John said his Mum is going to burn his orders, so he's trying to get them sent to me, then he can tell his Dad and leave without his Mum knowing when he's going, but only if she doesn't come round to the idea."

Wednesday came and went. Thursday was pretty much the same except that Dad and I were working close to Phil so we waited for him to finish. We all walked home together, larking about and having a laugh. Dad kept telling us to pack it up and stop messing about. Secretly, I think he was enjoying it as much as we were. It probably reminded him of when we were youngsters and we all used to have a laugh together.

When we all reached the door, we both said to Dad, "After you." Then for several more minutes, we stood there saying "After you," " No after you."

Eventually, Phil and I both pushed our way through the door together.

"Quick, coats off, boots off. Go into the kitchen to see Mum and then supper."

Dad was standing behind Mum who was sitting at the table. They were holding hands and staring at two brown envelopes laying side by side in front of Mum. Dad said they had arrived about mid-morning and that Mother had been sitting there since they came.

"She's hoping that if she sits there long enough, they'll go away. So, there's no supper ready but we'll all get stuck in and see what we can get."

Later, we sat down to eat a hastily-prepared supper, which considering the circumstances was not too bad. Although Mum never moved, her spoken instructions were a great help. She ate nothing though. She just sat there, staring at the envelopes. We finished eating and cleared away.

"It's no good just looking at them. Pass Bill's over and we'll see what it says."

For a short time, Mum never moved. Then Dad reached over, saying, "Come on, Mother, it's not going to go away."

Very reluctantly, she passed the envelopes to the both of us. I was the first to open my letter. I looked at Dad and then at Mum.

"Tuesday," I said. "I've to report to the training camp by 5 o'clock. There's a train pass, as well. It's up in North Yorkshire, I think."

And passing the envelope and papers to Dad, he confirmed what I'd said.

"Looks like you will have to get the bus to town, then walk right across to catch the ten o'clock, then change at Crewe junction for York. It says here you will be met at the station and then taken to the camp. There's also a list of things you can take with you - clothes, wash things, personal items, you know the sort of things.

Mum said hurriedly, "I'll have the list, so I can make sure you've got it all. We'll have to see if we can borrow something to put it all in. There might be something up at the hospital that I can borrow. I'll ask when I go in tomorrow."

Phil opened his letter and said it looked the same as mine, and again he passed it over to Mum to read.

The rest of the evening disappeared quickly. The orders were read again and again. Mum kept looking at the clothes list, saying what we had and had not got. She kept telling us what we would have to try on and what we would have to get. Eventually, Dad said, "Hold on, hold on. It says this is only a suggested list, as they will supply all uniforms, clothes and equipment that they'll need when are they get to camp."

"I don't care," Mum said. "I'm not sending my boys off to War without all the things they need."

Thinking back, I now believe we did the right thing by letting her carry on amassing all she could from sources that our new Quarter Master would be envious of, for this task kept her constantly busy and kept her mind occupied.

Both Friday and Saturday were normal working days, which turned out to be non eventful. Given that we would be going away on Tuesday, I'm not sure what I was expecting on these last few days at home but in my eyes it wasn't really normal.

After breakfast on Sunday, we chopped wood, cleaned and sharpened tools, as we always had done. Then, Dad found an old football round about, so we spent the next hour or so having a kick around in the garden. Every so often, I looked over to the cottage and saw Mum looking across at us. I don't know what she was thinking. I think maybe with us larking about, laughing and enjoying ourselves, she thought that it was all a dream and that nothing was going to happen.

"Food's ready," Mum hollared. "Wash your hands, I'm just putting it out. Come on."

Phil picked up the ball and we chased him back to the cottage. Filing into the kitchen, we washed our hands and sat around the table.

"Come on, Mum," Phil jibed, " I'm starving."

"You've never been any different," Dad said smiling. "You're the only baby I've ever known who cried and cried for a second lot of milk."

Phil looked down sheepishly as we all laughed at him.

"What are the mugs for, Mother?" Dad said. "It's not Easter yet, is it?"

"No," she said. "Mr Moore brought round some of his home-made cider. He said he wanted the lads to have a drink on him before they go, and he said to wish you good luck and he'll see you when you get back."

"Well, well," said Dad. "He makes some of the best cider around these parts. It's very kind of him. You can go and thank him yourselves, boys. Now Phil, go and get it, I can't wait to taste it."

As we ate our food and drank the fine cider, the heavy atmosphere that had been with us started to lift. We were now behaving more like a family should behave in these troubled times, with an unknown future that faced us all. Our strong family bond was getting more resilient and our feelings for each other could not have been stronger. Whether or not these feelings had more to do with the cider we were all enjoying, it mattered very little. The main thing was that we were all pulling together, so we couldn't fail to come through.

As we cleared away, Mum surprised us with the request that we all go to the evening church service together. She knew none of us would be too happy at this request, but she said it would mean a lot to her if we made the effort. Surprisingly, without any thought, we all said yes at the same time. This pleased Mum greatly and all afternoon, as we all relaxed around the fire, she seemed to be in a joyful mood.

It was nearly dark as we walked towards the church but by the dim lights coming from inside, we could make out quite a large crowd, with more families just like us approaching from different directions. We all seemed to be drawn to the hazy, warm glow. We were greeted by so many people outside the church. Some we knew better than others, but the warmth in their voices said it all.

71

The little church was full. I've never heard, or on the odd occasion when I have attended, seen it like this. There were so many people, families, and even some soldiers and nurses from the hospital. People had come from all the surrounding villages, both near and far; many faces we knew, many we didn't. I looked on in great wonder and contemplated why is it that only at times of great trouble or in War times are people drawn to the church, but in normal times when the crops fail and people are poor and starving, the church is empty?

I was just trying to find an answer to this question when the vicar came into the church and walked up the aisle to the pulpit. The service started and after a number of Bible readings and hymns, the vicar then read his own sermon condemning the War and our enemies. He asked for mercy for all the innocent people caught up in the War; all the sick and the wounded, and that they may be granted a speedy recovery. He asked that all the troops, from both home and abroad, be spared the horrors of the battlefields, wherever they maybe. Finally, may God in his wisdom grant victory to the righteous. God save the King.

After a short pause, another hymn was sung, which I hoped would be the last. While the singing was taking place, I couldn't help but wonder if by chance, somewhere in a small village in Germany, a similar service was being conducted. I wondered which God they prayed to and more importantly, which God would win the War. I was brought back to my senses by Mum, who was shaking my arm. I looked at her and she motioned me to look to the front. On doing so, I saw that standing in front of the vicar were Peter, John and Harry, and Phil was walking up to join them. Two other lads, who I didn't know, were also walking towards them. I looked down at Mum and she quietly said, "Didn't you hear your name called? Go on, up you go and join them. Go on, go on."

Looking around again at the large number of people, I hesitated. This was not for me. I didn't like this kind of thing and was very put out and nervous. Mum knew this and took hold of my cold, trembling hand. Clasping her warm, soft hand, I looked down at her again.

"I know, I know," she said. "This will probably be the hardest thing you'll have to do. Just follow your brother; your friends are waiting for you. Just fix your eyes on them and you'll be fine."

I let go of her hand and headed towards the front. As I got closer, I noticed that the vicar was smiling at me. He knew what I was like at times such as this. He knew he would have to give me a little extra time as he had in the past, many times before. I came alongside Phil and he looked sideways at me. He smiled and winked and then we all looked forward towards the altar. The vicar stood in front of us, looking at the congregation.

"You all know these lads and their families. In fact, I can say with pride, I baptized all of them and have watched them grow from boys into fine men. On Tuesday, they are going away to fight in the War. Now, only God knows what is going to happen to them over there, as it is beyond our human minds' capacity to try to imagine the kind of horrors awaiting these young men. I have a little prayer, which I think says it all. So, let's pray together. God, we ask you to look over our young sons as they fight the evil trying to take away our homes and lives. Grant them the strength to be courageous, brave and strong; to show mercy and compassion to our enemy and all human beings. May they come through their darkest times and return home to their families and friends, untouched and unscarred in any way. May your love and kindness flow over our loved ones left behind, and grant them strength to carry their load until the final Day of Judgment arrives. Amen. I want you all to know that the church will never be closed for prayer from now on.

There will be candles burning until they return and you can always come to see me at any time, night or day."

He then came to each of us, saying our name and touching our shoulders.

"May God speed your safe return home. Now go back to your families."

When this was all finished, he looked out over the packed church.

"Now, before you go, I shall expect to see all of you who can be there in the tavern tomorrow night so that we can give these boys a good send off. Bless you all and good night."

After we'd passed through the crowd of well-wishers and had shaken many, many hands, we passed the lads with their families. Stopping for a short while, just to make sure they were coming tomorrow night, we said our goodnights and carried on towards home. It was a very cold night and the sky was clear and full of stars. Phil said, "There's a good frost on the way tonight. What do you think, Dad?"

"You could be right," was his reply. "Might even snow over the next day or two. Still, it won't bother you two. You'll be in nice warm army huts with big hot stoves and your own bed. No more sharing, either."

"Don't say that," said Mum, "or they won't want to come home."

Walking up to the door, Mum stopped, turned around and looked up at the sky saying, "Do you know, I'm going to look at the stars every night at the same time. It'll remind me of tonight, our last night together as a family and if both of you do the same, wherever you are, we can pretend we are a family once again."

She gripped a hand of both of us as tightly as she could, "Don't forget to look at the stars. I'll always be here. Now, come on, let's have our supper and early bed. There's a lot to do in the morning."

"Come on, you two! Time to get up! Just because there's no work today doesn't mean you can lie in there all day."

"What time is it, Mum?" I groaned as I raised my head up to see Mum standing in the doorway.

"Turned eight o'clock. Your Dad's gone out to work and your breakfasts will be ready in ten minutes. Now wake your brother and have a wash. Come on, hurry up. There's a lot to be done."

At that, she turned and clattered noisily down stairs and carried on preparing our food with just as much noise. I think she wanted to make sure we got up out of bed. Turning over, I gave Phil a couple of shakes.

"Breakfast's nearly ready. Come on, time to get up."

I pulled on my shirt and trousers and looked out of the window over the fields. With my hand, I rubbed away the ice, which had formed on the inside of the glass. Just as we had predicted last night, there had been a hard frost, and now there was also a light covering of snow. In the distance, I just caught sight of someone going into the woods, and looking out over the fields I could make out footprints coming back towards our cottage.

Must be Dad. I wonder why he's gone that way. I'll miss this view in spring and summer. The colours are glorious. The trees and hills in the distance – there's no finer place to be. Then everything changes for autumn and winter, different colours all over. Crisp winter mornings, snowy winter evenings. Oh, how I'll miss this place. Mum and Dad, as well. All this is my life, I don't know that I want anything else. There is so much for me here, I know in my heart though that I will come back.

I was still daydreaming when Mum came back into our room.

"Look at you two," she said. "One still fast asleep and the other staring out of the window. Fine pair of soldiers you'll make. Wake up Phil! I'm putting your breakfast out now, so hurry or it will be cold."

I spun around, "Sorry, Mum. I was just thinking about..."

"I know," she said softly. "It'll all still be here waiting for you to come back to."

With that, I jumped on Phil, grabbed a pillow and spent a few minutes waking him up!

It certainly was a busy day. After we'd cleared away from breakfast, we had a great many visitors call to wish us well. Most of them brought small gifts for us, useful things like socks, hankies, tooth brushes, tin and bottle openers, all sorts of things that would be handy. The rest of the time was spent sorting out what clothes to take and trying things on. Mum was busy fussing around but eventually we managed to get everything all together.

"What can we put it all in, Mum?"

"Just a minute, I've got just the thing. One of the officers at the hospital got them for me."

A few minutes later, she came in with two brand new army kitbags. Here you are, I think these will do just fine."

"Thanks, Mum. What will we do without you?"

By the time we'd packed all our stuff, we heard the back door open and Dad's voice shouted upstairs, "I'm home, Mother! It's going to be a bad night. It's freezing now and just starting to snow. Lads all done ready for the morning?"

"Just about," was the reply. "Can you bring in some more firewood before you take your boots off?"

When we came downstairs, Dad was filling up the wood box with an armful of logs, saying, "That'll do you for the night while we're out."

Mum looked over her shoulder and smiled at him. "It's all right for some, enjoying themselves while I'm stuck at home mending clothes."

" You know it's just for the men. It's tradition in the village."

"I know," she said. "I know, I'm just pulling your leg. Now come on, sit down and we'll have supper, it's nearly ready."

Supper finished, we cleared away and set off down the hill towards the pub. It was a bad night and both Phil and I slipped and fell several times, much to the amusement of Dad who never slipped once. As we approach the pub, we felt we were being drawn into a warm, safe and loving place where we knew everyone, and they knew us. From birth, they had watched us grow up and they were part of our lives now, possibly talking to us for the last time. But however much sorrow and apprehension they had there was a determination not to show it, and instead to make our last night one to remember.

It certainly was one to remember as they talked about that night for many, many years later. We, the brave soldiers, never paid for any of our drinks. As soon as our glasses were emptied, they were refilled. There was singing, games and fooling around. Some of the old men told us tales of the earlier campaigns that they had been involved with. Others told stories of local heroes, long ago passed away. There were tales of girls and women they had known in their youth and as the night wore on, the tales and songs got saucier and saucier.

When the time came to eventually leave, even with all the drink that had been consumed, the mood quickly changed from jollity to sobriety. As we shook hands and exchanged best wishes and goodbyes with everyone, traces of sadness could clearly be seen in the sympathetic, smiling faces that we passed by on our way out. As Dad opened the door, an icy blast, which instantly chilled you to the bone, hit us hard. There was a heart-warming cheer that came from within, one which I was never to forget and in the dark days to come it would bring me comfort at some of my lowest times.

Getting back home proved to be quite a tricky feat. After many slips, slides and falls by all three of us this time, we finally got to the door which was opened by Mum who was standing, larger-than-life on the doorstep. She looked at Dad saying, "I haven't seen you this bad since Phil was christened. What sort of a father are you bringing your son's home like this? I heard you as you came out of the inn, and I bet so did most of the village. Come on, hurry up in before you freeze to death. Look at your clothes, they're soaked - been swimming, as well? These are your best clothes. You're wearing them when you go tomorrow. What am I going to do with them? Right," she said, "get them all off and up to bed, all of you. Now, no talking back. Come on, come on, don't be shy you two. I've seen it all before. Now up to bed, you've got a long day ahead of you tomorrow, so get as much sleep as you can."

A brave new world

Chapter 3

I won't say it was one of the best night's sleep I've ever had, but once I had dropped off it wasn't until Mum came to wake us that I realised just how heavily I had slept.

"Your clothes are downstairs by the fire. Breakfast's nearly ready. You've got about an hour before you have to catch the bus."

I woke Phil and told him the same. We both lay there for a few minutes just staring at the ceiling.

Phil said, "I suppose we'd better get up or Mum will skin us alive again."

"Race you," I shouted, and we both shot out of bed, dived downstairs, still getting dressed and sat at the table arguing over who had won.

Dad came in with more logs for the fire.

"You're up then? I thought you might miss the bus. Your Mum's been up all night pressing your clothes."

We hadn't noticed, we were too excited at the thought of what lay ahead.

"Thanks, Mum," we both echoed. "Is breakfast nearly ready? We'll miss the bus if you don't hurry."

"No you won't, more's the pity," she said. "Here it is. Now take your time and don't rush it."

"Aye," Dad agreed, "it'll be the last good meal you'll get until you come home. Now, listen you two. Me and your Mum have been talking about this day and we've decided we'll say our goodbyes here at the cottage. We won't be coming down to the bus to see you go. We both think it's for the best. Hope you two can understand our reasons?"

I looked at Phil, then said, "Whatever you and Mum want to do is fine by us. It's such a cold day anyway we wouldn't want you standing around waiting."

With that, we finished eating, cleared away and went upstairs to get our stuff.

Bags and coats by the front door, we turned to Dad and faced a barrage of hugs, back-slapping and handshaking.

"Where's Mum?" Phil asked

"Just coming, just coming," she said as she came noisily downstairs. "I nearly forgot something. I know you've never been interested in the Church, just like your father," she said, glancing sideways at Dad, who moved uneasily on his feet, "but I want each of you to have one of these as a good luck charm." She handed us both a small silver cross and chain each. "They should fit. They belonged to my mother and before that her mother. They've brought us all good luck in some form or another, so hopefully they'll look after you two. Now, promise you'll wear them and bring them back home safely with you when the War is over? Now come here both of you."

We hugged and cried as we said our last goodbyes, then it was off down the path to the road. We both stopped, turned and waved as the top of the hill was the last place we could see them clearly. We stood waving and shouting for a few minutes, then Phil touched my arm, "Come on, the bus is coming."

At that, we turned and ran, slipping and sliding down the bank and through the village. People who saw us shouted good luck, hurry up back, but we had no time to stop and thank them, so we just waved and carried on running.

Jumping onto the bus, we made our way to the back as usual and as we drove off I just caught sight of the cottage roof and smoking chimney but it was soon gone as we sped on our way. This morning's memories would stay with me for a long time to come, with the added uncomfortable thought that possibly one or both of us may not be destined to return home. With these and many other thoughts flooding through my mind, I only subconsciously acknowledged the others getting on the bus, and it was only when we came to the end of the journey that I became more aware of my surroundings. As to be expected, the lads took the mickey out of me as we got off the bus and started the long walk across town to the station. It took nearly an hour to get there and as we walked onto the platform you could not help but notice how many young lads were there waiting. Phil said, "I wonder if they're all going to the same camp as us?"

"Probably," replied Harry. "I think this train is pretty much non-stop to the camp from here."

After we'd stood around for a while, a platform guard made his way through the crowd looking at everyone's travel tickets. As he got closer, we could hear him telling some people that the train was already very full and that the first passengers to get on would be army recruits, and only then if there were any spare seats others would be let on. One posh-looking man and woman started to complain. The guard looked at them and said, "Are you going to fight for your country, sir?" There was a brief pause when nothing was said. "I thought not, sir," said the guard and walked away. Moving over to us, he grunted, "Can't stand those types. Always moaning. Still, that shut him up. Now, travel passes, please lads. Are you all going to the same camp?"

We nodded at him as he checked our passes.

"Thanks lads and good luck to you all. I'll look out for you when you come back."

Then off he went making his way up the platform. A short time later he came back down again.

"Stand back, please everyone. The train's coming in. Stand back, please"

Through a huge cloud of smoke and steam billowing from the engine, the carriages slowly passed the platform and came to a halt. We all stood staring at this huge monster. We'd never seen a train so close up nor had we ever ridden on one so this was going to be a rare treat for us all. We started to board the train and it was soon very clear there wasn't going to be enough room for all of us. As we'd stood back looking at the train, other people had bordered and there was now no room. At that moment the guard came over.

"What's up lads? No room? Hang on. I'll just check who's on board. Don't worry, it won't go without you."

He jumped on and after a few minutes we heard raised voices, and shortly after three men got off, closely followed by the man and woman he had spoken to before. As the guard stepped off the train, we heard him say to the man, "The station manager's office is just over there, sir. I'm sure he'll be delighted to see you."

Looking over to us, he shouted, "Over here, lads. Five seats in first class await you."

He then wandered off to the back of the train with a huge grin on his face. A few minutes later, with our luggage stowed away and sitting in the best seats, the whistle blew and we were on our way. The train pulled slowly out of the station and gradually started to pick up speed.

As we passed small towns and villages, people stood watching and waving. After about an hour or so, a ticket collector came through checking out travel passes again. After a look at our passes, he said there would be no need to change trains as this one had been re-routed and it was now non-stop to York to make sure that the volunteers got there before nightfall. We were now due in York at about 3.30pm. Even though we had never been on a train before, after about three hours we were all starting to get a little fed up. We had some food with us, which we started to swap and eat which took about half an hour, so there wasn't really that much time left after that. Peter had some playing cards with him and we soon became engrossed in a game. In fact, we were so occupied, we hardly noticed the train slowing down as it pulled into York station.

"Come on, lads," the guard said. "This is your stop."

Peter collected the cards and stuffed them into his pocket.

Grabbing all our things together we piled out onto the platform, and just like lambs we followed all the other young men making their way out of the station. As we came closer to the way out, we could hear a lot of shouting which became more apparent as we were led forward. There were a number of soldiers standing beside army trucks, calling out names from lists and getting people loaded into the vehicles. When the trucks were full, they were driven away. We stood by the station entrance for a few minutes and it wasn't long before a soldier came over to us and barked at Harry, "What's your name, soldier?"

Harry replied quite quickly and the soldier checked his list.

"Over there," he shouted. "Get your stuff on to that truck, and in future you call me Sergeant, got it?"

Then, turning to the rest of us he worked his way down his list. Luckily, we all boarded the same truck and were soon on our way. It took about two hours to get the camp and by the time we got through all the sentries and finally stopped by a group of huts, it was dark and you couldn't see much at all. The sergeant opened the back of the truck and shouted at us all to get off and line up with all the others who were already there. As we lined up, the trucks drove off and we waited in silence for the rest of the convoy to arrive.

After three more trucks had pulled up, the sergeant stood in front of us all and shouted, "Welcome to York-moore Amy Training Camp. On behalf of your King and Countrymen, I thank you for volunteering. Now that's out of the way, there are a couple of bits of bad news I have to tell you. First, we haven't got enough huts for you all, so would all city and town dwellers take two steps forward."

At least two-thirds of the men stepped forward. The sergeant looked at the line and shouted, "Thank you for your honesty. Corporal, march these townies off to the tented camp. The rest of you stay here in the huts. Oh, and by the way, the cookhouse is shut, so I'll see you at breakfast in the morning at 6.30. Fall them out, Corporal. They're in the army now."

Each hut had room for thirty men, so we divided up and a soldier took us to our new abode. He opened the door and lighting a candle, led us all in.

"Well lads, this is your home for the next six months. There are more candles on the table. Make yourselves at home. The wash hut and ablutions are over the other side of the parade ground. Don't forget breakfast is at 6.30 and don't be late - it's a long time until the next meal."

With that, he turned around, stuck the candle on a shelf and slammed the door behind him. Slightly hesitantly, we all started to spread about, taking a candle each. We then each claimed a bed and started looking around the hut. As well as the bedsteads, each one had a mattress stuffed with straw, one pillow also stuffed with straw and one very rough blanket. There were a couple of hooks on the wall and an old box at the bottom of each bed. There were three long rough wooden tables and about sixteen wooden chairs. There was a small wooden shelf by each bed covered in candle wax. At the other end of the hut, there was a second door and last but not least, in the middle of the building was a large, wood-burning stove.

"That'll come in handy," I said to the lads. "We'll soon find some wood when we get settled in."

And settle in we did over the following three to four weeks. In our spare time, we begged, borrowed and stole everything needed and turned our hut into a little palace that was the envy of the rest of the camp. Even the Sergeant and several corporals marvelled at our ability to always manage to acquire our little extras. In fact, when they got to know us better they would come round and join us at our late-night suppers. Rabbit stew being a favourite, amongst many other choices. With what little food the army gave us, our extras were a necessity and any surplus was always good for trading with.

The first few days turned out to be the hardest whilst at the training camp. Amongst other things, we were learning to march, run for miles, being shouted at from dawn-to-dusk, finding our way around and collecting army kit as and when it arrived. At the same time, we got the hut sorted out and we received most of our goods, although we still only drilled with wooden rifles. Getting real ones was still a few weeks away, yet most of us had worked out our left from right on the parade ground, along with who to salute to and who not, and gradually things were starting to become clearer. There were drills, running and PT during the day, then hut and kit cleaning at night. Gradually, you could see the change from civilian to soldier.

I wrote home a couple of times and had a letter from Mum. All was well, but they both missed us a lot. Mum said it had hit Dad more than she had realised. Some days he was very low and stayed around the cottage instead of going to work, but she hoped that this would soon get better, especially if we got home on leave before we went to France. Home leave, I thought - that would be good before we go as there isn't any leave from camp here, except if we want to walk into the nearest town, which is actually about fifty miles there and back.

The mundane and boring daily routine suddenly changed when about ten weeks into training we were issued with brand new rifles. As they were bigger and heavier than our wooden ones, quite a number of men dropped them on the parade ground. The reaction of the Drill Sergeants was explosive. Pay was docked, extra drills and running was ordered, even cutting the grass with penknives and cleaning the toilets was not an uncommon punishment. We were then issued with bayonets, which in turn led to another practice drill. I don't think any of us had really thought about killing someone close up, but when you're practicing with your bayonet and sticking it into straw dummies, it suddenly hits you, what if?

As ammunition was desperately short, we didn't have too many trips to the range. However, for us five lads it wasn't too bad. We were all crack shots and had been shooting all types of game from an early age, so after a few times at the range we were classed as needing no further practice. However, there were other weapons that we trained on for a number of weeks.

We were just over five months into our training and most of our talk was of home leave. We reckoned that after three more weeks of training, we would be on our way. There were rumours going around saying leave was anything between one and three weeks, so it was well worth looking forward to. I had just started to write to Mum one night and tell her about the leave when the hut door was roughly pushed open and the Sergeant and two corporals marched in.

"Stand by your beds. Officer present." At that, the Camp Commanding Officer marched in. Quickly looking around the hut he said, "Everyone here, Sergeant?"

"Yes sir."

"Right, stand easy men. As you know, you have nearly finished your training here and before you go to France you should have some home leave."

We all looked around the hut, smiling at each other. Then the Sergeant cleared his throat.

"Eyes front", he barked. "However, orders have come through that all new recruits are needed at the front. Transport has been laid on for in the morning. Good luck to you all. I'm sure you will be a credit to the regiment."

With that, he turned and was gone.

"Right," said the Sergeant. "Pack all your army kit for marching and your personal kits in your boxes. Make sure they are clearly marked as you won't be coming back here again. Once we know where you are, they will be sent on. Breakfast is at 05.30. Report at 06.00 for transport to the station. Any questions? No, good."

He turned to go, then stopped.

"If you want to write home, keep it short. Don't mention anything about your orders. Give your letters to me and I'll make sure they get posted after being censored. If

I don't get chance in the morning, remember all that you have been taught. Listen to what you are being told and carry out all orders. Oh, and good luck. God be with you all."

Off he marched with the corporals following, saying good luck and keep your heads down, and they slammed the door behind them.

We all moved slowly towards the tables and stood around not knowing what to say. At first, one or two thought it might have been a joke and we were really going to go on leave. This was soon passed over and many other theories were put forward but none of them seemed possible. After we'd been talking for a while, one of the corporals came in.

"Sorry I couldn't tell you earlier. There's going to be a big offensive in a few weeks and the Generals have asked for every available man, trained or not, to be shipped over and put in reserve. So you lucky so and sos are going to be behind the front line. Some nice cushy jobs to be had there if you look hard enough. Anyway, I'm off to get ready for the next lot coming in the day after tomorrow."

By the time we had packed and labelled everything, there was just enough time to write a letter home. What could I say? I just didn't know where to start. So, I said sorry for such a short letter but it was orders. Leave had been cancelled and we were going to France tomorrow. We didn't know where to but not to worry and I'd write again when we got there. I got Phil to scribble a few lines on the same paper, then signed off with love and miss you both, Bill and Phil.

The following morning was utter chaos. It was raining, which had turned most of the parade ground paths and roads into muddy areas. There was a huge queue for food and they were also issuing ID tags, which had only just arrived, and when we finally got to the transport area, there were no trucks in sight. A couple of sergeants turned up and told us not enough had been sent. They had already loaded up and gone but would come back for us, but they had decided we would march towards the station anyway and meet the transport on the road. This would take some time, but they were going to hold the train for us. If they felt it necessary, the awaiting boat would also wait, but they hoped that once we got on the train, they could make up some time. So, we all got in line and marched out of the camp, heading for an unknown destination and as to what fate had in store for us, we didn't like to think about it, especially as we hadn't got off to a particularly good start.

It seemed like an age since we'd left the camp. We were all soaking wet and it felt like our kit had doubled in weight. Everyone was so tired, and it was only our months of training and shouting from the sergeants that kept us going. Suddenly, there was a roar and a cheer from the front of the ranks as the trucks came around a bend, sped past us, drove up the road and turned around. As they approached us, we stepped in front of them forcing them to stop and load us from the rear first. We did this so that we got to the station and seated on the train before the rest arrived. As it turned out, there weren't enough seats anyway, so we ended up sitting on our kit bags in a baggage carriage. Still, it was dry and we could take off our kit bags and some of the wet clothes to dry them out. It took about another forty minutes to get the rest of the troops loaded. Where they put them, God only knows, but we found out later that as with the trucks, neither had sufficient carriages been requested. The baggage car that we were in had been standing idle at the station and had been hastily attached, so it was lucky for us that we had got there first.

As the train moved slowly out of the station, I managed to get to a small window and could see thick, grey smoke belching out of the funnel. There was a loud hissing noise and the whistle kept blowing. I began to wonder if as there were so many soldiers crammed on board, whether it would be able to pull such a load, but slowly we picked up speed. As our carriage left the station, we went under the small bridge, which joined together either side of the station and the platforms. The smoke from the engine was still clearing when I noticed some women with younger children. They were all waving and throwing flowers onto the train's roof. I could see their mouths moving, but I couldn't hear what they were saying. Still, I waved back. I don't know if they saw me but I thought it was the best I could do as they had gone to the trouble of seeing us off. As the train gathered more speed, we started to leave the built-up area and head out into the open countryside. I couldn't help but notice the beauty of the area and promised myself that if ever I got a chance I would come back. Maybe take a little holiday. Perhaps Mum and Dad might

come, too. We'd never had a holiday. Still, there was a lot to do before our time got better and things could get back to normal again. I just wished I'd been able to see Mum and Dad again before going off to France. It had been nearly six months now. I know I was grown-up and supposed to be a man but I did so miss sitting in front of a roaring log fire with my head in Mum's lap as she gently stroked my hair and we sat listening to Dad telling all sorts of stories for hours and hours until bedtime. Thinking about this and other precious moments in my young life was making me feel very sad and despondent, and I could feel the tears welling up in my eyes. Suppose, just suppose, I didn't come back. Where do you go when you die? What's it like? Do you see others there, your friends or family? It wasn't a subject that any of us knew much about. I could feel myself slipping into something and somewhere I shouldn't be going, when someone shouted, "Bill, Bill, come out of your own world and come and play cards. Let's see if we can take some of your money off you. You know, the money that you were saving for your leave. I hope you weren't going to spend it on that girl!" said Peter.

"I don't know what you mean," I replied.

"You know, the girl at the market," Phil said.

"She won't wait for him," Harry shouted. "She's probably got another boyfriend already."

Everyone started laughing, so I spun round and leapt on top of them and proceeded to rough up as many as I could.

The train stopped. No one knew where or why, but it all soon became clear when the sliding doors opened. A corporal shouted in that we could get out of the carriage to stretch our legs and relieve ourselves if we wanted. There was also an army field kitchen set up with hot food and drink. We were only stopping for thirty minutes whilst the train loaded coal and water, so we were told not to hang around.

It was so good to get out of the carriage, as the smell of wet kit and clothes, as well as thirty odd bodies, was pungent. As we jumped down to the ground, I said to Phil that I'd rather clean out the pigs than sit in there much longer.

"I wonder where we are? Can't see any signs."

"I'd say looking at the sun, it's around four-ish. We must be over half way to the docks, wherever they might be."

"South coast," said Peter. "Somewhere on the south coast."

One or two agreed with him, then Phil said, "Come on, let's go and get some food and drink. Knowing the army, they've probably only got enough for half of us."

Everyone laughed as we made our way to the ever-growing queue forming at the front of the train. It was mutton stew, bread and hot tea, and it wasn't too bad, either.

Then we just had time to go into the bushes as there was only one toilet, and the station master wouldn't let us use the ladies.

The whistle sounded loudly and there was a flurry of men trying to get back to their carriages, and then a huge cloud of smoke belched from the train once more. More hissing noises and we started again. Off we went on the final part of our journey, in England at least, to the docks.

As the miles clattered by and the sky turned from day to night, it felt like whatever destiny had in store for us was closing in ever faster with every clickety clack of the train's wheels on the track. We had long finished playing cards as there was no light in the carriage. One or two of us had thought to bring a few candles but decided to save them just in case there was no light whenever we got to wherever we were going. Some of the others in the next carriage were playing what sounded like a mouth organ and a squeeze-box, and quite a few soldiers were singing along to the music. Some of the lads in with us were just humming along to the sound, and although you couldn't see them, except for the occasional glow from a cigarette, you knew what they were thinking and in a sad sort of way, you also knew that many of them would not be coming back. It was a little distressing, but it was also a privilege to be in the company of such brave men.

As the train slowed down and then stopped, there was a final loud hissing from the engine, and then silence. We all waited in the darkness of the carriage. Then there was shouting of orders and doors being flung open. Coming towards us, we could hear the familiar footsteps of a British Army sergeant major. Unforgettably, the doors flew open,

"Come on my lucky lads, it's the end of the line. Grab all your kit and get fell in on the platform. Don't forget anything, now. Move it. You're already late for your pleasure cruise, so we don't want to keep the ship waiting any longer, now do we? Come on, move it, move it. You'll have to move faster than this where you're going or not many of you will be coming back."

We piled out as quickly as we could and formed up on the platform. Someone from the back shouted, "Sergeant Major? Do you know where we're going?"

There was a pause before he answered. "You're going on a package tour to France."

This raised a hearty laugh. "Do any of you remember your schooldays when they taught you about Europe?"

Quite a few soldiers shouted 'yes'. "Well, you might not know this place but I'm sure you won't forget it. You're off to an area known as The Somme. Now, attention. Left turn. Quick march."

As we left the station, I glanced at the overhead clock. It was just turning midnight and we were in Dover. As we marched out of the station and towards the dock, I thought, "I don't know as I have heard of that place - The Somme. The Somme - must remember to ask Mum to look it up when I next write. Still, at least we know where we're going now."

At that moment, the wind began to get up and it started to rain. Phil said, "Would you believe it! First time we get to go abroad, it bloody well rains."

All the soldiers who heard the remark started to laugh until out of the dark a voice shouted, "Quiet in the ranks. The next man who even sneezes will be up for company punishment. Now march, double time."

As we marched out of the station on to the cobbled streets of Dover, the sound of over three hundred pairs of hobnailed boots marching in step was a rousing tune. As we headed towards the docks, on the way a number of people opened their doors and windows and cheered, wishing us good luck as we passed by. I wondered how many times they had done the same, and to how many soldiers as they went off to fight. I had no time to dwell on this anymore though as we were marching through the gates into the dock area. The rain was getting heavier and the wind was also picking up as we came alongside what could only be described as a floating trunk of scrap iron.

"Halt," shouted the Sergeant. "Face the front. Right, let's get boarded. Front rank first. Fall-out and get onto the boat, quick as you can, men. We're late already. Hurry up there."

We could already see there were a lot of supplies on board and someone shouted that it would sink before we even got out of the harbour. The Sergeant replied quickly, "Oh well, if we all drown, it will save the Germans the job then, won't it? Now hurry up and get onto the boat."

It took about thirty minutes to get fully loaded and then shortly after we were making our way out of the harbour. The crossing took about two hours and from the minute we left the harbour until we docked, there were men being sick all over the boat. We ran into a heavy storm about thirty minutes into the crossing and it proceeded to get worse and worse. The boat crew was having a good laugh at our misfortune, saying it was a gentle crossing, when in fact it was the worst channel storm for several years. You can imagine how relieved we were when land was sighted and we finally tied up. Where we were, we didn't know or care, we just wanted to get onto dry land. As the gangplank was lowered into place, those who weren't too bad scrambled to be first off the vessel but the rest were either helped or carried off by their friends. The boat crew was leaning over the rails whistling and shouting at us. They certainly must have enjoyed the crossing more than we did.

We were some of the last off as we had to help both Phil and Peter who had not had a good journey. They had spent a lot of the time, as did many others, praying to God, and now we could hear them on the dockside thanking him in return. Coming down the gangplank, our thanks quickly disappeared when we started to look at the surrounding area. In the early dawn light, the docks were covered in a shroud-like light mist which made everything you touched feel damp. The whole place felt uninviting and eerie. One of the first things we noticed was the lack of organization, which by now we had realized was so typical in the British Army. I sometimes wondered how the great British Empire was created, especially if the army had anything to do with it.

As we stepped onto the dockside, we found a quiet spot and dumped Phil and Peter there with their kit whilst we looked around and got our bearings. The sight that greeted us was chaos. There were both soldiers and civilians running here and there, some were shouting orders to anyone who could be bothered to listen. Others were just standing around in groups, waiting for something to do. There were empty trucks and horse-drawn carts being loaded up with supplies and ammunition boxes. The whole place stank of horses, dampness and human sweat. We looked on in disbelief. When we heard our company being called to form up, we went back for Phil and Peter, who by now looked a little better. They were both up and getting their kit on.

"Never again," said Peter. "I'll never go on a boat again."

"Nor me," Phil said.

"What will you do when it's all over and we're going home?" Harry shouted.

"We've decided to find a way to walk home," they both replied. There was a roar of laughter from all around us, and someone shouted, "Don't you know England's an island?" There was more laughter, then Phil said, "I don't care, but I'm not going back on that old rust bucket."

"Stop talking and get fell in," shouted the Sergeant.

And within a few minutes, we had formed up and were marching out of the docks. It was early morning and just getting light. The rain was easing off and the sun could be seen behind the breaking clouds. There were not many people about and the sound of our marching was about the only noise to be heard. As we headed out of town, there was a rumbling that started behind us and was getting louder by the second. None of us knew what it was and it began to sound like something from hell coming up the road for us. Then they came into view.

"Clear the road! Clear the road!" the officers and the NCO shouted. "Stand back or you'll all get crushed."

Then the first of many appeared. Teams of horses with one rider came racing past pulling timbers and field guns. They stopped for no one and scattered all that lay in their path. Sweat was pouring off the horse's backs, their manes were being slashed about like sabers; their breathing was fast and torturous, and they looked just like they were breathing fire out of their huge nostrils, but it was their eyes that gave it away. They were so deep and dark, wild and frightened. I wondered as they all passed, did they know something we didn't?

There were shouts for us to form up again, but after the sight we had just witnessed, things took a few minutes to sink in. As we wound our way to the outskirts of the town, we passed on either side of the road huge stores, vehicles of all kinds, both horse-drawn and mechanical, and further on there were massive dumps of ammunition, heavy artillery guns, field guns and all other types of equipment we'd never seen before. These dumps occurred at intervals of two or three miles until we were well into the countryside again. After the last munitions dump, we marched on for another couple of hours and then began to notice some old farm buildings coming up in front of us with quite a number of tents around them.

Someone shouted, "Sarge? Is this our hotel for the overnight stay?"

"You don't want to stay there, lad. Just wait and see," was his reply.

As we got closer, it became clear that it was a large field hospital, as some of the tents had red crosses on the side of them and there was also a makeshift flagpole positioned in the centre of the camp with a red cross fluttering in the breeze. There was an air about the place and although we were still a long way away, the odour lingered and was getting stronger the closer that we got. Then there was the screaming. At first, we thought it was an animal being butchered. Then there were several piercing screams that made your hair stand up on end. The closer that we got, the more we could hear and then we knew for certain that they were not animals. Getting ever closer, you could identify individual voices calling out in desperation for water, doctors, nurses, in fact anyone who could hear them. The cries were pitiful. The screams were unnerving. The sweet, sickly smell, which was now so overpowering hung under our noses, and as we were soon to find out was always around where there was blood and death.

As the front ranks of the soldiers drew level with the barn, we could hear several soldiers retching and as the next rank drew alongside, more and more men were heaving and were starting to drop out of line, rushing to the ditch where most of them were violently sick. At that moment, the officers and NCOs started shouting for us to keep our eyes to the front and move over to the right hand side of the road away from the buildings. By the time we got level with the hospital, we couldn't see that much as most of the holes in the tents were being blocked up from inside. We later found out that one of our officers had gone inside and demanded that all the windows and openings be blocked off, otherwise he said that at this rate he wouldn't have any men fit for fighting when we reached the front.

All the troops returned to rank and we carried on past the site. At the end of the buildings there was what appeared to be quite a large field surrounded by a thick hedge. It had probably been used to keep horses in before the War. Now, there were soldiers, stripped to the waist digging huge pits. Looking around there were signs of a large number of these pits. Our column was halted briefly whilst we waited for the officer to rejoin us. I was so curious as to what they were used for that I swapped places so I could get a better view. Now I was closer to the hedge, I had a far better view and recognised the soldiers as Pioneers. There was also a pit quite close to where I was standing. My immediate questions and curiosities were about to be answered when I saw, coming towards the pit, a number of men carrying stretchers. As they drew level with the pit, they tipped their load into it. I was horrified, as one after another, they tipped their loads and went back for more. The nearest I can remember to a sight like this was when we had to kill and bury all the pigs in our area at home, but to treat human beings like this was unbelievable. I was standing just yards away watching what I could only describe as a barbaric way of disposing of brave soldiers. They couldn't even be bothered to clean and tidy the bodies. They were just dumping them like animal carcasses.

"Right, Sergeant. Move the men out. We've a long way to go."

"Yes, sir. Right men, by the left, quick march."

I now knew what he meant about that place, and also we found out later that only the dying went there and were made as comfortable as possible, as they could take hours, days, or even weeks to die. I decided there and then that that was one place I was not going to be sent to.

As we carried on marching ever onwards, the day was warming up. There was a noticeable upturn in the amount of traffic on the road. Most of the vehicles coming from the front were either half-empty or carrying wounded soldiers. Now and then, we saw what looked like prisoner-only transportation and, apart from a different colour uniform, the men looked just like us. It was totally different coming from the docks and heading for the front. There were all sorts of vehicles in all sorts of sizes carrying supplies, ammunition shells, wire, everything you could think of. There were the cavalry troops and their horse-drawn guns that we had met earlier. We even saw huge steam traction engines pulling massive guns with enormous shells. None of us had seen anything like this before and gawped in awe as they trundled past us. But eventually, they became such a familiar sight over the next few days that they lost their fascination to us. When we saw their smoke in the distance, we used to bet on how long it would take them to reach us. As usual, it was Peter who won most of the time and couldn't wait for our first leave so he could collect his winnings in beer.

We came to a halt alongside an army mobile field kitchen where there was food and drink for us. These areas, as we were finding out, were dotted about all along our marching route. Some were just for basic food, but others were kitted out with sleeping areas, washing and toilet facilities as well as food, but depending on how many troops and vehicles were on the move defined what you got and how long you had to wait for it. After our food stop, we set out again pausing briefly for a water break and then carried on to our first night's stop. As we approached the camp, we could see there weren't too many others there, so we weren't short of getting the better overnight facilities.

The Sergeant called for us all to fall out in front of the temporary camp and we then made our way through the rows of tents until we found an empty one. Collapsing on the floor, we were all just exhausted. In fact, we were so tired we didn't even bother to take off our kit, we just lay there, eyes shut. We all had all kinds of thoughts spinning around in our heads. None of us moved for what seemed to us as no time at all, when suddenly we heard the Sergeant shouting for us to move ourselves. He pulled back our tent flap, saying there was another company of soldiers coming down the road, so we had to go and get some food while there was some to be had. Unstrapping our kit, we decided that one of us should stay behind and guard the tent and kit. Peter said he would stay, as he was not feeling too good yet, so we unpacked our mess tins and went to find the kitchen, which wasn't too hard as there was plenty of noise and cooking smells to follow.

As we strode into a long tent, there were about sixty men forming a line in front of six long tables. The line was moving quite quickly and when it was our turn, we presented our tins, which were duly filled with something hot and a hunk of bread. Tea could be found on the last table as the Cook kept saying over and over. When it was Phil's turn, he said to the Cook, "What's on the menu tonight, then?"

Pausing for a minute, the Cook then said, "Don't ask, just move along." He then continued serving and saying to everyone else, "Bread and tea on the last table."

We got some food for Peter, then went back to our tent. By this time, there were a lot of soldiers milling around looking for somewhere to sleep, and as we approached our tent we could see Peter talking to someone. Throwing the tent flaps back, I ducked in and by the faint light of a candle that he was holding, I saw two unknown soldiers. The others followed me in and we all sat down. I passed Peter his food and nodded to the strangers.

"Who are these then?"

Peter was just about to speak, when one of the strangers butted in, "My name's Joe and this is Stan. We were told by the Sergeant to share with you."

Glancing at them by the flickering candlelight, I said, "Well, if the Sergeant told you, I suppose it's all right. My name's Bill. Pleased to meet you."

The others introduced themselves and they were all starting to get involved in chatting when I interrupted them saying they should go and get some food before it ran out.

By the time they got back, we'd finished our food, or whatever it was. We waited until they'd finished theirs and then the three of us wandered around the camp with all the mess tins to wash.

Finding a huge half barrel of greasy water by the side of the kitchen, we made do and cleaned them as best we could. On our way back, we came across the field toilets. They were well laid out with one long narrow trench about six feet deep with a plank of wood about two feet high that ran the length of the trench. I presumed that this was there to sit on. On the other side, there was a wider board about four feet high with a few metal bowls and one broken shaving mirror. Considering this was to be shared by upwards of three thousand men, for the army it wasn't too bad.

We reported back to the others and were told the Sergeant had been round saying he wanted us up, washed and shaved and in full kit outside the kitchen by 05.30 so as to avoid the rush for breakfast. Anyone not shaved or washed, or late, would be put on a charge.

We all started to unpack our kit and laid out the wettest of our gear in the hope that it might dry out a bit during the night. The two new lads were standing just outside the tent relaxing with a cigarette, as best they could. I was the nearest to the tent flap and could just make out their hushed voices talking about their march and the different sights and sounds they had come across. In particular, they both seemed very interested in the large steam engine tractors. By the sound of things, they must have both worked at the factory where these were made, but they had no idea that they were being used to tow such heavy guns across France. They then talked about their homes, families and friends. The only thing that wasn't talked about were the convoys of wounded heading back to the docks, and of course the field hospital, which I felt held many horrors and many sights that I wanted to forget. Maybe they hadn't seen what I had. Maybe they had come another way, who knows? What I didn't know was that there was far, far worse to face in the coming weeks ahead, and what I was about to experience was going to stay with me for the rest of my days.

I looked about me: my brother, who had suddenly grown much older, all three best friends, the finest friends anyone could wish for. In fact, we were just like brothers. I looked at each one in turn, lingering for a moment and wondering what was going through their minds. Knowing I was looking at them each in turn they would look at me, and a wide grin would stretch across their faces. They were all where they wanted to be, with whom they wanted to be with.

"I'm turning in now, lads," I said. "We've another long day ahead, so we'll need all the rest we can get. I think it's going to be like this for a number of days to come yet - it's going to be just the same."

I lay back on my makeshift bed and closing my eyes started to visualise some of the things I had seen today. However, this didn't last long as my mind and body were overtaken by the greater need for sleep.

I woke up several times during the night. The heavy rain was pounding on the canvas, I heard someone leaving the tent and then coming back again. Probably going to the toilet or for a cigarette. It was so dark, I couldn't see who it was.

After that, things settled down again and I slept heavily, finding myself marching back the way we had come today, but I was on my own. I kept looking around for the others but they were nowhere to be found. I was marching with total strangers. When we stopped, no one spoke. We just sat on the ground, staring down at the floor. Nothing was said but again we all lined up and carried on marching. It seemed an age since we had set off and I was beginning to feel that we were lost. I looked around for any landmarks but couldn't see any. We carried on a while longer and then I saw it and knew we were on the right road. It took about thirty minutes to get alongside and the column was halted. Suddenly, men from all the ranks including the officers and the NCOs started to turn and fall out. They walked along the road into the hospital where there were hundreds of men, all very pale faced with glazed staring eyes, all going the same way. I looked around me and at least half of the men had gone. I was starting to panic and then suddenly breaking ranks, I ran to the nearest part of the hospital.

Looking through a gap in the hedge, I backed off in horror at what I saw. Gathering the courage to look again took several minutes, but when I did I found I couldn't tear myself away from the gruesome sight. The whole area, as far as I could see was covered in deep pits. There were soldiers everywhere, hundreds of them. Some were dressed, some half-dressed and some had nothing on at all, but what they all had in common was that they were all badly wounded and covered in blood. Some had limbs missing, with others huge pieces of their bodies were gouged out, parts of heads and faces missing. The really bad ones were on stretchers and were being carried to the pits. As they got there, they were tipped in and the walking ones either jumped in or climbed on top. When a pit was full, it was filled in and another one hastily dug. This was going on all over the field. It seemed never-ending. As soon as one was filled, another one was started. I just couldn't believe what my eyes were telling me. I felt really sick and went to draw away, when suddenly I saw two soldiers come into the field. One was carrying the other in his arms. They started filling in a pit close to where I was standing and the two soldiers started towards it. As they got closer, I had this feeling I knew them, but with the condition that they were in it was hard to tell. Maybe, when they got to the pit I might see a little better. Slowly, they got nearer and nearer, and when they reached the side of it, the walking body gently laid his friend on the side and then lowered himself in, too.

It was in these few seconds that I gazed at the man on the side and I knew it was Harry. I stared on in disbelief when his friend reached out for him and as he gently lifted him into the pit, he looked at me. I think he smiled but I will never know, as I had so many tears in my eyes. But the one thing I was sure of was that this was John who was carrying Harry.

The pit having been filled with bodies, the Pioneers started to cover it over with earth. I screamed their names but no sound came out of my mouth. My tears had all dried up. All I could do was stand by and watch. It was then, in a blind panic that I headed for the barns and outbuildings. Tearing frantically at the clothes and blankets covering the windows and walls in the building, I wasn't sure what I was looking for, or even if it was there. All that I did know was that I had got to look. The last big window that I uncovered revealed a large barn, and laid out on the floor were row upon row of wounded and dying men. There were no medics, nurses or assistants, but there were other soldiers there, just like me, who were looking over them. They were either guarding them or waiting for them, I wasn't sure which.

It was with great sadness in my heart that I looked up and down the lines of soldiers who were lying on the floor. Now and then a soldier would pick up his friend and gently, like a babe in arms, carry him away. Other soldiers would also appear and go and stand next to their friend. As I carried on looking, I knew what I was going to find, and a few moments later there he was. I could see Peter. I could tell it was him as he lay on the ground. He turned his head and looked over to me. He tried to lift himself up but his strength failed him and he slid back down to the ground. He did manage a smile and half a wave, and as I stood there helpless, I watched him die.

As the sight was registering in my mind, the soldier alongside him gracefully knelt down beside him, and with very little effort, scooped him up and gathered the blood-soaked bundle in his arms. He started to walk away from me, towards the door where they all seemed to go. By this time, I could stand it no longer. I knew it was Phil I was looking for, but I couldn't let him or the others go on without me. Suddenly, I started shouting, "Phil, Phil! Wait for me! I'm coming, too."

I started to climb through the window, all the time shouting and ranting. When I was nearly through the window, I looked towards the door where the soldier had stopped. As he turned to face me, I knew all my fears were now coming true. It was Phil, my only younger brother. Time stood still for a moment as we both just looked at each other, soaking up every detail possible and committing it to the depths of memory. I felt a whisper of the breeze on my neck, which sent a tremor down my spine. I blinked and in that magic moment, I looked for him again, but he was gone.

"Phil!" I shouted. "I'm coming! Please wait for me, please"

As I lifted my leg through the window, someone grabbed me from behind and started pulling me back and then shaking me.

"Wake up, Bill. Come on, it's time to get up. Come on. Hurry up. We'll be late, hurry up."

I stirred myself from sleep and found myself looking up at Peter, who was still shaking me.

"OK, OK," I said, "I'm awake now, okay."

I quickly looked around and noted that we were all still together and I had only been dreaming. This was a nightmare that I would relive over and over for the rest of my life.

Within a few minutes, we were all on the way to the wash area. Luckily, there was hardly anyone else there. It was very rough and ready but we managed. We then chased each other back to the tent, got dressed and kitted out and leaving the other two fast asleep, we made our way over to the field kitchen. As we all lined up, there was a better atmosphere amongst the troops than there had been the day before. Some were larking about, others were chatting and telling jokes, running round tables, the sorts of things you'd expect when a group of lads got together. The rest and sleep had done us all the world of good.

When we were all finished, we went and stood on the road waiting to be formed up. It was just getting light, the rain had long stopped and it looked like it had the makings of a fine day. At that moment, the officers and NCOs came clattering up the road, shouting orders to get fell in. They then went into the kitchen and slung out the late arrivals. As we lined up and set off, I noticed several officers in a group at the beginning of the column. I nudged Peter and said, "Looks like trouble," nodding towards the group, and it was. The medical officer came along and asked everyone if they had any trouble with their feet.

"Make sure you check and wash them every day, and wash your socks, too. Got any problems with your kit straps? Any burns or abrasions? Make sure you drink plenty of water whilst marching. Any problems, speak to a medical orderly."

Then the NCO did a full personal and kit inspection. He tore over half of us to pieces for our sloppiness. He handed out company punishments like leaves falling off a tree. When he had finished, he stood on a box and gave the whole company a good dressing-down, finishing off with, "I know you're all marching to the front to fight and the conditions are not that good, but good God men, what do you think the enemy will think when they find themselves fighting a bunch of scruffs like you? Next time I inspect you, I want to see a hundred per cent improvement, or by God, heads will roll. Sergeant, get this scruffy bunch moving and out of my sight."

For the following five or six days all that we did was march, break, march, eat, march, break, march, sleep, eat. It was easy to lose track of the days and of time. Luckily, it was not too hot and we had a few heavy downpours of rain, which helped to keep us cool. The seemingly never-ending stream of supplies, ammunition and artillery never stopped. Even through the night you could hear the convoys rumbling past. I think it was obvious to all of us that our first taste of action was going to be as part of a big offensive. In some ways, we all felt excited about the whole thing. Just the thought of being there, mixing with so many brave young men, watching in awe. We saw convoy after convoy go past with all kinds of vehicles, all types of guns, things you had never seen before, or knew what they were or what they were for. There was just so much, you couldn't take it all in. Amidst the excitement, the only negative side I could think of at that time was the constant flow of wounded soldiers coming back from the front, and the now familiar sight of field hospitals and aid centres. However, many of the wounded would wave at us and wish us good luck as they went by. For me the spectre of death and the dying was always close by.

On the afternoon of the sixth day, we had just stopped for a short break. It was a good day, blue sky, sunny and hot with not a cloud in sight. We all collapsed on the lush grass at the side of the road, and unclipped our kit, which we used for a headrest. We lay back, staring up at the sky.

"I wonder what the weather is like at home," Phil said. "I bet it's not as good as this. Just look how lush and green the grass is."

"Aye," said Peter, "just think of the milk and butter you'd get from cows that graze in these fields."

"It won't last long," said a voice close by.

"What won't?" I asked the soldier sitting beside us.

"This weather," he said. "It'll be raining soon."

"Don't be daft," I said, "There aren't any clouds in sight."

"It'll rain soon," he said. "I can hear thunder in the distance. I heard it just before we stopped. Quiet now, and you'll hear it again."

At that moment, we all stopped talking and tried to concentrate on listening. For a short while, all around us there was a deadly quiet. First one, then another said they could also hear thunder. Then more and more soldiers said they could hear it, too. Someone shouted to stand up because you could hear it better. So, one by one, we got to our feet and just stood looking towards the horizon, waiting and listening.

"There it is, and again."

Then more and more soldiers could hear it, until finally all of our group heard it. It sounded like a low rumbling sound that was getting slightly louder, and then easing off for a short time. Later, it would do it over and over again.

"That's not thunder," said Harry. "I know we're in France but thunder is the same wherever you go, and I'm telling you that's not like any thunder I've ever heard before. Look at the sky, it's as clear and blue as you'll ever see. No sign of rain."

"Right, you lot. Form up. Get into line. We've still a long way to go before nightfall," shouted the Sergeant, walking up and down the line. As he came close to us, Phil said, "Will we get to the rest camp before the storm hits us, Sergeant?"

Pausing alongside Phil, the Sergeant replied, "What storm? It's a lovely day and will be a fine evening. Where's this storm coming from?"

"Can't you hear the thunder in the distance, Sergeant?"

Laughing out loud, he shouted, "That's not thunder. You'll all soon get used to that noise, lads. It's heavy artillery bombardment, softening the enemy up for you when we finally get there. Now, quick march, we don't want them to start without us."

Gunfire. I had wondered what to expect and at that moment it didn't sound too bad, but I knew that the closer we got to the front, the louder it would get. I was trying to imagine what it was going to be like when we were on the receiving end of the enemy barrage. What would it be like? Would I be able to face up to it? Would I try and hide, or even run away? All these thoughts, and more, were going around my head, and I suspect many other heads, as we got closer to the front, and the guns got louder and louder. It was as if they were calling you ever nearer, enticing you to face your worst nightmare. To see what fate held in store for you. For as you closed in on the front line, you knew in your heart this would be your Judgement Day.

After pounding the road for another four hours, we suddenly turned through a gate and onto a rough cart track. As it was not wide enough for our column, the two outside lines of men had to march on the ploughed field. This caused a lot of problems and there was a lot of tripping and stumbling, along with much cursing and bad language. Even with the bad ground we were marching on, there was no let up in the pace of the march. After about an hour, we came to a wider road, which led up a steep hill. This part of the march was murder. Quite a number of men fell by the wayside and even with the NCOs shouting at them, they couldn't get them back onto their feet.

As we came to the top of the hill, the Captain halted the column and told us to rest. I had a glance behind us and saw about seventy to eighty men had fallen and were either sitting or lying by the side of the road. Some NCOs were going around giving them water and helping some of them take their packs off. At that moment, the Captain and several other officers stood close to where I was and shouted the Sergeant over to join them. They all gathered around and there was a lot of shouting and raised voices. I heard one of the officers say it was a disgrace and how they had let the company down, and he would see to it that they were suitably punished. The Sergeant interrupted, saying, "Beg your pardon, sir, but the men have been marching now for over five hours without a break or any water. The sun has been scorching and they've marched over very rough ground, and then have been expected to tackle a very steep hill without a change in marching pace."

I know, Sergeant " said the officer. "Don't forget that we've all marched as well."

"With the greatest of respect, sir, none of us is carrying sixty pounds of kit as well."

"That's enough, you two," said the Captain. "See what condition they are in. We've only two miles or so, and then we can rest up. Report back to me in five minutes."

"Yes, sir," they all snapped and saluted. With that they turned and went down the hill, stopping by all the exhausted men.

Whilst the Captain waited, he turned his back to us and began to take in the terrain. To his right, he could see the flickering glow of fires on the edge of a small forest. He knew from his orders that this was our last camp before moving up to the front. However, he had not been expecting it to be so intensive. As the light was fading and his vision was not so good, it was difficult to hazard a guess as just how big it was, but judging by the number of fires springing up, many thousands of troops were down there. His eyes followed the road that we were on, and just as it got to the bottom of the hill, it split. To the right went to the forest and the camp. The left hand road wound its way through lush countryside and then disappeared into a small wood. Slightly further on, it emerged again and then continued until it stopped in front of a very large and very splendid looking house. The first thing that came to mind was the number of chimneys. I couldn't count them all in the failing light but there were at least eleven, and several of these belched out thick, dark smoke. I think every light in the place was on as it shone like a beacon in the night. You could make out a horse and the riders at the front and the staff cars coming and going. Ah, it would be easy to let your mind wander back to another time. You could be watching a great gathering for a ball, or Christmas, or a special wedding party. You could also imagine that the rumbling noise and coloured flashes on the horizon were a great firework display or an electrifying thunderstorm that was slowly getting closer and closer.

111

"Beg pardon, sir," said the Sergeant. Those few words soon brought him back to reality.

"Yes, Sergeant," and turning around, he found his officers and NCOs standing around him.

"Beg to report, sir, that there are sixty two men who are not able to carry on. The others will manage better if they get their kit taken for them."

They were all in conversation when Peter came over to me.

"Bill, can you see all the lights in the distance? They look as though they're coming our way."

I stood up just to see for myself.

"I think you could be right, Peter." I marched a few steps over to where the officers were in conference. Coming to attention and saluting, I said, "Excuse me, sir."

"Yes, Private."

"I think we might be in luck, sir. There's a large convoy of vehicles heading our way, and with a bit of luck, they might have room for our sick, sir."

"Thank you, Private. You might have something there. Dismissed. Sergeant, take the NCOs and stop all those trucks and see if we can get our men a ride to the camp."

We were lucky. All the trucks were empty, so we all rode the last miles, and within a couple of hours we were all fed and bedded down for the night. I went out like a light. I was so exhausted. I slept all night. Expecting an early morning call, I was determined to get as much sleep as possible.

The first thing I was aware of when I awoke was that the gunfire in the distance was far louder than it had been last night, and there was a lot more of it. The lads were still asleep and it seemed wrong to wake them not knowing the time, although I could sense it was later than normal. I couldn't hear the usual commotion of the camp coming alive either. I crawled over to the flap and stuck my head out. It was a lovely morning, warm and sunny, the sky was blue with little cloud and the camp was so quiet. I suddenly thought they had all gone without us. Unclipping the tent flap, I stood up and went out looking for signs of life.

Wandering to the cookhouse, I soon found someone to talk to. It seemed that we were not moving up to the front until tomorrow midday, and we had all been granted a rest period until then. I was told to make the most of it, as we would be moving to the Somme where there was a big battle about to start.

"Listen to those guns."

"I know," I said. "I thought they had stepped up the firing."

"Good luck, mate," he said. "I might see you up there."

"Same to you," I said, as he wandered off.

When I got back to the tent, the others were starting to rouse themselves.

"Thanks for telling me we had a rest day, you lot. I've been up for hours."

"No you haven't," Phil said.

"I heard you go out," Peter said. "Shut that flap," and then he threw his boot at me. That was it, the start of twenty minutes of childish behaviour, which helped to take our mind off what lay ahead. We spent most of the day just lounging about resting, sleeping, just taking it easy. I wrote to Mum but only a few lines just to let them know that we were all right. I couldn't say much because I think they opened our letters anyway. After we'd had our evening meal, we decided to go and check and clean our kit before we turned in.

Phil and Peter were talking about where we were going and when we might get there. I wondered whether or not to tell them what I was told this morning, but instead I thought better of it.

"Who's that with the Sergeant?" said Phil. "I haven't seen him before."

Could be a new officer joining us. Looks like he's showing him around our camp. Lookout," I said, "he's coming over to us next."

"Now, Sergeant," said the new officer. "Which one of these men is your best choice?"

Pointing to me, he said, "On your feet, Private. Officer present."

I sprang to my feet, stood to attention and gave a smart salute.

"He seems to be what we are looking for. Do you think he's up to the job, Sergeant?"

"Yes, sir. A first-class soldier who won't let you down, sir."

"Right, have him at the HQ by 05.30 with the others. That will be all, Sergeant." They exchanged salutes and the officer marched briskly away.

Turning to me, the Sergeant said, "First class turn-out. In the morning, Private, you will be parading in front of high-ranking officers. You can leave your kit behind, just bring your rifle and ammunition pouches. I'll wake you in time. Now get some sleep, it's going to be a long day tomorrow."

At that, he turned and marched off.

Sitting back down again, not knowing what to think, I looked around at my friends for some help, but no one said anything.

"Well?" I said. "Anybody got any ideas?"

After a few more minutes of silence, Peter said, "They might want you to try out a new weapon or show them how good you are at rifle drill."

At this, they all started to laugh.

"No," Phil said, "I think it's much more serious than that."

We all looked at him and waited with bated breath.

"You know, I think they want someone to saddle their horses for them so they can take early morning rides."

With that, he got up and ran off shouting, "Officers' groom, officers' groom boy."

By this time, everyone around us had joined in and they were all laughing.

Eventually I'd had enough of this and got up and wandered off into the forest for a while. It was such a beautiful place, I could have stayed there forever. The light was fading rapidly, so I made my way back to the camp, just in time to see the sun setting. Both the sun and the sky were such a fiery red it was like the world was on fire, and with the sound of the guns in the distance it felt as if I was looking into the centre of the world. I stood there as if transfixed at the sight and sound that I was experiencing. I was so taken by the moment that I didn't hear the Sergeant walk up and stand beside me until he spoke.

115

"It's like staring into the depths of hell," he said.

Startled, I turned sharply. "Sorry, I didn't see you there, Sergeant."

"Don't worry about it. We are on rest time. You know, I don't get much chance to see sights like these. I live in a town you see, in the Midlands. My father and his father were miners. I went down the mines when I was twelve. Been there ever since - well, up until the War started, then I joined up and if I survive I think I'll stay in, too. At least you get to see sights like these. Anyway, come on, get back and get some sleep. Got a big day tomorrow. Make sure your uniform and kit are spotless for the officers' parade. I'll be going with you, so I'll get you up."

"Thanks, Sergeant," and we both headed back to the camp in total silence

As I lay waiting for sleep to take hold of my weary body and take away the never-ending distant gunfire, I started to think of tomorrow's early-morning duty. I tried to think of all the things it could or couldn't possibly be, but even then came up with nothing. I think the most worrying of it all was the way the Sergeant had spoken to me, like a human being. Now that was worrying, or perhaps he knew what was going to happen.

Present arms

Chapter 4

Letting sleep finally take hold of me, I slept through until I was woken by the Sergeant.

"Come on, soldier. Twenty minutes until kit inspection over by the road. Hurry now, we can't be late for this one."

I grabbed my wash kit and sprinted over to the wash area, and was surprised to find that there were five other lads getting ready. No one spoke, but just got on with what we were doing. I took a guess that we were all strangers and must also be part of this morning's duty. As we each finished, we went our separate ways, next to meet up by the road. The Sergeant gave us a good going-over, adjusting this strap and that strap, tightening belts and buckles, shining buttons and boots, hat badges and belt buckles. Nothing was missed and we all caught a good tongue-lashing. Then finally, he inspected our rifles. As he was working his way along the line, out of the corner of my eye, I noticed a small truck coming out of the early-morning mist, heading towards us. It arrived to pick us up just as the Sergeant had finished his inspection. His only comment being that we weren't fit to serve in any army, never mind the King of England's army.

"Now get on that truck, smartish and let's get this duty done."

The truck trundled up the hill, making slow progress back into the mist. As we went through the curtain, it seemed to get much colder, although it would soon burn off when the sun rose higher into the sky later. It was certainly chilly now though. Appearing through the mist in front of us, came the army headquarters, and as we got even closer, the bigger it seemed to get. I was beginning to think it was a king's palace. It was so beautiful. I had never seen anything quite like it before. There were quite a large number of army staff cars and other vehicles parked all around the front. As we approached the building, the driver turned down the side and pulled up.

"Right, squad. Get down and form up in two lines," the Sergeant shouted. "Right, shoulder arms and quick march."

Following the Sergeant, we went round the back of the house, through a gate into a cobbled courtyard with a number of stables with horses in, and I had to laugh to myself. Perhaps what Phil had said about being a groom for the officers might be true.

As we marched across the cobbles, our hobnailed boots made a right noise, and even disturbed the horses. We were brought to a halt by a high wall on the far side of the courtyard. We fell out and were then led through a large door into a very large room with a few wooden tables and chairs all spread about. The Sergeant pointed to a table and told us to put our rifles up in the corner and then to sit down.

"I'll go and see if I can get some tea."

We all sat there in silence, starting to get a little nervous.

There were several doors leading off the room. We could hear footsteps heading towards us, but not approaching the door that the Sergeant went out of. A small door in the corner opened quietly and a young woman came in carrying a tray. As she came towards us, I noticed how pale she looked. She wasn't much older than me, quite pretty with dark hair, but too thin for her height, probably caused by lack of nourishing food. She placed the tray on the table, then passed around seven cups and some milk and sugar. She never once looked at any of us, nor did she speak or smile. She just picked up her tray and left the room. As she closed the door behind her, we heard the familiar hobnailed boots crunching on the stone floor, a brief halt to open the door and then the Sergeant came in carrying a large metal teapot. Banging it down on a table, he said "Come on, one of you pour. I'm gasping."

We all then sat round, sipping the hot tea, thankful that we had something to do rather than staring at the walls, not wanting to catch anyone's eye.

"I've told the cook that the Sergeant said you poor young soldiers have missed breakfast, so she said she would see what she could do."

"Can we smoke, Sergeant?" said one of the other soldiers.

"I don't see why not, but don't make a mess or we'll all be for it."

Upon that, three of the soldiers produced cigarettes. Lighting them up and taking several drags seemed to somehow relax and unwind them, and as they had something in common they started to chat amongst themselves.

A few minutes later, the far door opened and a fairly large lady came in carrying a tray. As she got close to the table, the Sergeant got up and took the tray from her and put it in the middle of the table. Turning to her, he thanked her for her kindness and in return she gave him a big, beaming smile. Flinging her arms around him, she proceeded to kiss him on either side of his cheeks. She also spoke to him in a language we didn't understand. When she'd finished, she turned and walked away, going out through the same door that she had come in.

"Tuck in then, lads," the Sergeant said, reaching over and picking up a handful of sandwiches from one of the several plates on the tray. He opened it before taking a bite, "Bacon," he said with a grin on his face.

"She's done us proud."

I said looking at the others, "I think she might fancy you, Sergeant. We thought she was going to pick you up and carry you off, all that hugging and kissing."

We all then started to laugh while we got stuck into the food. Sitting back down again, the Sergeant said, "Hold on, hold on. That's how the French do it over here and anyway, I couldn't understand her but at least we got a drink and some food out of her," which prompted us all to laugh again.

Just at the same time, the door from the courtyard opened and an officer came in. We all went to stand up to attention, but he soon responded with, "Stand easy men. Carry on with your food."

He walked over to the Sergeant.

"Everything in order, Sergeant?"

"Yes, sir."

"It's a bit of a chilly morning, so I've brought you and the men a drop of whisky for a nip in your tea." He then took a small bottle of whisky out from his coat pocket and placed it on the table in front of the Sergeant.

"From the men and myself, thank you, sir."

"Look, Sergeant. As you know, I need to brief you and the men." Looking at his watch, he said "We've still plenty of time, so I'll leave you to finish your food and then I'll come back in, say, ten minutes?"

"Yes, sir. We'll be ready by then."

"Thank you, Sergeant."

Turning on his heels, he walked towards the door, opened and closed it and then marched away. We listened to his footsteps until they could no longer be heard, trying to get a bearing on which way he went.

"Where do you think we are going and what for, Sergeant?" one of the lads said.

Getting to his feet, he picked up the bottle, took off the top and started going round the table, pouring a good measure into everyone's cup.

"I don't know what we're here for. You heard the officer, he's coming back, so we'll all know soon enough. Now drink your tea and finish off. He'll be back soon."

We all did as we were told, although no one said anything. I think we all thought the same, that the Sergeant did know but was probably under orders not to say anything. When we'd finished, we collected everything together and put it on one of the other tables, then sat there in silence, waiting for the footsteps to return.

We didn't wait long until the unmistakable steps could be heard again. Then the door opened.

"Stay as you are, men," he said, as he came in, shutting the door behind him. He pulled up a chair to the head of the table and sat down.

"Right men. There's no good or bad way to say this, so I'll be brief. Several months ago, an attack was put in further up the line in another sector. There was this service incident where a group of soldiers refused the order to attack. The officer in charge, along with several NCOs, managed to get all of the men to obey the order, with the exception of one. When the attack was over, he was taken back to company headquarters and was given a thorough medical examination by one of the army's senior doctors. He was found to be both physically and mentally fit for duty. Now, as you are all aware, failure to carry out orders is a court martial offence that carries a long prison sentence. Also, in extreme cases, it can also carry the death sentence."

As soon as he said those last two words, my guts started to churn. I felt sick and started to tremble. Now I knew why we had been treated so well. It didn't just happen like that normally. It had all been well planned. He continued and told us that as this man had disobeyed orders in the face of the enemy, he was court-martialed for cowardice against the enemy and failure to obey orders. He was found guilty on both charges and sentenced to death by firing squad today at 07.00 and us six soldiers were the chosen firing party.

He said no more for a while to let it all sink in, and then said, "I want you all to be very clear about this. You'll be given an order to fire. If any of you do not carry out that order, you will be court-martialed and either face a very long prison sentence, or a firing squad yourself. Are we all clear about that?"

He wandered around the whole of the table as we all replied "Yes, sir."

"Now, when you get there, a lot of high-ranking officers will be there to witness the procedure, so I want a good turnout. I'm in charge. There's doctor and a priest on hand, too. The prisoner will be marched to the firing post and then secured. He will be asked if he wants to be blindfolded, or not. A small piece of red cloth will then be pinned to his coat next to his heart. This will be your aiming marker. When the order is given, you will open fire. Myself and the doctor will move in to check the body. If there are still any signs of life, I will administer the fatal shot. The body will then be taken down, placed in a coffin and taken away for burial and you will all return to your various camps."

He reached into his pocket and took out a handful of bullets and put them on the table.

"These are the six bullets to be used. When you have discharged your duty, you will reject the spent cartridge and the Sergeant here will collect them up and give them to me. Just one more thing. It has been decided that one of these bullets is a blank, so when this is all over, providing that you all aim at the target, you will never know if you fired a live or a blank round. Now Sergeant," he said looking at his watch, "it's time to go. Right men, take a bullet, pick up your rifles and line up in the yard."

We all got up and carried out his orders whilst the officer went towards the door. I still to this day don't know why I asked the question, especially as I had a good idea what the answer would be.

"Excuse me, sir."

The officer turned in the doorway. The room and everyone in it seemed to freeze.

"Yes, Private?"

"Beg your pardon, sir. What nationality is the soldier, sir?"

He hesitated. I don't think he was supposed to say. He turned and stepped out into the courtyard.

"British, Private," he said, "British."

We scrambled out through the door and formed up. The officer led, next the Sergeant, then us. As we clattered across the courtyard, I could just make out a small door in the high wall. This was opened for us as we got nearer but it wasn't big enough for us to march through. Instead, we halted, shouldered our rifles and passed through one at a time. When we had all gone through, we reformed up again and began to march along the back of the house. The path was made of rough stone and didn't make as much noise as across the courtyard earlier. Moving quickly along the back of the house, which I noticed was a lot bigger than it looked, we came to a large grassed area. It was probably a well-kept lawn before the War, but it was now overgrown and run-down. At the back of the house was a large terrace and two flights of steps leading down to the lawn. There were two double doors leading into the house. These were open with quite a large gathering of army officers already standing on the patio and the steps. Directly in front of us was a small wooded area, probably used for shooting, and on our left hand side there was nothing but uninterrupted beauty over the valley.

We marched round the half circle lawn and came to a halt halfway round and in the middle of the two flights of steps. As we stood there, we could see the officers talking on the terrace above our heads. We then heard the order for a left turn, "Unshoulder arms, stand easy". As we looked away from the house, the beauty of the views was outstanding. The sun was coming up on clear blue skies with just a little mist still close to the ground in patches, mainly over by the wood. In my mind, I was desperately searching for something to focus on as a distraction from the coming event. However, it was very hard as the only thing directly in front of us was a large wooden post. It stood about six foot six inches high and was about twenty five feet away from our position. On the ground beside it were several small coils of rope. Looking to the right side, cleverly concealed at the edge of the wood, were what looked like two medical orderlies with a two-wheeled handcart and a coffin, which could be seen quite clearly, although an attempt had been made to cover it over with an old sheet.

A slight movement to the left of my eye made me move my line of sight just as two officers approached the post. One I knew as the officer in charge, the other was much older and the senior of the two. He carried a black bag with a cross on it. I think he was a doctor, but I couldn't think why they needed him at an execution.

We heard the prisoner before he came into view. I had this vision of him marching up to the post, hands tied around the post, blindfold put on. I never expected the drama that was unfolding in front of me. The sound coming from the far side of the house was like nothing I had ever heard, neither animal nor human. There were piercing, howling screams, then lower whimpers and sobs. Into view came four burly army policemen. They were trying to march in some kind of orderly fashion, but were being pushed and pulled in all directions. They were barely able to restrain their prisoner who continued to resist for all he was worth, until they finally got him to the post. He seemed to calm down a little then and the guards relaxed their grip on him slightly, as they tried to gently manoeuvre him onto the post. He made a last, desperate bid to get away, but the guards still had chains on him and soon wrestled him to the ground. It was at this point that I had my first look at him. He was only small and thin, not very old, maybe nineteen or twenty. He had fair hair and a pale complexion. I couldn't see his eyes, but I knew what they looked like.

He soiled his trousers as they dragged him across the courtyard. Pulling him to the post, they tied his hands and feet first, but he kept slumping forward so they had to strap his waist, chest and his head so that he was upright. As the guards marched away and he was left alone, he started weeping and screaming, trying to shake his head and body to try and get free. The officer in charge marched over to him and read out the charges and the sentence. He asked the prisoner if he had any last requests. There was no reply. I don't think he knew what was going on around him. The officer took a blindfold and a red patch from his pocket. Fixing the patch to his shirt over his heart, he asked the

125

prisoner if he wanted the blindfold. His head moved slightly to indicate that he didn't.

We were brought to attention and shouldered arms. The man was asked again if he wanted the blindfold, and this time he stopped sobbing just enough to say no. It was now that we were told to load our weapons. Remembering all that we had been told, I hoped that I had picked the right bullet. I would like to think I was lucky, but I knew that the other five were all thinking and hoping just the same.

An army chaplain joined the officer and stood in front of the prisoner, said a short prayer and then withdrew. The sobbing man's spirit was now broken and quieter. He was calling for his mother, begging to see her one last time.

"Present arms."

He started wriggling again and shouting, "No, no, Mum, don't let them take me away from you!"

Take aim.

His bladder emptied all down his trousers. His last word was 'Mum'.

Fire.

All six separate shots emerged as one, as if in slow motion. I thought I saw all the bullets going towards the target as they hit his chest, exploded, and then blood gushed out with bone and skin, fat and muscle. They all mingled with his shirt and vest. The red patch had long gone. Probably gone through his body and out the other side.

We stood down and ejected the spent cartridges which the Sergeant collected. I then looked over to the prisoner whose body now hung lifeless from the post. The three officers were standing around and the doctor was carrying out his examination. He removed several things out of his bag. After a short time, he looked at the other two shaking his head. From where I was standing, I didn't know what he meant. I was slightly puzzled with what was going on. All the bullets hit the mark, so why was there such confusion?

We all fell in and got ready to march off, when shockingly I saw the officer take out his pistol. The other two stood to one side while he put the gun to the man's head and looking away, at arm's length, he fired once. As most of the man's head shattered, the officer tried to avoid the mess but was not quick enough. His arm and part of his uniform were covered in blood and brain. As we marched away, I could see the medics with the coffin cutting the body down. The three officers were now standing around talking. The ones on the terrace had started to go back inside the house. No doubt believing that they had rid the army of a coward, when probably he shouldn't have been there in the first place. Just because he was frightened doesn't make him a coward in my books.

As we marched back through the gate and across the courtyard, I began to think if my courage would fail me when I first go into battle. What about my brother and our friends? It could happen to any one of us. We could be tied to that post in a few weeks. What a horrible, inhumane way to die. I wondered how many of those higher-ranking officers had been to the front and been involved in the fighting, or even ever been frightened.

We stopped by the entrance that we had used earlier. The sergeants said we could take a short break and those who smoked immediately lit up. No one spoke. We were all trying to find our own way to live with what we had just taken part in; some way to live with what we had done. Just then the door opened and the officer came out carrying a bottle and some tin mugs, which he passed around. When we'd all had one drink he came along the line giving each of us a generous measure.

"Sorry, it's only rum this time, but it might help to dull the feelings of this morning's filthy business."

While he was talking, I couldn't help noticing that although he had changed his shirt and tunic, there were still bloodstains on his boots, his trousers, and on the side of his face, and even in his hair. I thought to tell him but decided against it. He had had a worse day than us.

He thanked us for doing our job and wished us all good luck and then disappeared back inside. After we'd finished our drinks, we formed up and marched round to the side of the house where our transport was waiting to take us back to camp.

No one spoke on the way back and as we climbed off the vehicle, we wished each other good luck and went off to our various companies. As I walked back with the Sergeant towards our camp, I said, "What do I tell the others, Sergeant? They're bound to ask."

"It's been a really bloody duty today, not good for the British Army. I think you should tell the truth, son. You have nothing to be ashamed of. The people who allowed this to happen are the ones who must answer for their actions. Now go and get some rest. We've a long march ahead."

As I walked past row upon row of tents, there was something different about the camp. I stopped for a short while, noticing the distant gunfire was even louder and more ferocious than ever before, but it was not that that caught my attention, it was something else. Something closer. Then it came to me. I could hear the birds singing in the trees towards the back of the camp. There had always been too much noise coming from the men before, but now it was so quiet and so peaceful. I had to pinch myself to be certain that I was awake. All other thoughts forgotten for the time being, I began to panic. I rushed to the nearest tent, ripping a flap open. There was no kit and there were no men. I went to another and another, then many more. They were all the same; empty. It was looking like the whole camp was empty. They had all gone, but where? I began to run as fast as I could to where our tent was, and as I got closer I knew I had been left behind. I slumped on the grass outside, partly through running and partly through sheer desperation. My emotions were all confused. Tears were beginning to trickle down my face.

"The head groom's back, then," shouted Peter. I looked up and there they were, stripped to the waist, strolling through the grass, towels slung over their shoulders, just coming back from the wash-house.

"What's up?" Phil shouted. "Not good enough for the officers' horses?"

John joined in. "He's alright with the old cart horses back home though."

They all roared with laughter, but as they got closer they could see there were something really wrong.

I got up to greet them and threw my arms around them.

"I thought you'd gone and left me behind."

"No," Peter said, looking slightly startled, "Most of the other companies have gone but we aren't due to be sent out until midday."

I frantically looked around for Phil who was standing slightly away from the others. I moved over to face him with tears in my eyes. I hugged him as never before. We then all sat on the grass and it was Phil who spoke first.

"Now, what exactly was this early-morning duty then?"

Peter started to go on about horses but Phil told him to shut up and listen to me. I started at the beginning and told them everything; about the young girl with the tea, the cook and the sandwiches, the whisky for the tea. I even told them what the officer had said and about the choosing of the bullets. At this point, they were all staring at me in disbelief. I carried on and told them how the prisoner was dragged, kicking and screaming to the stake and how they had tied him to it. I told them about the coffin and the priest and finally how we murdered him, but that eventually it still took a single shot from the officer's revolver to finish the job, I explained about the rum to steady our nerves and then our journey back to camp.

"How do I live with that then, lads?" I queried in a slightly sarcastic tone.

"You don't have to. You were only doing your duty, obeying orders. Why it was done is not your business, that burden lies with others, not you."

Looking around, it was the Sergeant talking. He had quietly walked towards us and had overheard me telling my tale.

"But Sergeant," John interrupted, "we can't be made to kill our own soldiers. We all signed up to fight the enemy, not execute our own kind, no matter what they've done."

The Sergeant replied angrily, "When you joined the British Army, you agreed to come here under Army regulations which say you obey and carry out all orders. You do not question orders, under any circumstances. What you have just said could be looked upon as mutiny, which is a punishable offence and under Army regulations carries the death sentence. So if I were you, I would be very careful who you say things like that to. Anyway, I came to tell you that we're moving out to the front in three hours, so get all your kit organised and together, and then get some rest. It's going to be a hard march and we will be within range of the enemy's guns. Come on, jump to! Report on the road in three hours. If you haven't already done it, I suggest you make out your wills too, in the section provided in your pay book."

Then off he went to spread the news to the rest of the company.

Just after midday, we were formed up and marching at a steady pace towards the ever-calling of the big guns. Finally, after many days since we had set out from training camp, we were going to face the front line and action.

Shell holes and craters

Chapter 5

As we moved closer to the front, the ominous signs of War were becoming more and more visible more and more frequently. Huge store dumps camouflaged from enemy spotters were becoming more frequent the closer that we got. Munitions were now in smaller dumps, but there were a lot more of them than we had seen earlier on in our journey. Artillery shells of all sizes lay in rows along the side of the road. As the miles went by, there were more and more of these dumps, and also fields full of extra equipment. We could see miles and miles of barbed wire, stakes, tools of all kinds, spare vehicles, water carriers, all sorts and sizes of timber, small guns, large guns and tractors. Everywhere you looked there were Army stores. It seemed that we were now moving at an ever-quickening pace to the front.

As the light began to fade, we started to come upon artillery batteries dug in along hedgerows and in the natural hollows, and for the first time each salvo of fire made us all shake. There were shell craters all over the area where the enemy artillery had been trying to destroy our guns. Further on, we started coming upon first-aid stations. There were the all too familiar smells of the dying and the dead, accompanied by the screams and cries of the wounded and the sobbing of the dying. To the sides and rear were bodies piled high with sheets thrown over them, but despite the well-intended attempts to disguise such horrors you could still see arms and legs sticking out from underneath. I knew they were waiting for burial, but surely this is not the way to treat the heroic dead?

Although it was night-time, the horizon and the sky directly in front of me was lit up just like daylight, and then looking over my shoulder I was startled to see that it was exactly the same behind. We were totally surrounded by artillery fire. It came as a shock when we actually first came under shellfire. Without any prior warning, several shells came down in the field close to the road, then two more landed on the other side of the road. What followed was utter confusion. No one knew which way to run. The NCOs were shouting for us to get out of the road but in the fields was where the shells were landing. If we had done as we were told, we wouldn't have taken any casualties at all, but we didn't follow orders. A few seconds later, about twenty to thirty shells landed along the road and on either side of us. Before the second salvo hit, we had all scattered across the fields taking what cover we could find. I managed to jump into an old shell crater and curled up into a ball at the bottom and just spent my time praying that we would all survive. After about five minutes, the shelling stopped for a few minutes. All was quiet and then the cries of the wounded drifted across the fields. I scrambled out of my hole and was glad to see all the others in one piece. Together, we hurried across our field to where the cries were the loudest. We were met by a totally confused situation. There were wounded soldiers everywhere. We had to scrabble about in the dark as we had no sources of light. Most of the NCOs were either dead or wounded. In the middle of all the chaos, a couple of regular soldiers started to shout orders to go to the nearest wounded men. We were told to do what we could for them and also if we located any dead to mark them for collection for when it would get light. They also said they were going to send a couple of runners towards the front to try and find help.

Phil and I started to work along the ditch, feeling our way and it was not too long before we found a body. I remember thinking that I just thanked God that it was so dark. While feeling for any sign of life, it soon became clear that he was dead. The blast had caught him on his left side and his arm was gone completely, and also half of his leg, too. He also had a large hole in his head and quite a number of his ribs were sticking right out of his chest.

"Phil, see if you can find his rifle and use it to mark the spot."

As he searched for the rifle, I was trying to wipe off the warm and sticky blood that I had got all over my hands in the damp, dewy grass. We crawled further on in the ditch, finding several more bodies, and then we came upon a live soldier. I checked him out as best I could and apart from a couple of small cuts, he seemed to be alright. I tried to get through to him where he was and what exactly had happened to him but he wouldn't talk.

"Look," I said, "if you climb up onto the road, the rest of the company are just a little way on. There will be someone there to help you."

He seemed to have all his kit, and so we tried to help him get up.

"I'm not going without my mate," he said in a steady voice. "We've been friends for years. I'm going to marry his sister when we get home. Ken is going to be my best man. I can't leave him here, can I? He's my best man."

"Where is he?" I said. "We can help both of you if you tell us where he is."

Phil and I started calling his name, but there was no answer.

"Are you sure he's out there?" I said. "He might have gone ahead to try to find help."

"No," the soldier said. "He wouldn't leave me. No, he's here with me."

I knelt down beside him, softly asking him to take my hand and guide me to him. Slowly, he took hold of my hand and guided it towards his lap. I felt hair first, then an ear but running my fingers over the face, even though I could feel no wounds, I knew he was dead.

"Look," I said. "I will lift Ken off you and we can lay him to have a rest alongside you. Then, after a while, you can make your way to the front of the column."

His only reply was that he wouldn't leave Ken on his own. I stood up and stepped over him, and then bending over to feel for his friend's body, I couldn't find anything. So moving my hands up his body, I found what I was looking for, the only part of his body left untouched. The soldier was lovingly cradling his friend's head in his lap, probably not even knowing that the rest of him was gone. I tried several times to get him to let go, but he just wouldn't. So eventually, we decided to leave him for the medical people to deal with. We could do no more.

We carried on along the ditch but found nothing else, so we crossed the road and started working our way back towards the front. We patched up several minor wounded as best we could and also marked another three dead. As we approached what was left of our company, it was a great sight to see that none of our friends were hurt. There were also several officers who had come from a camp not far

away and had now taken charge. All the wounded were being carried out onto the road. Those in a serious condition
were left where they fell. An ambulance had just arrived
and several people got out and spoke with the officers.
Then they made their way into the fields with lamps and
started attending to the seriously wounded. One of the officers shouted for all non-injured soldiers to fall in on the
road with their kit ready to march. He then called for any
wounded who could either march to the aid post, which
was about thirty minutes away, or even up to about one-
and-a-half hours to our company command post. Quite a
few got to their feet and came over to join the column.

"Right, lads," said the officer. "Help them as much
you can."

As we dispersed ourselves amongst the wounded,
several more shouted for help.

"We can get to the aid station faster with a little help.
You men at the rear, go and help as many as want to go
down to the aid station."

We ended up carrying another six lads in what
turned out for them to be a grueling and painful thirty odd
minutes. As we trudged along the road, several ambulances
and trucks passed by driving on to where our wounded
were going, or at least we hoped they were. We had to dive
for cover several times as enemy shells were raining down
all around us. Then it started to rain. Slowly at first, but it
was not long before it was a very heavy downpour. Finally,
we came upon the aid post and left our wounded with
them. Some of the minor wounded were patched up and
continued on with the rest of us. Without the casualties
holding us back, the pace of the march was stepped up and
in just under an hour we arrived at our destination.

Looking around, it looked as though at one time it
had been quite a large farm with lots of outbuildings and
barns. Most of these had suffered some kind of damage.

There were now tents dotted around the place and quite a number of old wooden carts scattered randomly, too. There were batteries of light and medium guns on all sides which just kept on firing. From their flashes as they fired, you could see the gunners dashing about to keep the guns firing at maximum firepower. Behind each gun was a large pile of ammunition, and just a bit further away there was a team of horses. This assault on the enemy lines stretched both ways as far as any man could see. We could not hear ourselves speak. However the gunners managed, I'll never know. This bombardment had been going on for six days non-stop. God only knows when it would stop. Still, I suppose that whilst they were firing, at least soldiers were not being attacked.

The officer told us to fall out and try to get some rest wherever we could and to wait for further orders. We were also expecting new officers to join up with us in the near future, too. We all went off to scout around the place to try and find a dry place to rest up, but there weren't any, no matter how hard we looked. All the tents were occupied, but Harry did manage to come up with some food.

"Come on," I said, "I've got an idea."

I led them to one of the big barns. On the side of it was a large wooden cart.

"Look," I said, "if we lift the cart and let it fall against the wall, we can all get underneath it."

John said, "I've seen some sheeting over there, we can put it over the cart to keep the rain out. It should stop most of it."

We all looked at each other. "Why not?" said Phil. "Let's give it to go."

Within half an hour, we were home and dry. There was even a sheet put on the ground and another two that blocked off both ends. Harry got out a couple of candles that he'd brought from the training camp and he was just about to light them, when Phil said, "You can't light them, the Germans might see us."

"So?" Harry said.

"Well, they might see the light and start shelling us," Phil said.

"I don't know if you have noticed or not, but we are in the middle of a massive artillery battle. The place is lit up like a November bonfire. I don't think two candles will make that much difference."

With that we all burst out laughing at him.

"I suppose you're right," he said, "but you never know," he replied, smirking.

After about an hour, we had made ourselves very much at home. There were no leaks and we had created a dry area to sit on. As the shelling carried on around us, we ate all the food that Harry had found. I think we had all got used to the gunfire by now, or as much as we ever would. In the very brief periods of near silence, we would talk about the men who had been killed and wounded earlier. There were only one or two we thought we knew, but in all the chaos and darkness, we could not be sure. I wondered to myself if we would ever be told, or find out who had been hurt or lost. I was just starting to think back to the horrors that we had found back in the fields, when the end of our shelter cover was briskly pulled open. A familiar voice shouted inside, "I might have guessed you lot would find a nice comfy shelter. Now move up and let me in, it's wet out here."

Once the Sergeant had clambered in, we all tried to talk to him at the same time, as well as shake his hand.

"Hold on, hold on," he said. "If you would just listen, I'll tell you what happened."

He paused briefly and then continued.

"When the first shells hit, we knew these were ranging shots and that worse was on the way, that's why we kept

139

telling you dozy lot to scatter off the road. The rest is history. I came to as they were carrying me into the aid station. I was lucky. A shell blast knocked me out but it blew me into the fields, which probably saved me. I got a small piece of shell in my shoulder, which they took out."

He reached into his pocket and took out a small piece of metal.

"I'm keeping this for my kids, if ever I have any. I managed to get a lift up here. I knew you wouldn't start without me, so here I am."

While he was eating some of our leftover food, Peter asked about the injured and the dead. We waited patiently until he had he finished chewing.

"I don't know any names but there were forty six wounded, some seriously, others not too badly. They've found twenty-eight dead so far, but they're going to check the area again in daylight. They did find an unusual one in the ditch near the end of the column, though. A dead soldier was cradling another soldier in his arms, like you would a baby, only this was just the head of another soldier. There wasn't any body anywhere to be found. No one could work out how it could have happened. They must have been pals, I suppose. Funny that."

With that, he drifted off into his own thoughts for a few seconds. Phil and I looked at each other and I shook my head as discreetly as I could. That was the end of that, another of our unbelievable experiences that never in our whole lives would we forget.

"Anyway," said the Sergeant, "there's a huge offensive starting at six o'clock."

He looked at his watch fleetingly.

"That's in about five hours time. The first waves of infantry are already in the frontline trenches. Our job is to follow them up and secure the enemy positions already taken. It's as easy as that, lads. Okay? By the way, as well as our own kit and ammunition, we've also got to carry as much spare ammunition as we can to replenish the first wave's, so report at six o'clock at the command post. There'll also be new officers and NCOs. I'll be there as well, just to keep an eye on you lot."

Then off he went, shouting back to us to keep our heads down tonight as apparently this lot of firing was going to get worse. He was right. As the night wore on, the bombardment, both theirs and ours, got far worse. On a number of occasions, shells landed so close to us that if it had not been for the thick timber that the cart was made of, we would have been cut to pieces by the metal from the shells.

As we waited and rested as much as we could, time was our worst enemy. Dark soon became light, and although none of us had a watch, we knew it was nearly time for the off. We decided to leave our safe shelter and make our way to the command post.

The sight that met our eyes was like nothing you could ever have imagined, not even in your worst nightmare. The ruined farm and outbuildings were like an island surrounded by ploughed, muddy fields. Only they weren't ploughed, they were churned up by all types of guns, horses, tractors, vehicles of all sizes, but mostly by enemy shelling. There were thousands upon thousands of craters. As we got closer to the command post, you could see all over the area. Munitions dumps, supplies, first-aid stations and thousands of soldiers lining up, waiting for orders, just as we were about to do, too.

As we approached the group of tents, there was a distinct change in the sound of gunfire. I still to this day don't know what it was, but I was about to find out what it would mean to be on the receiving end. Other soldiers started to gather into a group, so we formed into ranks and waited silently in wonderment. After about five minutes, I was pushed into going to find out what was happening. Walking up to the main tent, I checked my appearance briefly before opening flap and then walking smartly in. There were about a dozen officers and NCOs standing around a table with a map on it. At first, no one took much notice of me, until one of the officers turned around.

"Yes, soldier? What do you want?"

As best I could, I came to attention.

"Beg to report, sir, but all the men are lined up waiting for your orders, sir."

"Wait a minute," he said, coming closer. "I know you, don't I?"

"Yes, sir," I said. "We met the other morning."

"Yes, that's right. Nasty business."

Someone at the table said, "Sir, last countdown."

"Right," he said, "Corporal, go and sort the men out. We'll be out shortly."

"Yes, sir," came the reply.

Someone I didn't know marched past me, saying to get fell in. We marched one behind the other to the rest of the company, I fell in with them and he then brought us all to attention. After standing there for several minutes, we could faintly hear something in the distance, quietly at first and then it grew louder and louder. It was a roaring noise just like at a football match, only much, much louder. Then, mass rifle fire and slowly, a build-up of machine gun fire. The surrounding batteries of artillery began to step up their rate of fire, and fresh guns could be seen being sent up to the front ready for action. At that moment, officers and NCOs came out of the tent and over to us.

"Right men. As you have probably heard, our main attack has just started. Our job is to take fresh supplies, dig in and hold against the counter-attack ground gained by this morning's attack. Right, Sergeant, get the men moving to the supply dump. Pick a couple of men out for runners. They can stay here until needed."

"Yes, sir," shouted the Sergeant. "Right turn, quick march."

I know it might sound odd but it was good to hear a friendly voice in a situation such as this. As we drew level with him, he said, "Who's the best runner amongst you lot?" We all pointed to John.

"Right, fall out and report to company command. Tell them you're the runners, and you, too," he said, pointing to another soldier.

There was no time for goodbyes or handshakes. Within the blink of an eye, John was gone. I thought at the time that at least he would be a lot safer at the rear and we would get to see him when he'd come with messages.

We were about four hundred yards away from the command post when fate dealt us its first of many cruel blows. The first shells landed short of their target. We scattered and found cover where we could. The full barrage of shells scored direct hits time after time, but only lasting for several minutes, and it was soon over. Phil, myself and Peter dashed back, closely followed by Harry to see if we could help the wounded, but as we got closer it was becoming more and more obvious that there would be no wounded. We all stood by the huge crater that had once been a command post, caused by so many shells. There was only smoke and an odd flicker of flame now coming out of the hole. I started to climb down into the crater just as the officer and several NCOs arrived.

"You can't help them now, soldier," he shouted. "The Pioneers will dig what's left of them out."

"Sorry, sir, but one of my best friends is down here somewhere, sir. Wouldn't you try for your best friend, sir?"

"Of course I would, soldier."

"Private, you stay here searching and I'll take the men to the supplies, and you can catch up later."

"Yes, sir. Beg pardon, sir. Can my other three friends stay and help? We'll be done quicker if they do, sir."

"Yes, Private. You know where to find us."

"Yes, sir ."

"Oh, and good luck to you all."

He took a glance down at me in the hole and we both knew there was nothing left of John to be found. As the others started to come into the crater, I stopped them and told them to look around the perimeter as he might have managed to get out or have been blown out. As I started to search amongst the rubble, the Sergeant came down to join me.

"Thanks, Sarge, but you don't have to. He's our friend."

"I know," he said, "but I'm the one who picked him. How do you think I feel?"

I just nodded and we both set about the gruesome task of trying to find anything that was either John, or that had belonged to him.

After a couple of hours of searching through limbs, parts of limbs, flesh, organs, hair, rib cages, shattered heads, hands, feet and everything you could possibly imagine, we had found nothing of significance to John. It was with sad hearts that we had to give up the search. We all stood in a line on the edge of the crater. There was nothing to be said and no words could describe how we were feeling. It could have been any one of us. It was just because he ran the fastest that fate had taken a hand in his life. We all shed tears and said goodbye in our own way. As we stood there in total shock, I couldn't help but picture his Mum hearing the news on her front doorstep. She would quickly go into shock and collapse with an unstoppable flow of tears. Friends and neighbours would be called to help her into the house. Someone would go and fetch his Dad who would make his way home in a state of total disbelief, only to see the look in his darling wife's eyes. Their lives, forever shattered, they would never recover. The word would spread quickly around the village and people would come hurrying over to offer sympathy and help. Last of all, would come our Mums, not daring to leave their homes in case there was a message coming for them and not wanting to go in case there was bad news waiting for them there.

As I gradually began to surface out of my state of shock, I walked across to each of the lads in turn. We hugged and said a few words to each other. No one wanted to leave, so I said as gently as I could, "Time to go now. John wouldn't want us moping around here now, would he?"

With heads slightly bowed, we each said our last goodbyes, then turned and slowly walked away, down towards the Sergeant who was waiting for us. We lined up and with British guns firing around us, and enemy shells landing all over the place, we marched down the muddy path and through the fields to join the rest of the company.

We rejoined the company at the munitions and supply dump. They had all been loaded up with as much as each man could carry. We were also quickly loaded like pack mules. Within a few minutes, we'd set off, marching as best we could through terrible conditions; mud, shell holes, ploughed up fields and no path to follow. We trudged on and on, the rifle and machine-gun fire getting ever closer. We were soon met by a runner who led us into a trench system, which turned out to be huge and still growing all the time. It was far beyond any civilian's imagination. Trenches weaved in and out. There were signs and arrows pointing the way to aid posts and officers' dug outs all along the way.

As we got closer to the frontline, there were signs ordering us to keep our heads down as we were now in sniper range. The chatter of machine-gun fire was almost deafening, and on top of that there was rifle fire, trench mortars and the non-stop shelling.

Some of the trenches were boarded but mostly they were either filled with water or mud. Stretchers with the wounded were pouring past us, non-stop. The cries and screams were pitiful to hear. We were halted by another officer, who looked like a captain. He spoke briefly to our officer and then they went forward together. While they were gone, we unloaded our extra supplies into a deep bunker. I thought that we were supposed to take them further forward to reinforce captured positions, but obviously someone had other ideas. We waited for about half an hour when, without any warning, the machine-gun to the front of us stopped firing. We could hear shouting, charge men were attacking, whistles were being blown and an ever-growing roar of human voices became apparent. The enemy's machine-guns and rifle fire eased off for a few minutes. Then it started all over again. As it started to grow in ferocity, it drowned out all human voices. The shelling started to concentrate more on the battlefield than the rear positions from where we were. Although we couldn't see anything, the sounds were like hell on earth. After about twenty minutes, the enemy shelling again switched to the rear positions. The constant chatter of enemy machine-guns never wavered and now with our machine-guns opening up as well, it was beginning to sound like an ongoing duel. Without having any time to think, our company was moved on, into the front line trenches. Nothing had prepared us for what we were to encounter.

It was a fairly deep trench, shored up with wood and props. The floor was probably made from timber duckboards, but we couldn't see for the thick mud and the bodies of the wounded that were sitting or lying waiting for help. The whole trench system was full of them, everywhere we looked. The mud was running deep red with blood. We had to make our way along the firing step in order not to trample them. We lost several of our company to enemy fire but it was the only way to assemble in preparation for our attack. Every so often, there were either old ladders or steps cut into the side of the trench. Machine-guns were dug in and were also sand-bagged for extra cover and protection. When we were in position, we knelt down and waited. I think we all knew what was coming. That's what we had all joined up for, to fight our country's enemy but we had never, ever thought it would be anything like this. You imagine as a child from books and pictures that you read about the glory, chivalry and brave deeds, valiant heroes and grand campaigns. Nothing is ever said about the dead, the dying, the wounded, the terrible conditions, the filth and the disease. This was no way for anyone to fight and die, drowning in a sea of filth, blood and bodies.

Glancing down there was a soldier propped up against the wall. His legs were under the mud but there was blood bubbling on the surface. His battledress tunic was seeping blood, his head was tilted slightly to one side, his eyes were closed and his face splashed with mud. Someone, probably a pal or even his brother, had lit a cigarette and put it between his lips. At first, I thought he was dead but every so often a trail of smoke would rise. This one thing sparked an urge in me to step out of line and help him. As I was getting ready to jump down, the order came down the line to fix bayonets and to stand to.

Fixing our bayonets, we all stood up waiting for the next order. I was quite close to a ladder, so I could get away quickly. God knows what waited for us and the thousands of others once that order was given. I glanced back to see how the wounded lad was doing but he was gone, probably picked up by some stretcher-bearers. Then I spotted a few odd, bloody bubbles floating on the mud and water. Had he died before he slipped under the filth? It was just one of the many questions that I would never find an answer to.

Looking up and down the line, I could see officers and NCOs getting onto the ladders. The enemy machine-gun fire eased off, waiting for fresh targets. The enemy's artillery was getting ready to switch targets, too. In a steady swell from man to man down the line came the orders: covering fire, friendly troops coming in. Caught off guard, it took a few seconds to register, but then we started to send a hail of bullets towards the enemy lines. Both machine-gun fire and artillery fire was brought to bear. Slowly at first, then it gradually speeded up.

The survivors of the previous attack came back. Some with minor wounds, but quite a few of these were having to carry the badly wounded themselves. Some used the ladders and steps but most just jumped back into the trenches, which by now were so crowded that it was impossible to move. It makes me feel sick when I recall that the only way to move around the trench was by walking over the bodies who were sunk in the mud at the bottom. But still, it was the only way to get the wounded out. As the attacks died down, the murderous enemy fire also eased off and finally stopped. Within seconds, their artillery started shelling our trenches, for they must have known there were more troops than usual crowded together. There was no cover to be had anywhere and no means of escape out of the trenches. The first shells landed just short of the frontline trenches, but we all knew they were just ranging in on their target. As we were waiting, you could hear men praying, others were sobbing and many were talking desperately to their mothers. I just knelt there with my brother and our friends, all huddled together, clinging to the side of the trench for protection.

The volume of the rush firstly came like the sound of dozens of fast trains, and then the initial shells started to rain down, exploding amongst a tide of human flesh, bones and blood. Initially, they hit the trenches further along from us. Accompanying the noise of incoming shells and explosions were the now all too familiar screams and cries of the wounded. I never heard the first shell hit our trench but the impact and explosion seemed to suck all the air from our lungs and caused great pressure deep down in our eardrums. The first shells bombarded us for how long, God only knows. But no one was shown any mercy, that I know for sure. I could stand to look no more. Every shell bought misery, pain and suffering. More flesh and limbs were ripped from an already choked trench, and then ceaselessly scattered its grisly load all around the place. I tried to force myself into the side of the trench and blamed Mum for making me too big with her good cooking. I don't know who the man behind me was, but I could feel his fear as he gripped my shoulder. I reached for his arm and just lightly gripped him and held on for a few minutes. I think it helped him a little, if only to reassure him he wasn't alone.

There was a slight lull in the shelling when a number of soldiers, for whatever reason, tried to get away from the carnage. One of our company jumped off the firing step, sobbing and ranting. He started to try to get away but our Sergeant stopped him, gave him a drink and calmed him down. Then one of his pals came and took him back to his position. Shortly after, the shelling started again. Luckily, it didn't persist for as long as the first bombardment, and as we still huddled together, waiting for it to restart, the minutes were ticking away. We began to relax our muscles first, and then gradually our shattered minds followed suit. The vision of the trenches was one of utter carnage. Never in any one person's life could such a sight be fully absorbed.

I've never been a strongly religious person, but if God exists why did he allow this all to happen? Why did he let all the survivors witness such horrors that would live with them until they died? Why did he allow all the mothers of these brave soldiers to go through untold pain and sadness when they received the dreaded letter? If all mothers around the world could see what we saw, they would never let their sons go to war.

"Stand to. Stand to."

The order came down the line and everyone who wasn't wounded took up their position on the firing step. At first, I couldn't see much as the whole of the battlefield was shrouded in smoke.

"Stay alert and keep your heads down," shouted the Sergeant. "They might try and sneak through to our lines under the cover of all this smoke."

I kept down as low as I could and watched whilst the smoke slowly drifted away. The sight in front of our trench was as I had thought it would be. The ground was churned up and covered with shell holes and craters. There were rows upon rows of barbed wire, damaged in places by shell-fire. There was what looked like army uniforms hanging on the wire in a number of places. Not knowing what they were for, I asked the soldier next to me.

"They're bodies, mate, " he said. "It's too dangerous to bring them in, so they stay out there."

By this time, the smoke had almost cleared and the enemy lines could clearly be seen. Their barbed wire was far thicker and deeper than ours, and it looked like they had machine-guns positioned every few feet. Their sandbags were piled far higher and wider. In all, I thought their defences looked a lot more substantial than ours. Between the barbed wire was what I got to know as the 'killing ground'. What was probably once good farming land was now covered in craters and muddy ploughed up furrows, just like it had been prepared ready for planting, but then the War had started. The ground was littered with bodies from the earlier attack, and I suspected that there were even more in the craters, unseen.

There was a bit of a commotion in the line to our right as a British soldier climbed out of the trench and started running up and down screaming, crying, and shouting. It was probably because he couldn't stand any more. Soldiers were calling him back in but he couldn't hear them. I thought fearfully to myself that it wouldn't be long before a sniper shoots him. He dropped to his knees and started crying like a baby. The spectacle was incredibly unnerving for everyone witnessing it. He clambered back up onto his feet and ran in front of us and then fell onto his knees once again, howling and begging for help. Amidst the mayhem, suddenly a single shot rang out, exploding the back of his head. He slumped forward, his face landing in the mud. He twitched several times, and then he was finally still. Word soon spread down the line that it was one of our officers who had shot him. I suppose you could say that it was a mercy killing. No one in their right mind would want anyone to suffer like that. As it turned out, officers had been told to shoot in similar circumstances and were under orders to do so in order to prevent desertion, cowardice, or even mutiny.

For the rest of the day, very little happened. Every so often, the big guns would fire a few shells but they mainly landed behind us. The stretcher-bearers had to start to clear the wounded and dead with the help of some Pioneers, but there were so many they finally agreed to try to deal with the wounded first, leaving the dead to sink slowly into the mud. We had water and food brought round, which we ate whilst still on duty, and we eventually stood down just after dusk. The Sergeant posted the guards and informed us of the duty roster.

"Now, get as much rest as you can. There's an attack planned for dawn."

Brotherly love

Chapter 6

I don't think anyone actually got much rest. We all stayed up on the firing step; it was unthinkable to step down into the mud. It wasn't too long before the cries of the wounded stranded in no man's land came drifting across to us. Flares were sent up by both sides so that the battlefield was lit up for the majority of the time. The stretcher-bearers tried on many occasions to retrieve some of them, but were fired on whenever they were seen. Several minor wounded managed to crawl back to our lines, along with quite a few who had taken cover in the craters. The time up until midnight was uneventful really. You could hear the reinforcements moving up behind us and ammunition was being restocked. Hot tea came round and the Officer and Sergeant came to confirm our next planned attack.

The barrage started at midnight and was aimed at hitting the enemy's trenches and barbed wire. Shellfire was returned but it was going to our rear. The shelling lasted till daylight, then more shells started landing in our barbed wire fortifications to open up some through routes. It was quite light by now. The battlefield was covered with a mixture of mist and smoke, and when the shelling stopped it became so peaceful, so tranquil that it was hard to understand why all around us was about to be turned into a living hell.

"Fix bayonets," came the order. The click click of bayonets being fixed onto guns up and down the trenches was deafening. We had a few minutes to make peace with our God, and then a colossal artillery barrage began, aimed at the enemy positions. Flares went up, whistles began sounding and officers accompanied by their NCOs were on top of the trenches, urging us to attack. A deep roar started to rise from the throats of thousands of English infantry as they clambered over the top of their trenches and headed for the enemy's lines. The ferocity of our bombardment must have stunned the enemy briefly as there was very little defensive fire, but once it did start it was murderous. They concentrated their machine-guns on the top of our trenches and their shellfire was spread across no-man's-land.

There were so many young men who got no further than the top of the trench. They either fell back or were pulled in by others waiting impatiently to go up and over. Most were either dead or dying, and not many would survive the day. It was chaos trying to get out of the trench. With us in the first wave still not all gone, the second wave was crushing in behind us. As I grabbed the ladder, a pair of hands reached above mine from behind me.

"Me first," he shouted. Looking up, with a big grin on his face, I could see Phil. He winked at me cheekily.

"Good luck," I shouted, and then he was gone up the ladder. I was only one rung behind him as he stepped off, out into the unknown.

He wouldn't have felt anything. As he stumbled back, I tried to catch him but he ended up pulling us both back into the bottom of the trench. We sank into the mud and for a few seconds I thought I was going to die there. It must have been fate but our Sergeant had seen all that had happened and jumped back into the trench and pulled me from the mire. Between us, we carried Phil away from the firing step, barging past the second wave who were still pushing forward, until we managed to find a side trench which was not as filthy and had a wider shelf on one side. We laid him down and the Sergeant unbuckled his ammunition pouches. He put his hand on my shoulder.

"I'm so sorry," he said. "I know you were very close. Look, get a stretcher party to take him to the rear. At least he will be buried respectfully and recorded in a mass grave. If you leave him here, he'll just be left in the trenches. I've got to go now, so good luck."

I looked up at him and tried to thank him but the words just wouldn't come out.

"I know, son," he said. "I know. Now, you see to your brother and do as I've told you."

With that, he turned and went. I only found out later that he went over with the second wave. He managed to get as far as our barbed wire, got tangled up and was brutally machine-gunned down.

I unhooked Phil's water bottle and started to clean him up as best I could. He'd been hit several times in the face and neck, but although he was disfigured, I could only see Phil as he had been. I spent what seemed like an age cleaning the mud from his uniform and boots, talking to him all the time about nothing in particular. I'd done the same when he was young. He used to be scared of the dark and would only go to sleep when he knew I was there with him. When I'd finished my cleaning task, I went through his kit to see if there was anything to take home. I didn't know why but even now with only three of us left, I still had the feeling that I would be going home.

Searching through his pockets, I came across one of Mum's homemade handkerchiefs that we had had when we were young. The edges were frilly with patterns stitched around them. I remembered how the other children would laugh at us when they saw them, but we didn't mind, they were special to us. In his top jacket pocket I found an envelope addressed to Mum and Dad. To be honest, I was a little surprised to find it as he was no good when it came to writing letters. He usually left them to me. The envelope was almost covered in blood but I could just see a piece of paper inside. I couldn't get it out at first as it was too wet and sticky and I didn't want to damage it.

Feeling through the blood and ripped flesh around his neck, it took me a while before I found what I was looking for. Gently, I slipped the chain round his neck until I came to the clasp, and cautiously unclipping it, I took it off. The cross itself was actually stuck in one of the bullet-holes, so gently opening the wound up a little I managed to prise the cross free. I put it in the envelope and placed it on the delicate hanky, folding them all together. Then, unbuttoning my tunic, I put the package into my shirt pocket. I could do no more for him, so I hesitantly knelt down in front of him.

"At least it was quick and you didn't suffer, Phil. You know, Mum will be heartbroken when she gets the news. I wish it were me telling her. Still, when I see her, I'll tell her how brave you were and how you didn't suffer any pain. I don't know where you go from here but I would like to think that we'll all meet up in a time and a place where we go on forever. I'm sorry I can't shed any tears for you now. I fear they will come later though, much later."

Slowly, the sounds of battle once again began to filter back into my head. Standing up, my eyes were fixed on looking down at him, lying in the mud with half of his face and skull shot away. But I could still only see him as I had always known him. I wasn't shocked or sickened by the horror in front of my eyes. I merely touched his other cheek, bent over and kissed his forehead.

"Sleep well, little brother. Sleep well. The darkness won't hurt you now. I have to go now but look for me when the time comes."

Walking a few steps back to the main trench, which was now in a state of sheer chaos, there were soldiers trying to get down to the front. Ammunition carriers were pushing their way through, stretcher parties were trying to get to the front and then were returning with the wounded. I shouted to a stretcher party who followed me up to where Phil was lying. The Corporal in charge just looked at Phil without any emotion.

"Sorry, mate. We can only take the wounded back until we're ordered to do otherwise. Was he your pal?"

"No," I said, calmly, "He's my younger brother. I don't want him dumped in a mud-filled trench or shell hole, so please take him back to the rear for a humane burial. Please, Corporal. I'm begging you."

"Look, soldier. We're both sorry for your loss but we just can't take him while there's a wounded man left on the battlefield."

They turned to leave but I stepped in front of them, tilting my rifle towards their faces.

"Look, son. You don't want to go down that road. We both feel for you, honestly. I don't want to have to report you, so come on, let us pass and we'll forget all about it."

They moved towards me and I quickly loaded and shouldered my rifle.

"What's going on here?" a voice roared behind me. No one answered.

"Corporal, give me a full report and be quick about it."

The Corporal sprang to attention and told him all that had happened.

"Private, put your rifle down, now."

"No, sir."

I heard him take his gun from its holster.

"Private, I have a gun pointed at you. Do you know you have committed a court martial offence? That means you could face a firing squad."

"Yes, sir. I know all about firing squads."

For a brief moment, time stood still. Then he walked up the trench and stood beside me. Looking at me sideways, he put his gun slowly back into its holster. Then, reaching for my rifle, he said, "It's all right, Corporal. I know this man."

I let him take the gun and he lent it against the side of the trench. He walked over to Phil and gazed down at him.

"Your brother you say?"

"Yes, sir."

"I'm very sorry to hear that. How many of your group are there left?"

"There's me, but I don't know about the other two. They went over the top with the first wave, just before dawn."

"Corporal, this man lying here is still alive. Get him onto your stretcher and you know where to take him."

"But, sir..."

"No buts, Corporal. I know your orders and this man is alive, so hurry and get him out of here. Any questions, tell them I ordered it." Turning to me, he motioned, "Don't forget your rifle, Private, and see if you can find something better to aim at next time."

Turning sharply, he marched off briskly towards the front line trenches. They carried Phil off and I stood and watched until they were well out of sight. Then, I made my way down to the front line in time for the next wave to be butchered whilst trying to capture, what? Nobody ever told us what, so we just came, obeyed and carried out our orders. Consequently, most of them died and were buried in places we'd never heard of.

Crouching on the firing step, the all too familiar battle calls started up again. Whistles, flares, and then the almighty roar from thousands of sheep being led to the slaughter. I finally stepped onto the battlefield and not caring whether I lived or died, charged towards the enemy lines. Young men were being mercilessly cut down all around me, but I was unaware of what was going on about me. All I could see was the goal in the meadow. I had the ball and was running up the middle of the field. Phil was on my left and John on the right. Both were calling for the ball but I just kept on going. There was my goal. I swerved past one defender, then another. Phil and John were still calling for the ball but I only had the goalie to beat and then it was mine. I ran towards the goalie, who came out to meet me. I sidestepped him and put the ball in the back of the net. Jumping with joy, I looked around for the others but to my dismay there was no one there.

"Get down, get down you fool, get down."

I don't know who shouted at me but it jolted me back to the battlefield. Realising I was out in front and the enemy's fire was concentrated on another wave just forming up, I quickly looked for cover and dived headlong into an older drainage ditch. The smell was terrible but it wasn't coming from the ditch itself. There were dozens and dozens of rotting corpses scattered all over the place. I took out my trench spade and as the shells rained down and the enemy machine-guns sized down more infantry attacks,

I dug myself a shelter and shored it up using wood, dirt and bodies. I was determined to somehow come out of this alive. I crawled into my makeshift cover and pulled a body over the entrance and this is where I stayed until nightfall. The guns from both sides kept on firing, shells landed in the distance and occasionally within a few yards of my makeshift grave, sending mud, dirt and bits of soldiers up in the air, landing on top of me. I was terrified beyond belief. I was so scared I cried myself dry. I couldn't help wetting myself. I lay there curled up like a newborn baby. I screamed for my Mum and begged for a quick death. I now think I know how the executed man felt, only my death just went on and on. It was endless torture.

There were several more attacks from our trenches. I couldn't see anything, but I could hear the flares going up and the whistles being blown. The most devastating moment was when the roar of thousands of troops went up, for within minutes the enemy machine-guns opened fire and cut them down in their tracks. Fortunately, none even came near to my shelter and when the guns died down, the screams, the crying, the begging and praying from the wounded started again. It was pitiful to hear and not be able to do anything to help. I tried to block it out by covering my ears. I screamed as loud as I could to try and drown out the sounds of human suffering, but it was impossible. I'll carry those sounds with me for the rest of my life. Eventually, after a while, it started to quieten down and then as if it were cyclical, it started all over again.

As darkness shrouded the battlefield, I crawled out from my hell-hole and took my first breaths of clean air for many an hour. I didn't know how long I had been in there but I know I'll carry the memory for a lifetime. I unbuckled all of my kit, my ammunition pouches, and bayonet holder and ditched them all, except for a few personal things which I stuffed into my shirt pockets. I must have smelt terrible, for as well as lying amongst the bodies in the ditch, the ones that I had used on top had been dripping all kinds of fluids onto me. I gladly dumped my rifle, bayonet and helmet and thought that if I didn't get back, I wouldn't need them, so why bother dragging them around with me?

I moved along the ditch a little way and came to another, which looked like it was going towards our trenches. It wasn't very deep, so I got down onto my stomach as flat as I could and started inching my way forwards. By now, both sides had started firing flares all over the battlefield, which meant there were no dark spells, so I just moved along with extreme caution. As I got closer to our lines, the ditch was filling up with dead soldiers who must have tried to find a scrap of cover. Their torn, mangled, twisted and distorted bodies were forcing me to leave the little cover the ditch had given me and move out into the open. I don't know how long it took but I managed to get within about a hundred yards of our barbed wire.

Whatever luck I had ran out when the ditch leveled off. The barbed wire was damaged in many places, so after looking at several of the nearest openings, I picked what I thought might be the easiest route. The wire was about twenty five yards thick and about a hundred and fifty yards to the trench, and hopefully, safety. Slowly, very slowly I edged my way around large shell holes, which were mostly half-full of water and bloated bodies. Suddenly, one of our machine-guns opened fire then the German gunners joined in, so I rolled into a shallow crater, convinced that they had seen me. As I cowered there, hugging the dirt for cover, I noticed something moving opposite me. The feeling of terror ran through my whole body. Realization dawned that I had no weapon with which to defend myself. I groped around in the half-light, searching for something to protect myself with. I was in such a blind state of panic. I was prepared to kill with my bare hands to survive if I had to. If I hadn't lost all reason after my ordeal, I would have known that it couldn't possibly be the enemy. They hadn't left their positions and it was us who were attacking them in this direction. As I wondered what to do next as a flare burst overhead and floated towards the ground, I could see that the moving body was wearing a British uniform. When the flare had extinguished, I carefully worked my way around the side of the crater until I was alongside him. Leaning over him I whispered, hesitantly, "Are you alright, mate?"

There was no reply. Poor sod, he must have died just as I got here. I started searching his body for anything useful, when I came across a revolver. He must have been an officer, I thought. He won't need this now, though. So I stuffed it down my trousers. I found his spare ammunition and put a handful into my empty pockets. I was just about to go through his pockets for personal articles, which could be sent to his family.

"Water, water, please give me water."

Gently touching his face, I murmured, "I thought you were dead. I was just getting ready to go."

"Water."

Of course, I hadn't any with me. I had dumped it along with my kit. I thought for a while and then made my way back to the ditch. There were dozens of bodies, so it didn't take long to find what I was looking for. There was also a medical bag amongst them, so I threw that over my shoulder as well.

When I got back to him, he had passed out again, so I dribbled some water slowly over his face and lips. I searched the bag for a cloth or something that I could soak to put on his lips. Once I'd done that, I started to look for his wounds.

"It's the right leg that's the worst. My stomach hurts but it's not too bad. Can I have more water, please?"

Lifting the bottle to his lips, I let him take small drops that he could swallow easily.

"Not too much now. Let me look in your wounds."

He was right. His stomach had several small pieces of shrapnel sticking out of it but the injuries weren't really worth bothering with in comparison. His leg was shattered from just above the knee right down to his foot. It was really only hanging on by a few strands of skin. There was nothing suitable in the bag that I could use to help this. Offering him more water, he asked how extensive his injuries were and I told him with as much honesty as I could muster.

"You'd best be on your way, then. It'll soon be light and you want to be undercover by then. Thanks for the water."

"I can't leave you here, you'll die soon when the new attack goes in. The Germans will shell the whole area."

"I might not wait until that happens," he said, reaching for his revolver.

When he couldn't find it, he started to sob.

"Why can't I die with a little dignity, at my own chosen time?"

"Try asking those dead boys lying all around us. They never had your choice. I bet I know what they would have chosen," I said. "There are some things I need to get. I'll be back soon, so hang on. Stay quiet and we'll both get out of here alive."

I slid back out and made my way along the ditch where I collected a number of belts and webbing. Groping around among the dead, I was lucky to find some bits of wood for a splint. Crawling back on all fours, I could see the first signs of dawn appearing on the horizon. Dropping back into the hole, I hastily told him what I was going to do, and finished by informing him that needless to say it was going to be extremely painful for him.

"Don't worry, I won't cry out and give our position away, but I still say you should leave me and go on your own. You stand a better chance of making it alive."

I said nothing, but began my task of binding the splint around his leg.

The pain must have been too much and he soon passed out, which was a blessing as it meant that I could get on quicker. When it was well secured, I made a rough harness from the belts and webbing. After fitting this underneath him and around his arms and body, I was ready to go. I stuffed the water bottle into his tunic and began the hardest part of getting us out of the crater. By sheer luck, he stayed unconscious until we had gone about fifty yards. Then I felt him tugging on the strapping, so I stopped and slid back to him, offering him some water. I pleaded with him, "We've moved closer to our lines, so please try not yell out."

He nodded his head and I put the water away. Gathering my strength, I carried on and once I managed to get him moving. With his good leg, he began to help by propelling himself.

Progress was slow and I was getting tired. With still a long way to go, we had two further stops and I could tell he was getting weaker. I told him to save his energy but he took no notice. Finally, we passed through our wire and with only a hundred and fifty yards to go, it was the first time that I really knew we had a good chance of making it back. On and on we persevered. We got that close I could actually hear the guards talking at the listing post. It was now that our artillery opened up to signal the beginning of another day of slaughter. I wondered if Peter and Harry were still alive, and if the Pioneers had buried Phil in a rightful manner.

He was a dead weight by now, and was probably too exhausted to carry on pushing. As I edged ever closer, I could see the guards' helmets in our trenches. The sight was one I never thought I would see again. Spurred on by this, I went a few more yards until I could eventually go no further. I was totally exhausted. Collapsing face down in the mud, not knowing if my wounded officer was alive or not, I hadn't got the capacity in my lungs to shout out. I thought to myself, it can't end like this. I haven't fired my rifle at the enemy yet. I haven't even seen the enemy.

Scratching around in the mud, I found a clip of bullets and with the last ounce of my strength, I threw it towards our lines. I heard it clatter against something and then for a few seconds there was a commotion, then a challenge came forth.

"Who goes there?"

I managed to raise my arm as a signal.

"Are you wounded?"

I waved as best I could, then my arm slumped back into the mud and I just lay there, not really caring what would happen next.

I remember being dragged roughly into the trenches. I must have looked and smelled horrific. I could hear voices but I couldn't understand what they were saying. I was trying to tell them about the wounded officer but the words wouldn't come out. The last thing I remember was the familiar succession of noises that started just as the troops went over the top to mount another attack on the enemy positions. As their machine-guns started to fire, the screams of the wounded started to drift into my head once again.

I felt warm, clean, dry and comfortable. I knew I wasn't dead as my body, particularly my arms and shoulders, were giving me a lot of pain. I kept my eyes shut because I didn't know where I was. I was scared in case this was not real but just a thought in a dead or dying head. As I lay there, quite still with my eyes tightly closed, memories darted in and out of my mind that I couldn't cope with, and thus my body willingly shut down.

Memories and a reunion

Chapter 7

I raised myself up onto one arm. I looked around to find that I was lying on the floor of an aid tent. It was huge and there were so many other soldiers lying in orderly rows.

"Do you want a drink?"

Startled at first, I looked up and there was a nursing orderly standing over me with a tin mug. I nodded my head. As my mouth was very dry and caked up with mud, I couldn't speak. Dipping the mug in a bucket, he passed it over to me and as I gulped it down, he said, "We all wondered how long you would be out for."

Passing him the mug back, he asked, "Do want any more?"

Shaking my head, I managed to say thank you.

"I'll tell the Sergeant you're back with us. He'll be round to see you soon."

I lay back down again, just staring at the roof of the tent. I could still hear the sound of guns but they were in the distance now. I could hear all the goings on around me, but the most soothing sound of all was the gentle rain on the canvas above my head. I shut my eyes and was soon back home with Phil and Dad working in the rain in the forest, taking shelter under the trees. Phil and I were larking about and playing jokes on Dad. My mind knew Phil was gone and the pain would never leave, but I would rather think of him before we came to this place. However, in my dreams I would always see him in death.

The gentle patter of the rain on canvas must have sent me off to sleep until someone shook my arm.

"Wake up, soldier. Wake up."

I leapt up and was greeted by a burly Sergeant with a round, smiling, red face.

"Welcome back to the land of the living. I've some questions to ask you. You came to us with no kit or clothes on, just a few personal things in a bag, which I've got here for you. You stank to high heaven and apart from some deep gouges on your shoulders and a few cuts and bruises here and there, we can't find anything wrong with you. Now, let's get started. What happened?"

He asked me all his questions and then wanted to know how I got here. I had more water and then started my tale from Phil getting shot to throwing the bullets into the trench. From there, I didn't know how I had got any further. He looked at me and said, "Well lad, I'll tell you then. You were lucky that the attack was just starting. A stretcher party came out under the guns, thinking there was only one wounded. When they got to you they found the officer. They said you made them take him first. They shouted to the guards that there was another wounded and a soldier just ran out and threw you're over his shoulder and ran back. They say that everyone who could see it was cheering as he dodged the bullets and jumped headlong into the trench. The Lieutenant and you were taken to the first-aid post and then sent on to us. You seem to have caused quite a bit of a stir. The Lieutenant's father is a Staff Officer, quite high up apparently."

"Is he still alive?"

"Yes, but they had to take most of his leg off. He's waiting for transport, on his way home to a proper hospital. If he survives the journey, he'll be all right. Is he a friend of yours?"

"No, I just came across him on the battlefield. Could I go and see him before he leaves?"

"Yes, if you want. I've got you some clothes, new kit and a rifle over there," he said, pointing to a bundle in the opposite corner. "He's over there in the small brown tent with some other wounded officers. Thanks for all you've done though, and good luck." He shook my hand and then walked purposefully away.

As I dressed, I rummaged through the pile that had been given to me until I found Phil's things. I put them back into my shirt pocket and finished dressing. Having put all of my kit on and shouldered the rifle, I walked stiffly out of the tent. After a quick look around, I saw what I was looking for. Making my way over to the officers' tent, I had an empty feeling in the pit of my stomach. What was I going to find there? Opening the tent flap, I walked in. There were eight beds but only five were in use. They all looked like officers, and as I walked past the beds, for some reason I stopped at the third one. Even in the poor light, I could make out his face. I stepped a little closer and leaned over him. Yes, it was my officer. Looking down his bed, I lifted the blanket and saw that he had only got a small section of his leg remaining. I gently lowered the blanket back down. Although a great sadness came over me for his loss, at least he was alive and could start again with a new life. I stayed by his side for quite a while, hoping that he might come round so we could speak, but he didn't. Turning to go, the tent flaps were suddenly drawn back and an officer came in. I couldn't make him out in the poor light but I thought he must be a doctor. As I tried to get past him, he said, "What are you doing in here, soldier?"

"Just looking in on one of my officers before I go back to the front, sir."

"Which one, soldier?" he said.

"Sorry, sir. I don't know his name, sir."

So I pointed over to him instead.

"You must be the one who dragged him back to our lines then, eh? A brave thing to do. No doubt about that."

"Yes, sir."

At that moment, there was a vague movement and a little murmuring came from his bed. We both looked across and I could feel the excitement radiating from the other officer.

"Excuse me, please," he said. "Can I just get by? I must get to see him."

As he squeezed past me, he grasped my hand and shook it robustly, and with a tearful voice said, "Thank you for saving my son's life. I will never be able to repay you for what you've done. Does my son know your name and regiment? I'm sure he'll want to see you when this wretched War is over."

"Yes, sir," I said. "He'll know me. Wish him good luck when he comes round please, sir," and with that I left, stepping out into the bright sunshine. The only thing now on my mind was to get back to the front and try to find Harry and Peter, if they were still alive.

I never knew if the officer had lived until many years after the War had finished. I had, for a number of years, been asked to attend annual reunions. As I hadn't known too many of the others in my company, I usually didn't bother to go but this year I had a different kind of feeling. Something was telling me to go, somehow I felt like I was being drawn for a reason. As usual, it was going to be held in some posh London hotel. For me, getting there was going to be a great ordeal because after I'd returned back from the War, I hadn't been much further than the local town. I mentioned it to a few people and this year friends and family all said I should go as it might help me to lay to rest some of the ghosts of the past. So here I was outside the hotel, trying to pluck up the courage to go in.

After standing there for nearly ten minutes, my nerves got the better of me. Turning away, I started to walk back in the direction of the railway station, when someone tapped my shoulder.

"Excuse me, are you looking for the reunion? If you are, you've come to the right place."

I turned round slowly, saying, "Yes, how do you know?"

"Is your first one? I saw you out of the window pacing up and down. Don't worry, you'll be alright, we've all been there. Come on, I'll take you in and introduce you to some of the others."

The room was very large with tables of food at one end and a bar in the middle. There were tables and chairs all around, most of which had people sitting at them, chatting across to each other. He took me to the bar and bought me a drink, and then introduced me to various people, the majority of whom I either didn't know or had maybe forgotten. In fact, by now, all that I wanted to do was to go back to the safety of my own home and village. All that I had ever needed was there. I must really have looked the odd one out, standing all on my own in the middle of such a large, crowded room. I moved slowly towards the front of the room where the door was. There were also several window tables and chairs, so I sat down thinking that I'd finish my drink and then slip away when I got the chance, hopefully without too many people noticing.

They started serving the food and my new-found friend brought me over a plate full and another drink. As I was offering to pay, he commented, "No, you're ok, it's all free. Has been since they started it. The Gowers pay for it. They were both in France. Got loads of money - family's into banking, property, oil, you know that sort of thing. They'll be here soon for the speeches and all that."

I thought to myself that this felt like more than a coincidence, and my curiosity got the better of me. After about half an hour, an elderly man came into the room followed by two other men and two ladies. Everyone started clapping as the elderly gentleman slowly climbed onto a small stage. He spoke for a few minutes and then handed over to his son. There was yet more clapping and talking. I didn't recognise any of them really, although I did think that the son was limping when he got onto the stage. I couldn't be sure though, the stage was a long way off and my eyes were beginning to fail me.

Finishing my drink, I stood up and put my coat on, not noticing that the talking had finished. I was walking towards the door, when suddenly there was the familiar tap on my shoulder again. Expecting to see my new friend, I half turned, saying, "Sorry, I can't stay, I've..."

I choked on the rest of my sentence. As I looked into his eyes, I knew it was him.

"Mark Gower, Ex-lieutenant. Nice to see you. Is this your first reunion? They can be daunting until you get to know us. Did you sign in? We must keep in touch for the future. I run this myself, you know. The men enjoy it. Would you like another drink?"

Before I could say no, he has signaled to someone to bring me another.

"Let's sit down. Take your coat off, we should talk a little before you go."

After the drinks had arrived, he started asking lots of questions about France and what I was doing now. He told me a little of his time in France, but mostly about his life after the War. Then he asked a strange question.

"What was the worst part of the War for you?"

We were then interrupted by the older man and the other guests.

"Mark, my boy," the old man said, "we have to go now."

"Not yet, Father. I'm waiting for an answer to an important question from this gentleman."

They all looked at me with curiosity in their eyes. Again, our eyes met and he stared at me intently and said, "Well, Private?"

Without further hesitation, I replied, "The same time as yours, sir."

"I knew it was you," he said excitedly, grabbing my hand. Looking up at his father, he said, "Father, I believe you've already met this heroic soldier."

The old man looked a little puzzled.

"You'll have to forgive my father but he's getting on a bit. Father, the Somme, July 1916 in an army medical tent. I believe you shook this man's hand. The man who dragged me from the battlefield and saved my life."

For a few seconds, no one spoke. Then the old man offered his hand for me to shake.

"It's so good to meet you again. I never really thanked you properly the last time we met."

Standing up, he took my hand, and shook it warmly.

"Even after all these years, I cannot begin to thank you enough for what you did for my son and me. In fact, for all of our family."

He then introduced me to rest of the group and sensing I was getting a little overwhelmed, he looked at his son.

"I know you've waited and hoped for this meeting for a long time, so we'll leave you two to catch up. I will offer your excuses tonight, Mark."

He looked at me again, "You've made us all very happy by coming here today. This meeting will hopefully allow my son to put a close to that part of his life now." He paused, and looked at me thoughtfully.

"You and your family will always be welcome in our houses. It is the only way I know that we can begin to repay you for you heroic deed"

It was a very emotionally charged meeting for the three of us, even though many years had passed. For those of us who had lived through the War, meetings like this would always be the same. The old man stepped towards me, and reaching out he put his arms around my shoulders. As he patted me sincerely on the back, he said, "Don't leave it so long next time, will you?"

With that, he swept the group away and left us to talk further.

We decided to move to a side room where it would be quieter. We talked and drank tea all afternoon. He insisted on having my address and he gave me his in return. Finally, he took me to the station in a taxi and as I was getting out of the car, he said, "Now don't forget, if you ever need anything at all, please get in touch. It would give me a lot of pleasure to help out a friend and fellow ex-soldier."

After thanking him for his hospitality, we parted company, sadly never to meet again. For me, it brought back a lot of bad memories, but also meeting up again helped me come to terms with much of it, and consequently I managed to reach a different kind of peace in my mind.

I read about his father's death in the paper a couple of years later, which made me feel very sad, for I knew the bond between father and son was very strong. I had thought of getting in touch but decided against it. At times like these a man needs his family around him, so I purposefully kept my distance. I continued receiving invitations to reunions every year but I had decided that after my first and last visit they were not for me anymore. There's only one more reunion that I plan to go to, but the time hasn't come for me yet.

Frontline trench fire

Chapter 8

Making my way along the frontline trench, the shelling didn't seem to be nearly as heavy as it had been. There was very little machine gun or rifle fire now. There were no dead or wounded lying around and as I made my way along to where the remainder of my company were grouped, I wondered if the War was over. When I reached the company, I asked several soldiers if they had seen Peter or Harry. I was having no luck at all in finding them, and as I got near to the end of the company positions I was beginning to think that they might be wounded or dead afterall. It was then that I heard Peter's voice and I gladly followed the sounds to a small dug-out where both Peter and Harry were playing cards with three other soldiers, using only a couple of candles for light.

"Got room for another?" I said, cheekily.

Without even looking up, Peter said, "Have you got any money?"

"No, I'll pay you where we get home though. Can't say fairer than that!"

"You've never paid us yet," Harry retorted.

They both looked up with huge wide grins.

"Where the bloody hell have you been?"

They finished the game off and then cleared the dug-out. Finally, we were all alone and could talk. Peter told me about their exploits on the battlefield and how lucky they had been to always find shelter and get back to our lines. He told me how they took over the dug-out when the previous owners hadn't returned after a morning attack. Harry said that a ceasefire had been called until midnight to clear no-man's-land of the dead and wounded.

"Have you heard that we've been attached to another regiment along with several other companies who've lost a lot of men? With the few outside, and Phil that adds up to about thirty eight all together. Where is Phil, by the way? I bet he's landed himself a cushy job somewhere."

I looked down at the floor.

"Look lads. There's no easy way to say this but Phil was killed a few days ago."

Lifting my head, I looked at them both and told them how it had happened, taking care not to go into too much detail.

"At least it was quick. He would never have known what hit him and there wouldn't have been any pain at all."

It was to be quite a while before the full impact of what I had told them came to the surface. They'd seen so much over such a short space of time, it was too much to take in. I carried on telling them what had happened to me, and how I'd managed to find them. When I'd finished, a deathly silence shrouded us, only interrupted by the rumble of the odd artillery shell coming over. Really there was nothing more to say. The time we had was now ours to make the most of because none of us knew what the future would hold.

"Tea?" I said. "I could drink a gallon."

This snapped them out of it and we soon had a small fire going.

"There's nothing like a fresh, sweet, piping hot mug of tea to cheer you up. Don't you all agree, lads?"

Soon we were talking about our younger days, all the adventures we'd had. We were laughing at the things we'd done, and we talked about all the things we were going to do when the War was over. This bought a few tears to all our eyes, as we knew in our hearts that these things would never happen. Pooling our rations together we came up with a half-decent meal, and as we ate we talked about our families and how they would be coping, and how long it would be before they were told about our situation.

We were just making some more tea when the cover to our shelter was pulled aside and our new Sergeant strode in.

"Just in time, am I?" He sat himself down next to me, and asked, "Who's this one then? Another stray from your old company?"

Taking the mug of tea that Peter passed to him, he questioned me, "Are there many more of you lot left?"

"I don't know, Sergeant. I haven't seen any more on my way down here."

Then he wrote my details on a scrap of paper, saying he would pass it on to the Captain.

"Which one of you three was the best poacher at home?"

Harry said, "That depends on what you're stalking?"

Taking a swallow of tea, he replied, "German prisoners. The high-ups want a night patrol sent out to see if we can bring back a prisoner for the intelligence people to have a go at. I'm going and I need five more to come with me. I heard that you lads were good at catching rabbits, fish and game in your previous lives and I thought it might suit you."

I commented, "There's a bit of difference between animals and humans, you know."

"Yes," said Peter, "don't forget the whole of the bloody German army might not want us to have one of them."

"Steady on," said Harry. "You see sir," he explained patiently, "on our first day at the front, Peter there lost his lifelong best friend, and now we've just met up with another of our friends who lost his brother a few days ago. If you want all three of us to go, we won't. If you just want the best stalker amongst us to go, I'll be glad to come with you."

"I could order you all to go, you know?"

"And I could shoot you now and dump your body on the piles of the dead behind the trench. Besides, they'll be going over the top at dawn anyway. At least let them have these few hours to mourn together then," Harry begged the Sergeant.

After a few minutes of silence, the Sergeant looked back at Harry.

"0430 the attack's going in. 0030 they start the artillery barrage. We go out at 11 o'clock. If we're not back by 0030, we could be in trouble. Meet me at the Captain's dugout at 2230 for orders and to restock your ammunition. You two, get some rest. There's a long day coming."

As he was going, he said to Harry, "Would you have shot me, Private?"

"What for?" Harry replied, "The Germans are going to do that in a few hours anyway."

As we sat around the small fire, Harry was defending his stance on the night patrol.

"Look," he said, "for the last time, you both know I'm the best one for this kind of job. We all know the chances of getting back are slim, but I stand more of a chance than either of you two do. So let's stop going on about it. Just think, I'll have a brew ready for you when you get back from your early-morning walk."

We all laughed and agreed to stop bickering. For the rest of the time left, we just carried on cleaning and checking our equipment. Peter went out and came back with some fresh ammunition. Harry took out his bayonet and set to sharpening it. He also had a combat knife, which he sharpened with great precision. He wouldn't tell us where he got it from but it certainly wasn't standard Army issue.

Peter said, "Do you think you'll get close enough to use them?"

"I bet I'll get closer than you two will in the morning."

As time slipped away, the talk came round to home and families again.

Peter said, "I think we all feel the same and if any one of us should get home, it would be nice if they could visit the others' families. Tell them how much we missed them and how we love them dearly, and that when the end came there was no suffering and it was quick and clean. Also tell them that we had a proper burial. I don't think it would do any good us telling them the truth. What d'you think?"

After thinking it over for a while, I agreed with Peter, saying, "That also goes for Phil and John, too."

We all nodded our heads in full agreement.

Harry butted in, "Can you two just remind me of where you live for when I get home then?"

Even though it was a small dug-out, we both launched ourselves at him and spent the last thirty minutes doing what we had done for years - having fun.

The time had run out for us and Harry was just finishing getting kitted out. I think as we said our goodbyes, we all knew this was the last time we would all be together. We watched Harry tramp through the mud, up the trench and out of sight. We two who were left behind had tears in our eyes, and we knew that Harry would have, too. Getting back into our dug-out, we sat and waited, both of us silently hoping and praying he would get back alive.

It was just turned midnight when the enemy started firing. We heard only rifle and machine-gun fire at first. It wasn't aimed at us though. Several flares came down over the German lines. The firing went on for about ten minutes, then died down and it all went quiet again. We both knew what it meant.

"He might have been captured or wounded," said Peter, hopefully.

"He's probably found a hiding place, knowing Harry," I said. "He'll be crawling back right now."

"I'll make a brew," Peter said, "and get the last of the food out. He'll probably need it when he gets back."

As it turned out, Harry didn't come back. His body was never found either. His parents were told the usual, that he was killed in action, as were so many relatives when their sons just disappeared.

"Tea's ready."

At that moment, flares went into the air along the whole of the frontline, signaling the start of the biggest artillery bombardment I had seen so far. We both climbed onto the firing step to watch just as the first shells landed and thousands of fresh troops started to make their way into the trenches. Shortly after, the German guns opened fire on our trenches and it started all over again. I tugged at Peter's arm and we went back inside our dug-out. Here was as good a place as any, as you couldn't escape it completely. Besides, we had some food to eat and tea to drink, and we tried to ignore the reality.

The guns on both sides were tearing the trenches apart and the soldiers to pieces. We both got our kit together. We decided to leave some of it behind and put the rest onto our backs.

"Best to leave this place as you found it, then it will be ready for when we get back,"

Peter said, " If, you mean."

"No," I said, "when."

We pushed our way through the crowds of soldiers and reaching the firing step, kept our heads well down. There were plenty of ladders on either side of us, but we'd heard that once you got away from the ladders, you stood more chance. The order came swiftly, up and down the line.

"Fix bayonets."

The click click noise made when the bayonet is fixed in place seemed to echo far into the distance. Our guns were shelling our barbed wire again to open up even more through routes. The attack was now only seconds away. Men were crying and crying. Young lads were sobbing for their mothers.

"Stay close and we'll be all right," Peter said.

I didn't have time to reply, as the first of the whistles began up and down the trenches.

"Come on, lads. Let's have you. See who can score the first goal."

Then, a number of footballs were thrown over the top which helped to move the attack on. Once again, there was the huge roar of human voices as company after company, regiments and divisions, thousands upon thousands of men and boys clambered over the top and headed for the enemy's lines.

Quite a few of the young soldiers were kicking the balls along as they went, cheering and shouting the names of their favourite teams as they kicked the balls. Our artillery was now moving the barrage forward. We were just passing through our own wire when I glanced back and saw another wave of infantry coming in behind us. As we cleared our wire, we started to run, zig-zagging across the battlefield between the shell holes and craters. We couldn't believe our luck. There was hardly any enemy fire and their artillery fire was going to our rear. We couldn't see their lines because of the smoke and the ground that had been thrown up by our barrage, but we must have been well over half way by now. We seemed to be getting close to our barrage and our Sergeant signaled to us to drop back a bit. Looking back again, it was a sight that I'll never forget. As well as our own lines, there were two more waves of infantry moving up behind us, and yet another in the trenches getting ready to come over the top and advance in the first, early-morning light. Looking back over our front lines from the slightly higher advantage point, you could see this vast expanse of one small part of the front line which stretched on in both directions for God knows how many miles. How many men manned these trenches?

I glanced at Peter and got his attention. I shouted across to him, "Looks like we're going to get them at last." He nodded back and we kept moving ever closer to the enemy lines. Then, without any warning, we began taking enemy shellfire, which increased incredibly quickly, turning into a massive bombardment. After a few minutes, enemy machine-guns started to open fire rapidly, turning into a murderous solid wall of fire, which cut our lads down mercilessly. All the waves of troops were taking very heavy casualties but were still moving forward. The enemy must have been taking some casualties too, as our guns were now shelling directly on top of them. Slowly, it was getting lighter and some of the smoke was beginning to clear. You could now actually see the German soldiers in the trenches.

Some of our troops were kneeling and shooting at the machine gunners.

With my heart bursting and my lungs about to cave in, I made it to the enemy's wire. Soldiers on my left had moved through the wire, and with shouts and howls were throwing themselves amongst the enemy. The flare went up to mark the breach and fresh troops started to move quickly towards it. As more and more troops poured through the breach, the enemy fire started to die away. More troops were being directed towards us to exploit the small victory as much as possible. Calling Peter to follow me, we worked our way through the wire and charged up to the trench. It was just a frenzy of men slashing, stabbing, bayoneting each other with shovels, picks, butcher knives, anything that would kill, even boots and bare hands. I watched as one of our soldiers gouged out the eyes of an enemy soldier. We were just about to jump into the slaughtering pit when an NCO came over.

185

"You two stay on top and shoot anything that comes from the enemy side. They might try a counter-attack when we start to move up and down their trenches. I'll send over more men as soon as they get here. Look sharp! Use those sandbags to make a shelter and keep your eyes and ears open."

It took about five minutes to rig up a good firing position and once we had, we just lay and waited. Other soldiers came over and we told them to do the same. Looking back to our lines, I could see vast numbers of stretcher parties picking up the wounded. The main battle was slowly moving away from us. I was a little scared because I knew how many troops we had behind the main line. So where were the enemy reserves? At that moment, there were only about sixty to seventy of us. Still they must know what they're doing.

After a short while, Peter said, "I wouldn't mind one of those helmets to take home as a souvenir. What do you say? There's an officer just there, I could get it in a couple of minutes."

"Yes," I said, "and get court-martialed, ending up in prison for robbing the dead."

"No, I'll say he threw it at me just before I killed him. Keep watch," and down he went. He was back in a few seconds.

"What you think? Solid silver, I bet."

He was trying to clean the mud and blood off when I spotted an NCO on his way over. I nudged Peter who quickly stashed the helmet away in his backpack.

When he'd gone, Peter said, "I got you a little something, too," passing me the officer's pistol and ammunition pouches. "Should be worth a tidy sum when we get home."

"You're bloody mad. You'll get us both shot."

"By which side?" he said, with a big grin on his face.

I stashed my little something inside my jacket, thinking he was probably right. We might not get much further.

As more troops came forward, they were sent to either side of us to help clear the main trenches. We could hear the fierce hand-to-hand fighting going on and knew there was no quarter given or expected, as we could hear no cries from the wounded. As the troops fanned out, they were destroying the enemy's machine-guns, so at least if they counter-attacked and drove us back, we wouldn't have them shooting us in the back.

Although the sight and smell of the butchery only eight or nine feet below me was something I could never accept, to my shame I must admit it held a fascination for me. Looking down into the trench, the bodies were all distorted in unnatural shapes; arms and legs were all twisted and entwined together. Enemy and victor together, but only in death. The looks on their faces, some surprised, many shocked, few with hatred, but most had that look of sheer terror and horror. How could anyone inflict wounds which can only be described as sadistic mutilation on a fellow human being? The men and boys below, who we were told are our enemy, are just like us. They had mothers and fathers, sisters and brothers, and lives before this. Now they lay staring up at the sky, eyes wide open, warm blood leaving them and soaking into the soil, and for what? Probably nothing, but we would never know.

"Aye up," Peter said, "looks like something's moving."

And it was. As far as you could see in all directions, it looked like a gigantic grey wave moving up from the ground, gathering speed and getting bigger and bigger. Without any warning, the enemy counter-attack had begun along the whole of the front. As they got closer, their spiked helmets and bayonets glinted in the early morning sunlight. It was a sight to put fear into all who stood in their way. At about fifteen hundred yards, we opened fire. I looked back expecting to see reinforcements moving up behind us but they'd been held back. Instead, our big guns opened fire on them but to our horror they just kept coming. As they got closer, they had to manoeuvre around their own trench system, which slowed them down quite a lot but as we were shooting them they were still coming from their rear positions. Finally, the order was given for the whole front to retreat back to our own lines, in as orderly a fashion as possible. Still firing at the enemy, we moved backwards as fast as we could towards our lines, knowing that as soon as they got back into their own trench, they would bring up more machine-guns and their artillery would open fire on us.

The first section of trench that was re-occupied was to the right of us. Machine gun fire started within minutes and got heavier as more guns were brought up. The first enemy shells soon started coming down. I think Peter and I had the same idea, as we both turned and ran for it, as the machine-guns started firing at us. We were well over half way to our lines when I saw Peter stagger to his knees and fall onto his face. When I got to him, I saw a number of small holes in his backpack. Thinking he might just be winded, I grabbed his arms and dragged him into a shell crater. We both tumbled to the bottom, Peter landing on his back. It was then that I saw the blood oozing out of his battledress jacket. I crawled over to him and cut his straps and pouches off with my bayonet. Unfastening his jacket and shirt, I gently opened them up and was horrified at the size of the wounds. He must have been hit by at least six bullets, which had torn through his body and ripped chunks of flesh and bone away from his chest and stomach as they'd come out the other side. It was a miracle he was still alive. Blood was gushing out of his chest, so I closed his shirt and jacket to try and stop it.

In our packs, we both had some spare clothing, which I got out and placed directly onto his wounds, but no matter how much I tried, the blood kept soaking through. I think I knew he was dying and was glad he was unconscious. At least he was not in pain. As much as I wanted to, I knew I couldn't get him back to our lines, so I made my mind up to stay with him until the end. I took all my kit off and sat beside him. I lifted his head and put it on my lap, cradling him like a baby. I started talking to him about home, family and our friends. It was then that I heard him trying to say something. He started coughing up blood and suddenly reached up and grabbed my arm. Again, he tried to speak but this only caused more coughing. Slowly, his hand moved up my jacket and he started to pull it open.

"What do you want?" I said.

He kept pulling and pulling until I undid a few buttons. His ever-weakening hand reached inside and began trying to take out what he had wanted. I sat there, horrified. Now I knew what he wanted. I gently put his hand back by his side but as I let it go he began again. Staring at his face and the pain-racked eyes looking back at me, I knew he was fading fast. I felt his weak grip on my arm knowing that he could go no further. I reached into my jacket and took out the pistol he'd given me a only a few hours earlier. I knew what he wanted but I also knew he couldn't do it himself.

I couldn't imagine the pain he was in. It might take him hours to die. He knew I would stay with him and might even get wounded or killed doing so, if necessary. At least with our forces still falling back, I stood a chance but that meant I would be the one to end his life. I had already got more to live with than any one man should have, but to endure this as well. I didn't know if I could bear the thought. It was then that I felt Peter tug at my jacket. It startled me, as I was far away in my own thoughts. I gently took his helmet off and wiped away the sweat and dirt from his face. He strained to keep his eyes open and fixed them on me. He started coughing again, bringing up more blood. He tried to say something but it just sounded like a rasping noise in his throat. He tried several times more and then he went still and quiet. After a few minutes, I thought he might have gone. I leaned over to see if his breathing had stopped when he grabbed me and forced my ear to his mouth. He only said two words very clearly so I could hear. Then he let me go and slumped back into my lap. I checked the pistol was loaded and leaned over him.

"If you find the others, Peter, come for me when it's my turn. Goodbye old friend."

Kissing him gently on the forehead, I placed the pistol next to his temple and pulled the trigger. I also shot him through the heart just to be sure. Checking to see that he was dead, I threw down the pistol and pouches, grabbed my rifle and took one last look at the last of my friends, and as the tears began to trickle down my face again, I scrambled out of the hole and made a dash for our lines.

I'm not sure how far I ran. I didn't really know where I was going. I think I was hoping for a quick and painless death. I could have joined the others then. If not today, any time would do, just so long as I could be with the lads, so I didn't have to go home and see people thinking, "why did only you come back?" Why should I be the only one allowed to live longer and on my own?

As I ran and ran my mind was in utter turmoil, and I wasn't aware that I was heading into the German artillery barrage on our lines. I do remember the smoke and noise and smell from the exploding shells though. There was no pain, just a huge flash and then I was flying to where, I will never know.

A tearful homecoming

Chapter 9

As young lads, we'd never talked about dying or the afterlife, if it exists. The experience of death at first hand had only been forced upon us when we came to this place. It was back in this no-man's-land that I found myself, standing on my own on the battlefield, unhurt and in no pain whatsoever. Artillery shells were exploding all around me and bullets were flying over my head. Soldiers were still retreating but as they were running past me they didn't seem to notice me, but I suppose with all the commotion and smoke on the battlefield, it was easy to miss one more soldier. It hadn't struck me at first but I couldn't hear anything either. Perhaps the explosion had done some damage to my ears. I started to hunt around for my kit but couldn't find it. I wasn't sure what to do next when startlingly I saw several soldiers coming out of the smoke heading towards me. As they passed me by, I stared at them in total disbelief. I tried to shout at them but I couldn't get the words out. They walked over to the crater where Peter and I were and jumped in. They were out of my sight briefly but when they climbed out, they were all laughing and back-slapping another soldier who had joined them. Again, they came towards me, but didn't see me. I could see now who the other soldier was and as they drew alongside me, I said to them, "Don't forget me, lads. Don't go without me, please."

But they just carried on walking past me, laughing and joking amongst themselves, not hearing my pleas. As they carried on towards the thick smoke, I ran alongside, shouting, "Don't leave me, please. Don't leave me behind." Just before they moved into the smoke, they stopped and turned. First it was Harry, then John and Peter, and lastly was Phil. They all stood there as I begged and pleaded with them to let me go with them as well. No words were spoken as they turned and were lost in the battlefield smoke. I dropped to my knees, crying and screaming for them to come back for me. I was screaming so loudly that my chest and head felt as though they would burst. The smoke started to get thicker and darker until I couldn't see my hands in front of my face. I was so frightened and for the first time ever, so alone. I fell down on my face and cried out loudly once again for my friends to come back for me. Slowly, I became so exhausted that my cries were becoming racking sobs. It was then when I had almost given up that I heard a very soft voice coming from far away, telling me to calm down, I was in a safe place, nobody could hurt me now. It told me to rest a while. With those words echoing in my ears, I closed my eyes and a sort of indescribable calm came over me.

I don't know how long it lasted, I had no sense of time but when I came out of it, I was back to the screaming horrors I had seen before. I felt trapped. It was dark and I felt I had to run. It was my only way out but I was bound and could hardly move. I struggled and struggled and finally broke free. Moving away from my bindings, I started to fall and again found myself lying on my face but not on the battlefield. Again, I heard voices that I couldn't understand, and then it all went black again.

With a raging thirst, I opened my eyes.

"Water, water," I said in a faint voice.

I could see it was light but I had no idea where I was.

"If anyone can hear me, could I have a drink of water, please?"

I could hear voices but only very quietly. I was just about to ask again when someone put a wet sponge to my lips. I sucked on it greedily until I swallowed. The pain was tremendous, so I had no more. Although I couldn't see anyone, I knew someone was next to me, then a familiar voice spoke, very quietly.

"It's good to see you awake. I'll tell the doctor. He's got a lot to tell you."

It was a woman's voice, but I couldn't be sure where I'd heard it before. It seemed like a lifetime that I lay on my own until someone came back. Sensing the presence of several people now, I wasn't surprised when one of them spoke.

"Now young man. My name is Dr Wilson. It's good to see you awake. Don't try to talk. We'll tell you all you need to know for the moment. You've been here for just over three weeks. A shell exploded in front of you causing extensive injuries to your chest and stomach. Your legs have only minor shrapnel damage though. Your head, on the left hand side, gave us a lot of problems. There was quite a large chunk of shrapnel embedded in your skull. However, when we operated on it, we found it had missed the brain completely. We've done several operations on your chest and stomach but you'll probably have to undergo another one when you get your strength back. Just move your hand if you can understand me. Good, now just one last thing, then you can rest. We think your hearing has also been damaged by the blast."

I moved my hand briefly again.

"Good, that helps us a lot. Last of all, when you arrived here you were as good as dead. In fact, with your wounds, you should have died on the battlefield. You're nothing but a miracle. Someone was looking after you, so you keep going on as you are, destiny hasn't finished with you yet. I'll leave you now with Nurse Brooks who's been looking after you since you arrived."

I heard footsteps as he went away, then that now familiar voice whispered, "Rest now a while. You've had more than enough for today."

When I felt I was alone, I took my time making sure I digested everything that I'd been told. My brain could only come up with the same question all the time. Why me? Why save me, and not one of the others? They'd had as much right to live as me. I didn't want to live on my own, I wanted to be with them. This was no life for anyone to lead. Every time I closed my eyes, or when night fell, my dreams kept taking me back to the battlefields and I woke-up terrified. I couldn't speak of the horrors, my lips would move but the words weren't there.

After a few days, the horror of the whole situation was too much for me. I knew I could on go no further. The pain was so intense. I knew only one way to be free. I thought back to Peter and although my pain was not physical, it was just as bad to me. I waited until the Nurse came to see me and with hand movements, I asked for paper and pencil.

"Oh," she said, "you want to write down a request? I hope it's not cheeky. I'm a married lady with children, and probably older than your mother. If it's for food, sorry, not yet."

She paused.

"Still want the paper?"

I moved my hand to gesture 'yes' and off she went to get it. She came back and placed them in front of me and although I couldn't see because of the bandages, I managed to pick them up in the right hands. For a few seconds, I hesitated. Not because I had changed my mind but because I wasn't sure what to write. Then Peter's words came back to me and that's exactly what I wrote. Putting the paper and pencil on the bed, I waited, not knowing what would happen next.

"How can you lie there thinking only of yourself when there are thousands of wounded soldiers in a far worse condition than you who would never think such a thing? And what about all those young men who died out there? Given half a chance they would gladly change places with you. So I don't want any more of this nonsense from you. Do you hear?"

Over the next few days, she was still caring but also a little more concerned. I had the bandages changed and a smaller one was put on my head, which meant I could see for the first time. Nurse Brooks was, as she said, a little older and bigger than Mum with such a kind and gentle voice that it was so good to put a face to it. Over the next few weeks, she and the other nurses helped me through and taught me to cope with my wounds. I had several more operations on my chest to remove shell splinters and then that was that. Eventually the doctor came to tell me they could do no more for me and that although there were still a number of splinters, they had to be left in as they were too close to my heart, but that they shouldn't give me any problems in the future.

"I think another couple of weeks and you might be able to go home. Oh, and by the way, did Nurse Brooks tell you your mother is visiting you on Sunday? You'll be able to tell her your good news. Now, is there anything you want to ask me?"

I just lay there, screaming at him, "When will my voice come back? I can't hear properly, when can you fix that? What about the nightmares and memories? Can you take them away? Will I ever be able to sleep again after what I've seen and done? Please, what can you do to help me?"

"Nothing to ask then? Well, if you change your mind, you know how to get hold of me."

He wandered off in a sort of confused state. I wondered if he had the right patient. My mind was crying out to him to come back and help me. I was trying to shout at him but I couldn't make the words come out.

I felt a warm hand touch my head. It startled me for a few seconds until I saw who it was.

"I'm sorry I didn't have time to tell you about your mother coming. I only found out myself as the doctor came in. Your regiment got a letter from your Mum asking where you and your brother were. They must have already been told about you but they know nothing about your brother. These things take so much time. It can take months before good or bad news gets through. Where is your brother? Is he still out there on the front line, I mean?"

I was still letting all the news sink in when I realised the most dreadful thoughts. What if Mum didn't know about Phil, or any of the others? Maybe no one had been told. I couldn't see Mum if she didn't know. What would I say? That he'd had half his head shot away and died in so much pain, frightened and calling for her? And what about the others? Oh no, it's all too much. I couldn't relive all their deaths again.

I reached for my paper and pencil and wrote 'hanky in drawer'. She looked at the note and moved round the bed to the small wooden cupboard by my bedside. She seemed to know what I was looking for. Opening the drawer slightly, she slid her hand in and took out Phil's handkerchief. She laid it on the bed in front of me and then waited. Slowly, I unfolded the now dry blood-stained handkerchief and picked up the silver cross. It still had traces of mud from the battlefield on it, along with Phil's blood, which had poured down his neck from his wounds. I think she knew what was coming, and she lifted her hands to her face. Reaching inside my nightshirt, I unclipped my cross and pulled it from around my neck and put both chains together on the handkerchief.

"That's your brother's chain, isn't it? Is he dead?"

I wrote again on the paper. I scribbled our five names, then crossed them off one by one. My heart was crying, my head hung low but my eyes were dry. I could no longer cry. I passed a scrap of paper to her, not noticing her reaction, if any, as once again I was on the battlefield watching my brother and our best friends die such horrible deaths. I could see them towards the end again when they left me alone, as they went into the smoke and onto another great adventure together.

I was unaware that she had fetched a chair and was now sitting beside me, holding my hand.

"Bill, Bill," she said softly. "Have you lost your brother and your three friends?"

I nodded my head.

"Oh you poor, poor young man. What have you been through?"

She held my hand for a long time without a word being spoken.

"I am so, so sorry. I lost my elder son last year. He was about your age. We couldn't stop him signing up, though it would have been a great adventure for him. He was only out there for a few weeks. We were told he was missing in action, presumed dead, which didn't mean anything to us.

It would have been better if there was a body or grave, but no, not for my Tom."

We both returned to our own thoughts for a few minutes, she wondering if her son may still be alive or wounded, or even maybe a prisoner, whereas I was thinking of all the mass burial pits, the shell craters, and the mud and water-filled trenches. What if he had been blown into tiny pieces. What if he was shot by an officer, or even firing squad? My firing squad. I might have killed her son. I killed someone's son. What I wouldn't give, if only I could go back to before the War when we were all still alive. Maybe I could have changed things before all this happened. I know I was only trying to make myself feel less guilty because when I would go home, people would be saying, 'Why has he come home and none of the others?' Would Mum and Dad be bitter towards me for coming back instead of Phil? There were so many thoughts and questions going around my mind. I still wished for only one thing, to be with my brother and our friends. There's nothing left for me here now.

"I must go now," she said. "We must try and find out if your mother and your friends' mothers will have been told before Sunday."

As she walked away, I carefully folded both crosses back into the handkerchief and put it under my pillow. From that moment on, I decided that I would neither eat nor drink until I was united with my pals. By the time Sunday came round, the nurses were getting very concerned at my stubbornness to neither eat nor drink, but most of all in my lack of will to go on. With this and not eating, my health was getting worse by the day.

At about midday, Nurse Brooks came down the ward, and stopped by my bed.

"Bill," she said, softly, "I know you can hear me. Your Mum's here with another lady from your village. They're just talking to the doctor about your condition. There's another thing, too. Nobody can tell us if she's been told about Phil or the others. Now, the doctor thinks it would be better for you not to say anything, unless you want to. It's up to you though. I won't be far away if you need me. Here they come now, so I'll leave you alone."

I recognised Mum's footsteps coming towards my bed. Rolling onto my back, I propped myself up on my elbows to see her coming towards me, smiling widely, tears running down her cheeks. She carefully and gently embraced me. By this time, I was crying, too.

"I never thought this day would come. It's so good to have you home, Bill. So good."

I tried so hard to speak but could only hug and cry with her, and then what I think was a turning point for me, I suddenly said, "Love you, Mum."

"I know, I know. Now, let's have a good look at you." She let go of me gently and stepped back.

"Your doctor has spoken to me and told me about your wounds. Now they are mending fine. He also said that they had hoped to send you home in a few weeks, until you stopped eating and drinking. I said you'd probably gone off your food but you would be fine when you come home and I can cook your favourite meals. He says he thinks that the noises in your head and ears will stop when your head starts to heal. He says they aren't sure why you can't talk, though. There's no injury that they can find that might have caused it. He thinks it will come back in time. Well, I can tell him it already has and when you get home, who knows."

The lady with her was Peter's mother. She came over and kissed me on the forehead, saying how glad she was to see me and how worried they had all been as they hadn't heard any news from the front about us or how we were getting on. She went and sat down with Mum and they started talking about me going home. It was only then I also knew that I actually would be going home. In fact, I thought, I must be fit and go home, not for me but for all the mums and dads, but especially for mine more than any other. To lose one son was going to be heartbreaking for them, but to lose both sons would be a far greater pain than they should have to bear.

As the ladies chatted away, I knew it wouldn't be long before they would start talking about the others. Nurse Brooks came over to offer them a drink.

"Nurse, he spoke to me. He only said three words but it's a start."

She looked at me and smiled. "I knew you could do it. Now, how about a drink? Only water mind, tea for the ladies and water for the patient."

I could sense that all their thoughts were on me, willing me to say the right word. I knew I must, so with the lads egging me on in my head, I managed, "Water, please, water."

There, I had said it. No big fuss was made but the look on their faces was enough.

The drinks arrived and Nurse stayed to help me. The general talk carried on for a short while.

"How are the others getting on? Do you know where they are? I don't think there's anything wrong in telling us, then we can tell the others. What do you think, Nurse?" Peter's Mum said.

"Well, I think it's up to Bill, if he feels strong enough and don't forget he has been away from the front for over five weeks now. Things will have changed. He may not be able to remember. He's had a very serious head wound, you know."

"Well, perhaps he could tell us what he can then, any news would be welcome."

I knew they were desperate for news. It was in their eyes as they sat looking and waiting. I also knew the Nurse was trying to give me a way out but I didn't know if I would be able to live with myself if I didn't do the right thing.

Sitting up in bed as high as I could get, I gazed back at them, all the time trying to find the words to tell them the news that would shatter their lives. In the end, it was Mum who made a move. I think she knew there might be some bad news. She got up and came to my side and took hold of my hand.

"There, now you tell me how Phil and the boys are getting on then."

Pulling her close to me, I managed to say, "Oh God, Mum. Harry and John won't be coming home."

Her grip tightened on my hand and she started to tremble. She turned round to Peter's Mum.

"God help us. Harry and John are both dead."

Both of them seemed to go into a sort of state of shock. Mum went to leave my side but I clung on to her hand. She turned, looking at me,

"There's more, isn't there?"

I nodded my head and she leaned over me once more.

"Peter will be staying there as well."

Her eyes started to close and she let go of my hand, slowly raising it up to her mouth. She went and sat down next to Peter's Mum. I didn't hear what she said, but the onset of crying and sobbing spoke the worst news yet. I reached under my pillow and brought out Phil's hanky.

"Mum," I said. She left Peter's Mum with one of the nurses and came back to my side and I gave her the blood-stained handkerchief. She knew straightaway and put it down on the bed and just stared at it. You could see her life draining away in her face.

"Mum, please unfold it. It's what he wanted."

At first, she hesitated. Then carefully, so as not to damage it, she unfolded the cloth, staring at the two crosses. She lifted the blood-stained one up and let it fall into the palm of her hand. She turned away and went back to comfort her friend.

After a short while, Nurse Brooks asked them if they wanted to be on their own.

"We have a small room where you can have a drink and spend a little time together."

As they both got up, Mum passed out and had to be helped up. Two nurses went with them and I found myself alone again. The tremendous pain I had just gone through had completely drained me and I drifted off into a restless sleep until I was woken by Nurse Brooks.

"Bill, Bill, your mother's coming to say goodbye. They have to go for their train now."

Poor Mum. As she came down the ward she looked old and hunched. I'm sure she'd been taller when she had arrived earlier. If this is what war can do to you, I hope there are never any more so nobody has to go through this ever again. When she saw me looking she tried to force a smile and look a bit more cheerful. She came and wrapped her arms around me.

"Now, you make sure you eat and drink properly so you will soon be home. Your Dad and I, we need you more than ever now. God bless you, Bill. I think I understand some of what you have been through and what you'll have to go through in the years ahead. We'll get through it though when we're all together. We'll help one another. You've had another of your worst days today, so have some food and rest. Don't go upsetting the nurses. What they ask you to do is for your own good."

She held me tight and kissed me several times, then she was gone, off home to finish the worst day of her life.

Later on, Nurse Brooks was helping me to feed myself.

"I thought your Mum was so brave today. She looked after her friend in spite of her own distress, and when the Sergeant from you regiment spoke to them telling them that none of the deaths had been confirmed from the front, she looked straight back at him saying that her son wouldn't tell lies, and that you had been there and had seen it all happen."

The next two weeks went by very quickly and after instructions from the doctor and a tearful goodbye from all the nurses, especially Nurse Brooks without whom this day would never have come, I set off on my long journey home.

Little had changed as I crunched up the path to be greeted by Mum and Dad, who had probably been standing there for hours. It was a very tearful homecoming. Full of emotions of sadness and joy, and as I shut the door I felt all the love and happiness that makes a home close in around me. I had longed for this moment many times and now it was here. What more could I say?

I don't know if it was the first night at home or the long journey but I was worn out and slept like a log. Mum had borrowed a small bed from the Manor House and had set it up downstairs, so after a little supper, I turned in. When I finally awoke, it was so good to hear the early-morning sounds of Mum getting breakfast. I just lay there, enjoying it all, soaking it up.

"I see you're awake. Here, I've made you a drink. Your Dad's got a big job on today, so I'll get his food first. We can eat later, so just rest a while longer."

Dad came down the noisy old stairs and came straight over to me and sat down.

"How are you this morning, Bill? Sleep alright? Feeling a little better? It's really good to have you home."

Then he went on to tell me about his job, have his breakfast and then set off for work. He and Mum had a quiet word on the doorstep as always, she kissed him and then off he went. It was like this nearly every morning for a very long time. I tried to talk to him about me, Phil and the others but he always made an excuse and left.

"Leave it until another day when I have more time, then you can tell me everything."

Much later on, Mum told me that he blamed himself for Phil's death. He said that if he'd been stronger with him and stopped him going, he would still be here today. She said he wouldn't talk about it with anyone, not even her. It was probably the only way he could try to come to terms with his loss, but he never did. At night, he would come home and do his jobs for Mum around the house. At meal times, we sat on either side of the table but hardly a word was spoken. Then, he either sat by the fire or went out and chopped up logs. On some fine evenings, he and Mum would take an old blanket to the far end of the garden and stay there until the sun had gone down. Then, if the sky were clear, they would stay a little longer pointing out the stars. When Mum told me what they were doing, I soon found myself copying them.

The only time Dad showed his grief was at night. You could hear him sobbing gently and Mum's quiet voice soothing him long into the night. He hardly ever went out any more and cut himself off from most of his friends. Although I would have loved to have worked with him again, it was not to be. He was a loner now and that's how it stayed.

Mum and I sort of fell into a routine. After Dad had gone to work in the mornings, she would come and sit by me with some tea and we would just talk about lots of things – the village gossip and what was going on up at the Hall. I would talk about the training camp and all the tricks we'd got up to, then the train ride to the docks. I had her laughing so hard when I told her about the rusty old ship we'd gone on and the terrible crossing with everyone being sick. But I couldn't go any further with my story, not yet.

She would then change my bandages and clean me up. We'd have some breakfast and then she'd make me have a rest. Some of Mum's friends had lent us books, so I found myself starting to read a little. This went on for a week or so and then I started to have visitors in the afternoons. I think Mum was arranging it all. She had temporarily given up her job to look after me but she still went out most days with her basket to the village when she thought I was resting, which was actually most of the time. Occasionally, I would watch her from the window. She was still young but now her features always looked older and more frail, and at this moment in time she would only go out dressed all in black.

Sometime in the third week, the letters came from the War Department. They were put on the kitchen table and then we both sat down and ate breakfast. Mum cleared away and bustled around them and finally sitting back down again, she slid one of the letters over to me. She ripped hers open first and smiled to herself as she read its contents.

"They're just telling us that you've been wounded in France and when you come home, they will tell us which hospital you're being sent to."

She looked up at me and smiled, " I didn't need anyone's help in finding you and bringing you to the best hospital - that's your home, here."

We sat there for a few minutes, just looking at the other envelope. Knowing that we already knew what was inside, and that it was just the words to confirm the details, Mum picked it up.

"Come on, let's go and sit in the other room."

I followed her and sat on my makeshift bed, and she on the chair next to it. She opened the envelope and passed me the folded piece of paper.

"Please read it to me, Bill."

There wasn't a lot of writing on it. It was fancy paper with the War Department title and then our regiment underneath.

"Dear Mr and Mrs Stokes, We regret to inform you that your son Philip Stokes was killed in action while carrying out his duty assaulting the enemy's positions. His actions in the face of the enemy were both heroic and courageous. It is little comfort to you but you can feel very proud that he died the way he did, in the service of his King and Country."

It was then signed and that was all. I passed it over to Mum who glanced briefly at it and then put it carefully back into the envelope.

"I'll let your Dad see them both when he gets home."

She got up and went into the kitchen, put the envelope with the other one and then came back with a drink and sat beside me on the bed. We both sipped our tea in peace and then she turned to me.

"Do you know why the other lads' families haven't been to see you yet, even though they ask about you and send their best wishes? Don't you think it's strange that they haven't called round?"

I thought for a while.

"Is it may be that they wonder why I came back and not their sons? Why wasn't I killed instead, or maybe something like that? How would you have felt? How do you feel? Would you rather Phil had come back instead of me?"

The questions tumbled out of my mouth in a flurry. All the queries that I'd asked myself since I'd come round in hospital all those weeks ago.

"I don't know what to think myself any more, so I certainly don't know what others are thinking. Every day I feel guilty for being alive and all the others are gone. Every day I just want to be with them, as we all used to be. It's so hard Mum, and at night-time when I lie awake so afraid to sleep because of the horrors that come as dreams. I see their faces. I watch them die over and over, and I just wish I could have died with them all. That I'd had the courage to take my own life but I'm afraid I might never see them again. I just go on day-by-day, not knowing what else to do."

Mum reached out for me and I laid my head on her lap once again.

"My poor boy. What have you been through? I've heard you in your sleep, talking, crying, whimpering. Sitting beside you as you experience the horrors in your dreams has been so hard for me, knowing there's not much I can do unless you want to share your pain and suffering with me. Then, maybe it will make it all a little more bearable to live with." She paused and looked into the distance, thoughtfully.

"Anyway, I can help you to stop thinking about your friends' parents. It's not that they think any of those things you said. What they're hoping is that you might have been mistaken and there might be a small chance their sons might be alive, or even wounded and in hospital unrecorded but still alive. Until they receive the official letter, this hope is what they cling to. They can't bring themselves to see you for fear that you are telling them the truth."

I thought very carefully about what she'd just said and could understand what she meant. Looking into her eyes, I confided, "You know I haven't told any lies, don't you, Mum?"

"I do, and I think that they know that deep down, too. You know that when they do get their letters, they'll want to know all the details of their sons' deaths. This will be something you'll have to prepare yourself for."

"But what if I can't, or if their death was too horrible to recall. How can I tell them that?"

"You'll find the right words I know but remember that the complete truth is not always the best."

"Mum, is there anything about Phil's death you would like to talk about?"

"You know, when you came home I had to stop myself all the time from asking you but as the time has gone by, it seems less important how he died. I thanked God that you came home. Phil didn't suffer at the end and his brother and best friend was there to comfort him, and I think for the moment that's enough. I know that in the future, I'll make a decision about hearing the details of his death, and you'll be here to tell me. Anyway, you rest now whilst I go to the village. I shouldn't be too long."

She gathered her things and quietly shut the door on her way out whilst I lay back on my bed, thinking about all sorts of things. My mind kept going from one awful memory to another. I'd only just managed to shut out some of them for a while, but thinking about what Mum had said about the letters was going to bring it all back again. What should I say to the parents when they come, which I know they will? I just know I can't tell them the truth. It's bad enough to have lost your son, but to learn of the horrific way in which he died and the horrendous conditions he spent the final days and hours of his life would be far too much to live with.

I don't know what came over me but I felt trapped and suddenly started to shake and sweat. I needed to get away and be on my own. Going the back way out of the cottage, I hastily crossed the garden, struggled over the low hedge and crossed the track into the fields opposite. I couldn't breathe properly and despite the early winter chill,

I was burning up and my clothes were soaked with sweat. All that I could think of was getting away. I knew I couldn't relive the deaths of my friends again, especially with their mums and dads. Not yet. Maybe, not ever.

I ran over the fields stumbling and falling, and crawling on my hands and knees at times. When I couldn't go any further, I just lay there in the mud, beating my fists on the ground. I thought I was nearly going out of my mind but I got up and carried on, not knowing or caring where I was going, as long as it was as far away as possible. Somehow I got to the river, not too far from one of our favourite play spots. So I rested a while and then persevered on further. Lying down on the wet grass, I was so exhausted I couldn't continue any more, so that's where I stayed, drifting in and out of consciousness, my mind playing tricks on me all the time. One time, we were playing in the river on a gloriously hot and sunny day, and the next I would be searching through all the bits of human remains looking for something of John that we could bury, remembering Peter's head and brain shattering as I shot him, Mum coming down the meadow calling us in for supper. That's how it went, on and on for as long as I could recollect. I was sure this was going to be the end and I was so glad. No more dreams, no more pain or endless nightmares. Just endless peace.

Elizabeth

Chapter 10

"Here he is, Mother. Hurry with the blankets. He's frozen stiff but he's still alive. I'll go and shout the others and we'll carry him to the Manor and the doctor can see him there."

"Oh Bill. Why did you leave the cottage? We could have talked about it. Most of the village has been up all night, looking for you. Here we are. Now, let's get him on the stretcher. Careful, it looks like there's some blood on his shirt. Now wrap him up, Mother."

"Right. Lift him. Steady. Right, let's go, quick as we can. There's plenty of help if anyone gets tired. There's the bridge, lads, not far to go. Here we are. Thank you for your help. We'll let you all know how he's getting on."

"This is Bill Stokes. The doctor's expecting him. Where shall we put him?"

It was only after receiving treatment from the doctor and nursing staff that my parents were finally informed of my condition.

"Well, I can tell you that the good news is he's still alive, just some of his old wounds have opened up on his chest and we've drained fluid out of his lungs. His head wound is fine, too. The real problem we have is that he may be developing pneumonia, which is serious. I'm going to put him in a room on his own for now and we'll keep an 'around the clock' eye on him. Now, once we get him well again, from what you've told me about his state of mind and what's just happened, I think that there are more wounds to deal with in his head than there are physically. Now it may be coincidence or just luck but we've been told to expect far more patients in the very near future, so we're opening up more rooms. Anyway, they're also sending more nurses and three more doctors, one of whom is studying psychiatric medicine and I'm sure he'll be able to help Bill. Now there's nothing more that you can do for him at the moment, so go home and rest. It's going to be a worrying time for us all. If there's any change, don't worry, I'll get a message to you as soon as I can."

Although I was sometimes aware of what was happening to me, most of my time was spent in a semi-conscious state. It was to be many weeks before my body was recovered, although my mind was still in turmoil. Thankfully, I couldn't remember much of the detail that had led to me being brought into hospital. Mum had started back at work here as they were desperately short of workers and I think she was more than happy to have the opportunity of being close to me. It was around this time that one of the new doctors, Captain Conner, came to see me. He was taking over my case as the other doctor now had more urgent patients to look after.

Christmas came and went, and the winter weeks rolled by. My body and physical strength were mending well but unless my mind could be helped, I would never be able to lead any sort of normal life. Over the last couple of weeks, Dr Conner had been spending quite a bit of time with me just talking about nothing in particular. Things like when I was young and school and my Mum and Dad, those sorts of things. It was strange though, he never asked about the Somme.

I began to like him and found him easy to talk to and to share the memories of things that we had both done. It was about six weeks after Christmas that I had two new visitors. They only stayed a few minutes and after they'd gone I was so angry and full of emotion that I threw the paper and money that they'd brought across the room. Staggering out of bed, I started to kick and bang my fists on the walls and the door. The Doctor and two nurses came in and forced me back to bed, strapping me in unceremoniously.

"What's got into you, Bill?"

"Doctor, I've just found these on the floor," added one of the restraining nurses.

"Who gave you these, Bill? Come on, Bill. Tell me so I can help. Come on, Bill, you were doing so well. Talk to me."

"How do they know I'm unfit to fight again? Who said I wanted to be discharged, not me? I want to go back to where my friends died. They came here to give me a scrap of paper and a few pounds back pay for all I've been through. They could have waited until I was better, or even better dead, then it wouldn't have cost them anything."

"Don't talk like that, Bill. It's not their fault. They only carry out army regulations. They shouldn't have been allowed to see you anyway, and it won't happen again. Now, I'll give you something to relax you and I'll be back to see you later."

True to his word, he came back, and also two or three times every day after that. By the end of April, I had told him everything. He never judged me or passed any comments. He was there when I cried and even he cried a little when we talked about Peter's death. He knew that a big problem for me was going to be facing the mums and dads of the lads. He also knew that once I had spoken to them it would be a big leap forward in my healing time. So, between him and Mum, they arranged for them all to visit me one by one at the hospital, but only if I was feeling up to it.

It was Harry's parents who came first, and with Mum and Dr Conner sitting beside me, I was able to tell them what they wanted to hear. A lot of tears were shed and when they left, I sensed that they were glad to have learnt the truth. When it was the turn of John's parents, I stuck to the truth, except I omitted the part that he was blown to pieces but instead told them that a piece of shrapnel pierced his heart and he died in no pain as it was instant. As they were going, they wished me well and thanked me, saying it was comforting to know that he hadn't suffered.

Peter's mother came on her own and started asking questions before even sitting down. She hardly gave me the time to answer and most of the questions actually had nothing to do with how Peter had died. I think the doctor felt the same as I did, and he soon stepped in, saying the reason that he had agreed to allow her to see me was to listen to my account of the death of her son, and that was all. Any other details would have to wait until I had recovered. After a moment's silence, I told her how we attacked the German trenches and drove them back, then prepared to defend our gains against the counter-attack, if one was to come. I told her that when it did come, it was of such force that we were ordered to make an orderly withdrawal and it was during this time that Peter was killed by heavy machine-gun fire. He was only a few yards away from me but by the time I reached him he was dead. I told her that I had said a few words from the Bible over him, then closed his eyes, got up and carried on retreating. It was then that I was hit and I couldn't remember anything else.

Although she was a strong lady, hearing how her son died reduced her to an outpouring of grief with floods of tears. Mum went home with her as the doctor suggested and we were eventually left on our own.

"Well, how do you feel after unburdening yourself of those memories? You've helped the family's come to terms with their loss as well, you know. Maybe not now, but in a little while, you'll feel great relief and it was good that your mother was here to listen to a small part of what you've been through. Hopefully, she'll start to understand why you are as you are and learn to help you find your old self again now. You know, your old self is locked away in your head. It is there. Now, I think that's enough for today. A good rest is what you need."

He went, leaving me to think about the day and in particular his parting words to me.

Over the next few weeks, I began to feel better, as he had said I would. I was well enough to go home at the weekends and by mid-June I was living at home full-time. Although I was recovering well, I was still very weak and tired a lot of the time, and because of the dreams I was not sleeping well at night. Instead, I would take a blanket and sit in Mum's spot, star-gazing on clear nights or just thinking about what I was going to do in the years ahead. On hot days, I would lie in the sun and sometimes Mum would come and sit by me and we'd talk and talk and talk about nothing in particular until I had dozed off. I went to see the doctor less and less over the weeks ahead but he always said that if ever I needed him he would always have time for me.

It was after one of my visits that I came home to find that my makeshift bed in the front room had gone. Mum explained that they needed it back at the hospital as they had run short which meant I would have to sleep in Phil's and my old room. I hadn't even been in it since I came home. The memories it held went back far and deep in my mind, and I wasn't ready for such a big change. Instead, I took to sleeping in the woodshed until Dad caught me coming back into the house one morning.

"Oh, it's you Bill. I thought you might be a tramp stopping the night. Your Mum knows you don't sleep in your old bed, you know. She worries about you such a lot. I sometimes think there's only you left in her life. Me and her, well, you know, since Phil died, we won't ever be the same again. I blame myself. I should have stopped him from going. I should have tried to stop you all from going, but I didn't and now I live with it every day, and will do for the rest of my life. Your Mum has always been the strongest and she seems to be managing well enough on her own. I know why you can't face your old room, but remember that good memories and dreams of loved ones, alive or dead, won't hurt you. Not facing them can, and will, tear you apart. Now go and see your Mum, she's waiting for you."

That was one of the only talks that I had with Dad, as he was going deeper and deeper into himself, and there was nothing much that anybody could do for him.

I spent all of that afternoon in our old bedroom, sitting on the bed, going through all our old things. Although we hadn't got a lot, each object held its own cherished memory. I slept in our room from then on and Dad was right, nothing in or about the room ever hurt me, in fact, it was quite the opposite.

Mum received a letter from the Army about Phil's back pay which could be collected from the local recruiting office in the town, the same one that we had signed up at.

So, she arranged for the day off and as I was getting ready, my shoe went under the bed. Reaching underneath to get it, I caught my finger on one of the floorboards. The sharp pain made me pull my hand out quickly only to find a large splinter sticking out and a little blood. I removed the splinter with my teeth and sucked my sore finger. Then, pushing the bed out of the way, I found the problem. I went and fetched a hammer and some nails to fix down the loose floor board when, for no reason, I lifted the board and looked underneath. There was nothing there at all, only dirt and straw, probably part of a field mouse's nest. As I started to put it all back down, I saw a scrap of paper. When I picked it up, I could see it had been nibbled by the mouse but there was enough writing to recall what it was about.

The bus ride into town was full of memories and I just sat there and let them flow over me like time. It was coming up to a whole year since the battlefields had claimed my mates and my young brother. Although to me, it felt like only yesterday. Time had moved on rapidly, and now I thought I should, too. As we made our way across town, taking the same route as we had done previously, before long we arrived and sat down, waiting our turn at the recruiting office. In front of us were several young lads who had come to join up, so eager and excited just like we had been. When they went into the other room, probably for their medical, the clerk called Mum and she showed them the letter. After the clerk had read it, he got up and went and knocked on another door. Someone shouted to come in and he opened the door, saluted and disappeared inside. A few minutes later, he came back out, walked over to Mum and took her back into the room. He came back to his desk, sat down and shouted "Next" and as there was only me in the room, I tried to explain, "I have only come with..."

"What's up? Scared of a bit of action are we?"

Before I could speak, another soldier came behind me.

"You're not a coward are you? You know what the girls do to cowards? They pin white feathers to them, it tells everyone that they are too chicken to sign up. Are you one of them? Are you a chicken, then?"

I thought for a while about all I had been through and what the lads would want me to say or do. So I got up and walked over to the table. The other soldier followed me and went behind the table to join his fellow soldier. Sitting down, I said, "What's it like then, at the front? You must have been there. Both of you can tell me what it's like. If it sounds good, I'll sign up now. So, what's it like?"

They both went very quiet, then the one sitting down said, "Don't be bloody cheeky. We all do our duty for King and Country wherever they send us."

"You haven't been, then? You must be just regular army to land this posting. You know that lady who you just saw? Well, she's one of four mothers who will be coming here to collect their son's back pay, dated the day they died on the battlefields of the Somme. They all joined up here. One of them was his brother and was the only badly wounded survivor to get home alive and to be medically discharged."

Standing up, I took my coat off and unbuttoned my shirt.

"That lady in there is also my Mother. It was my brother and three of my best friends who died, and this," I said bitterly, opening my shirt, "is what a German field artillery shell can do to flesh and bone when it explodes at close range. In future, I would be very careful who you call names at."

I had just finished putting my coat back on, when Mum came out with the officer walking alongside her. They came over to where I was standing and reaching for my hand the officer said, "I'm really sorry about your brother and friends. Your mother says all your wounds are healing well and I wish you all the best for the future."

He stepped back and saluted Mum once again.

"On behalf of both myself and the British Army, we offer you our deepest sympathy for the loss of your son. Now, if you'll excuse me, please, I have much work to do."

As we were about to leave, the young lads joining up came bowling out of the room full of laughter and excitement at all being signed up to the same regiment, destined for the killing fields of Europe. I hoped for their sakes and their families' that they all came back alive.

Mum had a few places that she wanted to go whilst we were still in town, and I was quite happy to just follow her around. We had a lot of time before our bus home for me to hatch my plan that I had made as we had ridden in. As I fiddled with the piece of paper in my pocket, little did I know then how much it was going to change my life.

"Mum, shall we go down to the market and see what they've got to eat? I'm a little hungry after all this walking about, what you think?"

"I suppose so. We've plenty of time."

So we made our way through the narrow streets until we came into the square, which was alive with people and dozens of stalls selling everything you could imagine, except what we were looking for.

"Come on, Mum. Let's go and look in the Old Market Hall," not knowing whether it would still be there.

I half dragged Mum passed all of the stalls and eventually there it was, right at the far end. I wasn't sure how it had looked before as my memory wasn't too good yet, but it was here so that was a start. Looking through the window, there were several empty tables, and one by the window a little way away from the rest.

"Come on, Mum. This looks good. You order a drink and something to eat and I'll get the table."

"But Bill...."

"No buts. It'll be my treat. Don't forget I have my back pay to spend. Only the best for the best Mum in the world."

As we walked in, it all started to come flooding back to me. Sitting with my back to the counter, I began to drift back and could still see all the lads sitting around, laughing and joking whilst they drank their tea. We were talking about the girl who served us and they were ribbing me because I liked her. It was a glory to just sit there once again in their glow. I could have stayed there forever.

Startled by Mum's hand on my shoulder, the daydream was broken.

"Sorry to startle you, love. Are you alright? Only you seemed as though you were somewhere else."

"No, I'm fine. I was just remembering one of the good times that we all had together."

"Well, it looks like it must have been special. It's the first time I've seen you smile since before you went away."

"Pot of tea for two?"

I knew straightaway that it was her. I think I would have remembered her voice, no matter what. She came and stood by my side while she put the cups and plates on the table, and then put a large teapot and milk next to Mum.

"Your food won't be long. I'll bring it over to you when it's ready."

I turned and looked up at her, "Thank you very much, Miss."

Her eyes lit up and a broad smile came across her face.

"Well I never. Didn't think I would ever see you again. I'll go and tell Mum. She'll be really pleased to see you. We often talk about you and your pals and wonder how you'd got on. Didn't your brother go with you, too?"

"Elizabeth, customers to be served!"

"Coming, Mother. I'll be back with your food. It's good to see you again, though," she said as she disappeared down the passage into the kitchen.

"I think you have something to tell me about this place and that young lady! It's funny, but I had the feeling I was being taken somewhere."

Mum smiled at me with a glint in her eye.

I quickly told her all about my first visit and showed her the note that I'd written. She sat there looking at me in amazement until I had finished my tale.

"So, when you came and sat down, it only holds happy thoughts with no fears or worries about coming here? This must be a good sign for you at last."

Mum was interrupted by both Elizabeth and her mother coming back to the table.

"It's so good to see you safe and sound." Elizabeth's mother leaned over the table, kissed me on the cheek and gave me a big hug. I introduced her to Mum.

"Look, you eat your food while we close up, then we can talk a little. Are you on the bus? Plenty of time then, so don't rush."

We ate our sandwiches and cake without talking.

"I don't know what I'm going to talk about. Mind you, that cake was very nice, maybe she'll give me the recipe. I can't think what else we have in common."

"I know something, Mum," I said quietly. "You both lost a son in the War. She lost her only son in 1915, too, probably fighting in the same muddy fields."

At that moment, Elizabeth's mother came over with fresh tea and cups. A few minutes later, Elizabeth herself came across and sat down. With tea in the cups, the general chit-chat started and it wasn't long before the painful questions were about to begin.

"Look, to save anyone any upset about questions they want to ask, I'll tell you all there is to know. We came into town today to collect back pay owed to my brother who, along with my three best friends, was killed in action on the Somme battlefields."

Both mother and daughter were visibly shaken, and sat looking at me with their mouths half open.

"And fortunately for me, I wasn't killed alongside my brother and friends. Instead, I was wounded and discharged from the Army, so I can't even go back and have another go at joining them, wherever they are now."

I paused as my eyes misted over once more.

"If you don't mind, I need to be on my own for a little while."

Getting up, I let myself out of the tea shop and went to the rear of the market where there was a small area of grass and trees. Sitting down under a tree, I started gulping in air. My heart was pounding in my chest, my body oozing sweat all over. My nerves were so taut I thought I was going to shatter. I had been doing so well until now. I thought I was coming to terms with it all, but just look at me now. I lay on my side and curled into a tight ball and started to shake violently. With tears now rolling down my cheeks, I lay there helpless, unable to control my emotions or my life. However long I lay there, helpless as a newborn child, I will never know, but it was sometime before I became aware of the sweet, gentle voice calling me. Again and again the call came into my head but unable to move, all I could do was listen. Thinking I had died and maybe gone I know not where to, I opened my eyes and gazed into the most beautiful face I could ever imagine. My guardian angel had come to help me recover my sanity.

"Oh Bill, your mother is worried sick about you. We've all been looking for you for ages. I'll just go and tell them that I've found you, then I'll come back."

What felt like hours must have been only minutes before she came back. Sitting beside me, Elizabeth cradled my head in her arms, neither of us saying a word. We stayed like this well into the evening until my self-control started to bring me back to normal. Gently easing my head from her arms, I sat up, trying to recall what had been happening to me and what had started it off. One minute, I was drinking my tea, the next I couldn't remember anything, until now. As I sat there, confused and angry, she started to stir and then awoke with a start. She reached out and touched my shoulder.

"Did I make you jump? Earlier, when I couldn't feel your head in my arms, I thought you'd gone."

"No, I'm still here and I'm very sorry for how I've behaved. I don't know why it happened. It's never been as bad as this before."

"Don't worry, it's not your fault. Your mother told us what happened at the recruiting office and a little about your brother and friends. It's bound to upset you. Now, come on, you can sleep in my bed until you're feeling up to going home. Your Mum has already gone home and she says it's fine for you to stay. I'll sleep in with mother. It'll be just like it was when my brother was alive."

We made our way in the breaking light of dawn, back to her house. Just before we went in, I stood watching the sun rise slowly in the sky. I would never again enjoy this part of the day. By now on the front line, an assault would be under way. Hundreds of men would either be dead, dying or wounded and by the time it's over, there would be thousands of casualties with nothing more gained. Elizabeth held my hand and also watched the sun rise.

"It's such a terrible waste of all those young lives, but for you it's all over and you've now got to rebuild your life, whilst not forgetting your lost loved ones, of course."

I must have been worn out as I slept for most of that day, although being in a strange room and in Elizabeth's bed with no constant reminders of Phil and the lads also helped. Sitting up and looking around, it was bigger than my room but didn't have much furniture. There was a small table with a cracked mirror leaning against the wall. A brush and comb along with some small, wooden toys and a cloth doll. These few treasures were all laid out neatly on the top.

Just then, there was a knock at the door and Elizabeth came in carrying a glass of water. I grabbed the bed cover and pulled it up under my chin to cover my wounds. Laughing gently, she put the water by the side of the bed.

"I've seen a lot more than a bare chest, you know! Don't forget I had a brother not much older than you. There's not much I haven't seen before."

"You haven't seen me."

"Why are you different to anyone else?"

"It depends if they've been wounded or not."

"But your Mum only told us about your head wound, nothing more."

"I'm afraid I've not healed very well and I suppose she thought there was no reason to tell you."

She came over and sat on the bed.

"You may as well show me now because I'll see it on our wedding night."

Speechless, I allowed her to pull down the bed cover, uncovering the full extent of my chest wounds. Nothing could have prepared her for the sight that met her eyes.

"Can I touch the scars?"

"If you want to."

She started to run her fingers all over my chest and stomach.

"I'm not hurting you, am I?"

"No, I can't feel anything but the doctor said I might get some feeling back in time."

She stood up and walked to the door.

"I'll get some food ready for you downstairs and shout up when it's done."

Opening the door, she was half way out when I called her.

"Will you still marry me now you know some of my secrets?"

She thought for a few seconds, and then smiled at me.

"With a handsome face and a lovely chest like that, I would be foolish if I didn't marry you," and off she went.

After we'd had our meal and cleared away, we went out for a walk by the river. Although it was late autumn and quite chilly, in her company I was warmed by the aura that she exuded, the way she spoke and laughed, and by this feeling of being safe and wanted. She did most of the talking but we never talked about the War. She had me laughing many times, something I never thought I would ever do again. As we headed back to her house, I spoke about going home to the village.

"Only if you feel up to it. Mum won't mind how long you stay, but it's up to you."

"Don't get me wrong, I'd rather stay with you and your mother, but I know my Mum will be really worried about me, so I'd better go home tomorrow."

We hardly spoke as we went into the kitchen. Her Mum was baking cakes for the shop.

"Bill's going home tomorrow, Mum."

"As long as you feel strong enough to make the journey, and besides your Mum will be glad to see you're feeling better."

"Thank you for all you've done for me, both of you. I don't know what I'd have done without your help."

Feeling the tears building up in my eyes, I hastily said good night and went to bed.

Lying there wide awake, I was trying to remember all that Elizabeth and I had talked about. I wanted to remember every tiny detail. The sound of her voice and her laughter. Every little thing about her. I don't know why but I was beginning to think that our meeting was somehow meant to be. Sleep finally overcame me with my dreams in a swirl of emotion. I was flitting from Elizabeth to the War to home and my childhood and then back to complete darkness. Artillery fire was bursting all around me, screams from wounded men, dying men begging for a priest and for their mothers. It was the stench of rotting corpses next to me that made me realise that I was hiding under a pile of bodies. I was covered in putrifying flesh and body fluids, and there were rats everywhere eating as much as they could. There were maggots crawling in and out of the bodies. I tried to get from under the pile but I couldn't as something kept pulling me back. I tried and tried so many times, but even kicking out didn't help. Suddenly a flair burst above me, so I tried again. It was then I saw what was holding me back. I was being stopped from getting away by the corpses. They were gripping my legs and lower body, pulling me back deeper into the pile. Panic-stricken and terrified, I started kicking and lashing about, screaming for help. Summoning up all my remaining strength, I reared up and threw the corpses off my back. Suddenly, it was black again. No, there was a lamp on the table. I was trembling all over with fear and dripping with sweat. I didn't know where I was until I heard Elizabeth's voice.

"You're all right. It's only a bad dream. Nothing can hurt you now. Here, have some water, it'll help to calm you down."

"Thank you," I croaked hoarsely, taking the glass she offered. I was so thirsty that I emptied the glass and then downed another one.

When I'd settled a little, I looked across at her beautiful face that was lit up by the glow of the lamp. She smiled shyly and looked away.

"Look at me in my night clothes, alone in a man's bedroom. What would people think?"

"How long have you been here?"

"I heard you crying out about an hour ago, so I sat with you in case you might hurt yourself."

"Did I say much in my dream?"

"Yes, but it was all mixed up. I couldn't tell what it was all about, only that it was upsetting for you."

"Do you want to know what the dream was about?"

"Not unless you want to tell me."

"I do, I mean, I want to tell you but I can't, not just yet. The wounds are still too deep and the pain never goes away."

"I know. I had the same experience when my brother was killed. I can now talk about him with you, not only because you lost your brother and your friends but because you saw it all happen first hand. You've witnessed all the horrors of war and were badly wounded. If you never speak of it again, I will never ask if you want to talk about it. I'll always be here for you. Now, try and get some sleep for the journey home."

I settled down in the bed and she pulled the covers over gently. Kissing my head, I asked her softly, "Please could you leave the lamp on, just in case. You never know."

"I'll do better than that. I'll stay with you. I'll only lie awake worrying about you anyway," and she sat in her chair, awake until the sun came up.

She left me to dress and went downstairs to the kitchen where her mother had made some tea. She smiled as I went in and sat down. Passing me a drink over, she sat next to me.

"Do you get many bad dreams like that? Only, when my son died, at first I used to have them every other night. They were so real and terrifying, I was afraid to close my eyes. Then, they began to get less and less until they eventually stopped. I still think about him and sometimes dream about him, but in a nice way now – it's totally the opposite."

Just then, the door opened and Elizabeth came in, all dressed up in her best clothes and sat opposite me. She poured herself a drink and then said, "Only half an hour to the bus. If you want something to eat, I'll get it for you now."

"I'm not hungry at the moment, thank you."

"No, I'm not either."

So, we just sat there drinking our tea in silence. There were things I wanted to say to her because I didn't know when or if I was going to see her again, but with her Mum there it was all rather awkward. I thought that she must also be going somewhere all dressed up. I was panicking as to what to say.

"What time does the bus leave? We'll have to leave now or we'll miss it."

"We?"

"Yes, I promised your mother that I would bring you home safe and sound. That's, unless you don't want me to come with you?"

"Of course I do. It's just, well, I thought as you were all dressed up, you were going somewhere special."

"I am. I'm going to your village and may meet your Mum and Dad, and maybe some of your friends, too. That's special, isn't it? Now, come on or we won't be going anywhere."

I turned to her mother.

"I can't thank you enough for your understanding and sharing your home with me. You'll never know how much it has meant to me."

She came round the table and hugged me.

"You'll always be welcome in our house, and I know Elizabeth will always be happy to see you."

"Oh Mum, must you?"

"Yes, I must. I haven't seen you looking so happy since your brother was at home. Now off you two go, or you'll miss the bus."

All the way home, I talked non-stop about the village and all the people who lived there. I told her about all the surrounding villages and places where we'd played when we were children. I told her about the Hall before the War and it now being used as a hospital. Then I told her about our cottage and garden, and just as I finished the bus stopped and we hopped off. Although it was cold, at least it was dry. After I'd showed her around, stopping to talk to people along the way, we finally went to see Mum at work who was so pleased see us, especially Elizabeth. I think she had taken a special shine to her.

"Have you two had anything to eat yet? No, I didn't think so. I'm going home now, so when you get there I'll have something ready for you. No arguments."

We walked around the village, looking at all the places I'd talked about, and then we walked up the hill to the cottage where Mum was busy in the kitchen. I showed Elizabeth around inside and then left her to explore the outside and the gardens on her own.

"Food's ready. You'd better go and look for your young lady."

"Oh Mum, she's not my young lady."

"Haven't you seen the sparkle in her eyes when she looks at you? She knows it, even if you don't."

I looked around the outside of the cottage for her but I should have known where she would be. As I walked quietly to the end of the garden, she was sitting on the grass in Mum and Dad's favourite spot, just staring at the countryside before her. Putting my hand on her shoulder, I said, "You'll get your clothes wet sitting there."

"I know, but I don't care. It's such a magical spot I could sit here for ever."

We stayed a while longer until Mum called us in, and then I helped her up. It was then as I gazed into her eyes, I saw how they sparkled.

As we ate, Mum dried her clothes ready for the journey home. We ran down the hill hand in hand and as happy as the moment allowed us to be. As she got on the bus, she called back to me, "When will I see you again? Soon? Don't think you can put me off that easily - I'll be back at the weekend, your Mum says I can stay overnight, if I want. Would you like that?"

"Yes, of course! I'd like that very much."

She smiled and leaned forward, kissing my lips so softly, like a mother kisses a newborn baby. Then she was gone. I stood there and watched the bus trundle off out of sight. I didn't know what my feelings were telling me, but I did know that was the first time I had been kissed by a girl and it felt so good.

The changing of time

Chapter 11

Over the coming months, we saw as much of each other as we could, and during the spring and summer months spent a lot of time sitting in that special place in the garden. Slowly, I was able to talk to her about what I'd been through without holding anything back. We would sit holding hands, or I would lie with my head resting on her lap and she would listen as I retold the horrors that haunted my mind. When I cried as the scenes came back into my mind, she would wipe away my tears, along with many of my fears, for it was true that since I had begun opening up to her and getting closer to her, I was beginning to feel that my mind was coming back to me.

The War ended with no real winners or losers, only millions of ordinary people dead and just as many maimed for life. Our village, with others close by, had suffered badly with nearly every family losing at least one loved one. It was decided to make a small garden to remember the lost loved ones by and a plot was fenced off part way up the hill overlooking the village. Each family made a cross and it was hammered into the earth. Dad took several days over Phil's. It had engraved into it his name, the date he was born and the date he died. The whole surrounding area came to the service that Sunday to pay their respects to the lads. None were over the age of twenty three who had died in this war to end all wars. That's what we were told, anyway.

Within a year, the hospital was closed down and sold to an ex-army officer who wanted to return the Hall to its former glory and to start farming again. Both Elizabeth and her mother were taken on by the General and were given a small cottage on the estate to live in, which meant that we got to see each other every day. The time had now come for me to decide what I was going to do for a living. My army money had long run out and Mum and Dad were keeping me. I would have loved to work with Dad again but his life had changed so much. He seemed to shun human contact, even me and sometimes Mum. As it turned out, my life was about to take an unusual turn.

I was just walking to meet Elizabeth, when I came across the new owner of the Hall.

"Who are you? Do you know this is private land? What's your business here?"

I told him who I was and what I was doing.

"Oh, you're the Stokes' boy. I've heard about you. Had my only son killed just before it was over. Still, enough about that. Do you remember how the gardens, lawns and flowerbeds were laid out before the War? I would so love to restore the old place to its former self. The inside is coming on really well, but the army people made a real mess around the outside. Most of the old gardeners who worked here before the War have moved away or were killed in France. I can get labourers and some gardeners but I really need someone who can lay it out and oversee the work."

"We used to play all over the estate when I was young. As the owner was never at home, he left it to an overseer to run the estate, and then he left as the War started. When I left school, I went with my father, who's a woodsman, and we were always on the estate and so was my brother. So yes, I suppose I can just about remember most of it, and I can ask Dad what he can think of, too. I could also ask around the village, plenty of people used to work at the Hall. Whenever the owner was back, he used to have big house parties and garden parties. People came from up and down the country."

"And what about your brother and any friends who played there? They might remember some details."

It was then that our conversation went hushed for a while.

"What do you think about me gathering together all the information that I can and doing some rough sketches, and then we can take it from there?"

"I'll leave it with you then. Just come and see me any time. Oh, and feel free to come and go as you please."

As he turned to walk away, I said, "Excuse me, sir, but you mentioned my friends and brother. All four of them were killed at the Battle of the Somme in July 1916. I was the only one to come home, although I was severely wounded by artillery shell fire in my head, chest and stomach, so I'm afraid that I won't be doing much manual work for you."

"I can't tell you how sorry I am for your losses. I too was at the Somme and witnessed the massacre first hand. I was one of a number of officers who wanted the offensive halted but we were overruled. Now, as we both know, the battle will go into the annals of history."

He wandered off across the field, waving his stick as he went out of sight. And left me to contemplate the unexpected future that I had just been offered.

Everyone was really excited for me to be given a chance to work at the Hall. Even Dad gave me all the information he could remember and offered to help if ever I needed it. After about three weeks, I went up to the Hall and spread out my drawings in front of the ex-officer. He took his time browsing over them and asked a lot of questions. He went over to his desk and came back holding a few photographs.

"Just found these in a box in the attic. You were right, you can't draw but the detail is incredible. Your scribblings show far more than these images. When do you think we can get started?"

"You mean, you want me to carry out all the gardening?"

"No, not the manual work. I want you as my head gardener, to look after the whole estate, the crops and all. You'll report to me alone. You can tell me what you think is a fair wage for the job. I can't let you have a cottage though, as they're all occupied, but I want you to run everything." He paused, pondering what all of the plans would mean.

"This had always been our dream, my son and I, to live in the country and farm. My wife died years ago and you know about my son, so I know I'm too old to live my dream alone. I know nothing about the land and I know you don't know that much either but I feel that we've already got a bond that will be with us until we die, and besides, I trust you. You look after me and I'll look after you. Now, what do you think? Take as much time as you want, then let me know."

I gathered all my sketches together, folding them neatly and then put them carefully into my pocket.

"You really mean what you say, don't you?"

"I'm not in the habit of telling lies, and besides, I know you are the right man for the job and for me."

"If I take the job, I won't let you down you know."

"I know that."

"When do you want me to start?"

"As far as I'm concerned, you started the day that I first met you in the fields."

We shook hands warmly and toasted our new-found friendship with a small glass of sherry.

"Just a couple of things before you go. Now, I will want to come round with you every week to see how things are going, so I would like to suggest that in front of the men you call me General and I will call you Mr Stokes, but when we are alone, I'll call you Bill and you can call me Howard. Will that be all right with you?"

"I think that will be just fine, Howard."

"Good, good. Now," he picked up an envelope from his desk and gave it to me, "that's your payment for all your work to date and when we next meet, we can deal with all the money matters at the same time."

It was over two and a half years until it was all completed and the farm was making a profit. The General had very few family members who visited him but he did have quite a few ex-army officers and their wives came down to see him. Unbeknown to him, deep in one of his woods, I had started breeding pheasants for shooting. One day, we were on our usual inspection when I was talking to him about the previous owner.

"I remember before the War, when the owner would have big shooting weekends with parties the night before. We all used to beat for him, driving the pheasants into the guns. It was here in these woods. There would be as many as fifty or sixty guns lined up which would fetch down four hundred birds at a time."

"Ah, what a sight that would be, Bill. All those birds and guns; the smell, the excitement. What do you think? Could we do it again? It would be the event of the year for me."

Making our way deep into the wood, Howard was too busy planning a shoot to notice the breeding huts that I'd built and that were now full of young birds nearly ready for shooting. Stopping by the side of one of the sheds, I said, "Howard, what do you think of these?"

Lifting the roof, you could see about thirty or forty birds.

"You crafty young devil. I wondered why we came this way and all that talk of shooting. How many birds have you got then?"

"About twelve hundred and about forty beaters lined up with sixteen gun dogs, if we need them. It just means that you need to invite your guests."

"By God, if my son had lived I'd have hoped he would have turned out like you. Come on, I want to get back and start my guest list."

The hunting weekend was an out and out success and became an annual event, as did the villagers' party that he arranged as a thank you for all the work. It was on the evening of the first party that Elizabeth and I were sitting on a blanket a little way away from the frivolity itself. We were just enjoying the atmosphere and laughing at all the funny goings-on. Turning to Elizabeth, I leaned over and enjoyed a long lingering kiss, just as sweet as the first one that we'd ever had.

"What was that all about?"

"I was just thinking how much I truly love you. With you and your strength, we've come such a long way. Without you, I wouldn't have survived. It's you, and only you that believed in me and shared your love with me that gave me the will to carry on. You've helped me to shed the many horrors that I faced, and with your love and strength I've come through the darkness. I think you know there's still one dark secret buried deep in my memory though. I feel you have a right to know before we can carry on together with our lives any further."

I continued, describing the scene up to Peter getting wounded, then how he begged me to end his life and how I killed one of my best friends. It was a very emotional time for both of us. I don't think I will ever know what she was thinking, but after a while, she said, "Bill, if you ever had to face that again, what would you do? If, say, it was me and not Peter?"

I had to think long and hard, and it was a difficult question.

"I think I would be forced to do the same but..."

"No buts, you would do it as would I because it was the only thing you could do for him. I feel proud that you had the character and strength to do the right thing. Now, let's go dancing before it's all over."

She got up and dragged me off the blanket.

"Wait a minute. I have something I want to ask you."

"I know, I know. I've waited long enough and the answer is yes. Now, come on, I want to dance."

"But how did you know?"

"No buts, I can't let you into all my secrets. Now hurry up, the night's nearly over."

We got married the following year and it was one of the best days of my life. My love for Elizabeth never stopped growing. Preparations started months before and nearly all the village was involved. Elizabeth and her mother made her dress and the bridesmaids' dresses, too. Mum made her own dress, and Dad and I had to go and buy our clothes, as we only had our work garments. We had decided that after the ceremony, we would all come back to the cottage to celebrate. We were also going to live there too until we found a place of our own. The village women arranged it all, and it seemed to lift everyone's spirits no end. Although the War had been over for a few years, the villagers had struggled to come to terms with the devastation that it had inflicted. This was the first wedding since before the War and everyone was invited. They all wanted to give a little something.

The week before the actual wedding, I started to feel nervous, which Mum soon noticed. A few nights later, I was helping to tidy away in the kitchen.

"Getting more nervous as it gets closer?" she questioned.

"I didn't think it showed that much."

"Elizabeth will be the same, if not worse. It happens to all couples just before they get married."

"I'm also a little upset, Mum that I can't afford to get her a ring. We've talked about it and Elizabeth says she's marrying me, not a ring and that we can always buy one later, but I don't think it'll be the same. What do you think?"

"Just a minute." She went upstairs and when she came back down, she was carrying a small cloth pouch.

"Here you are. I've been cleaning it for days, just in case it might be needed."

I opened it and tipped the contents into my hand.

"It's beautiful, Mum. Really lovely, but I can't take your ring."

"It's not mine. It was my Mum's and her Mum's before that. It's always gone to the first daughter to get married but as I only have a son, I want you to give it your bride – my new daughter. It would make me so happy. She's as near to me as any daughter could be and she's been so good for you. I don't know what things would have been like without her. So take it to give to her, with my blessing."

I thanked her and gave her a big hug.

"Why aren't all Mum's like you? The world would be such a better place for us all to live in."

"Get off with you. I've got to finish my dress."

"Before I go, I've just one more thing that I really need to talk to you about, Mum. I've asked Dad and he said better to ask you, but I feel a little foolish about it, as though I should already know, but I don't."

"I think I know what you want to know about. There's no set way of loving each other, only do what feels right for both of you. Be kind and gentle with her. Only do what comes naturally to each of you. Always talk to each other about what you think is nice and not nice, and when you fall out, which you will, always make friends again before you go to sleep. The rest you can find out for yourselves. Now go away, please. I have a lot to do!"

As I went out the back door, I was thinking about what good advice Mum always gave, but I still didn't know what was supposed to happen on the wedding night. Still, I was sure Elizabeth would know more than me.

On the wedding day, I was up at 5.30am, even though the service wasn't until three o'clock. I thought I would cut some logs, so I went to the shed but that was already full. As I was hunting around for something to do, I came across an old football that we'd played with when we were lads. I sat on the chopping block, bouncing it up and down, thinking of all the games it had been in, all the scuffles and fights it had been involved in. Then, without thinking, I picked it up and headed off across the fields for a kick around on our favourite pitch.

It was a perfect day, sunshine, blue sky, warm but with a gentle breeze. I thought I would kick the ball around until I was tired, take a rest and then start again. I hadn't done this for quite some time and was enjoying myself immensely. The stream nearby provided me with water and I had plenty of time on my hands. Lots of funny, odd things kept coming in and out of my head, and for as long as I remember, all my thoughts were of the better times and the time ahead, being able to share my love with someone who loved me as much as I loved her.

For a while I lay on the grass, just thinking of the day ahead. I suppose if you think hard about certain things, it can sometimes be true that something good can come from something bad. If the War had never started, Phil and the lads would still be here but I probably wouldn't have met Elizabeth, or if I had, she would probably have gone out with Phil because he was better looking than me.

I must have fallen asleep, as the next thing that I remember was that I was being shaken awake.

"Come on, Bill. You'll be late. Your Mum's getting all worked up."

Half asleep, I saw it was Dad.

"Oh, I must have nodded off. I couldn't sleep and got up early and came here. How did you know where to look?"

"The football was missing and there's only a couple of places you'd go."

"Fancy a kickabout before we go back?"

"There's no time for that and besides, your Mum would go mad if she found out."

"Well she won't, will she? So come on."

We played for about twenty minutes and then kicked the ball home.

"Just like old times, eh?"

"Yes," I said, "but I bet I'll beat you back to the cottage."

"Oh, fancy yourself as a runner now do you? You never beat me before."

Scooping up the football, I shouted, "There's always a chance" and off we went, neck and neck across the meadow, heading home.

We were still arguing about who won when we burst into the kitchen.

"Where have you been? Just look at you! We have to set off in ten minutes or we'll be late."

"Never mind us, Mum. Just look you. Aren't you the prettiest Mum in the whole world? I can see why Dad fell for you!"

"Oh, get on with you, both of you! You won't get round me that easily. Now hurry up and get ready."

As we walked towards the church, the sight that met our eyes was like a fairy-tale. There were flowers and ribbons everywhere, all over the front of the church and up the path, with arches of ribbons and flowers covering the walk way. The small gates at the front had the most beautiful arch of mixed roses that I'd ever seen.

"Everyone in the village has been helping to grow flowers and make the decorations and things."

"Oh, Mum! It's so, so beautiful. I can't wait for Elizabeth to see it."

Everyone was going into the church as my bride would soon be here. I heard the distinct sound of the General's carriage approaching, and thought he must be late. I began walking up and down in front of the gate, my nerves starting to get the better of me. The carriage suddenly arrived and drew to a stop outside the church. Caught unawares, it took my breath away. It was decked out with ribbons and flowers, even the horses were decorated. The General was in his best uniform and was climbing down. He went to open the door as I slowly walked towards the carriage, making sure I didn't miss anything. Elizabeth's mother stepped out of the carriage first, then just as I got there, Elizabeth followed her. Words cannot describe how beautiful she looked. I was so taken aback. She was just like a princess. I took her hand and walked up the path behind the General and our Mums. Mum let all the others go in and then turned around to us.

"This won't take a minute," and she took out an old cloth. Unfolding it, there were the two silver crosses and chains that she had given to myself and Phil before we went to France.

"I want you both to have one for luck."

She put one on Elizabeth and the other on me. Looking at Elizabeth, she said, "The one that you've got is the one that Bill wore and it kept him alive."

Then, looking at me, "That's the one Phil wore. It's done its worst now. It'll act as a reminder, if ever you need one."

Then off she went, to take her place in the church.

We waited a few minutes in quiet contemplation and then turning to my bride, I whispered, "You look so beautiful. Every star in the sky is so envious, they might not come out again."

She looked at me, "Nervous?"

"Very."

"And me. So come on, let's go and get wed."

The inside of the church was like walking into a fairytale castle. We could have stayed forever but we were soon pronounced man and wife, and so we turned away from the altar and into our future together. Elizabeth was so pleased with her ring. When she cried at the altar, I didn't know if it was because of fear or pleasure.

We had to run down the church path while the whole village threw dried flower petals at us. Climbing into the carriage just past the lych gate, the General told us that he was going to take us the long way home.

"Have a bit of time on your own. It won't hurt them all to wait a little while."

Then, just as we eventually drew closer to home, he turned towards the Hall.

"Just got to pop back home. Forgot something, you know. You don't mind, do you?"

After we'd pulled up outside the Hall's huge front door, the General climbed down.

"Won't be long. I'll just pop in and get it," and off he went, striding around the side of the imposing building.

About ten minutes later, I suggested to my new wife that we should go check that everything was alright.

"Come on, let's go and find him. Mum will be worried where we are. He's been gone ages."

"Hey, don't forget that there are two Mum's now who'll be worried!" chipped in Elizabeth, with a bright smile across her face.

We peered in through the large Gothic windows along the front of the Hall, but there was no sign of life.

"Come on, let's see if he's round the back somewhere." As we walked hand in hand across the driveway and around the side of the Hall, with the gravel crunching under our new best shoes, we began to hear voices. Not just one or two, but what seemed like a whole crowd.

"What took you so long? We all began to think that you were both going to sit in the carriage on your own all evening. Anyway, glad you could make it - this is my wedding gift to the both of you. And by the way, you're also staying overnight. I've had the best guest room made up for you, so no arguments. Now, come on. You're the special couple that everyone's been waiting for. It's your day, make the most of it."

And what a day and night it was. The villagers talked about it for years after. It was such a fabulous day, something we often talked about and never forgot. As we stood by the window of the balcony of the guest bedroom that night, gazing at the stars, Elizabeth said to me, "You know what you said to me, by the church about the stars? Well, they have come out. I thought you said..."

"Ah, well. You had your wedding dress on then but now, well, you know..."

"Are you saying that I'm not good-looking with fewer clothes on?"

"No, no, I don't mean that. Oh, you know what I mean."

She laughed, "I was only teasing. You do know what comes next, don't you?"

"Well, actually, er, Dad wouldn't tell me. He said to ask Mum. Now she told me quite a lot but I'm still not convinced that I know everything. What about you?"

"Mum told me not to worry. She said that you would know everything."

We paused hesitantly and then I took hold of her hand. Drawing the curtains, I gently picked her up and we kissed lovingly. Carrying her to the bed, I laid her down gently and looked deep into her eyes.

"I think, my love, this is going to be as much fun as the whole day has been so far."

"Mmm, you may be right, but don't forget that we still have the rest of our lives to keep trying."

That whole day was one that we treasured in our hearts forever, and often reminisced about on long, dark, cold winter evenings. We found that although our lives flew by so very quickly, our love for each other grew stronger everyday. The General was as good as his word. Even though he passed on in late 1928, he made provision for me in his will, which meant that I had my job for life, whoever bought the Hall. Things did change somewhat when the new owners moved in, but it wasn't too bad and they spent most of their time up in London, so I was left to look after the place on my own.

Times were very hard in the Thirties, with lots of people going hungry and many jobs disappearing. I think we were luckier than most though, buried deep in the country. At least we could grow our own food and rear livestock, and we all shared what we had and looked out for each other. There were more troubles beginning to surface again in Germany though, making many of us War veterans uneasy. You would think they would have learnt their lesson from the last War, but no, they were soon fighting again. It lasted longer than the first War had and millions lost their lives. Our village and the others around us were luckier this time and only lost fourteen lads. Even that was heartbreaking though for their families, and it all brought back many upsetting memories for most of us in the village.

After many long years, we were finally blessed with a beautiful baby daughter. We had given up hope and then suddenly, there she was. We had her christened Sarah, and with her mum and two grandmothers she was never short of love and attention. The Second World War finally finished after six long years and the troops started to come home. A lot of damage had been caused in the cities, which needed to be put right in order that many people had a decent roof over their heads. There were thousands of homeless and food continued to be rationed for a few more years, but a least the fighting had stopped.

Sarah was about four when Elizabeth's mother died. She had been born with a weak heart and it just stopped beating. That's what the doctor told us afterwards, anyway. We were all so upset, as it had happened so suddenly and unexpectedly, with no warning at all. Elizabeth took her loss very badly as she had no other family of her own. It left her feeling lonely and very down. They do say that time is a great healer and certainly with a four-year-old daughter who was so full of fun and mischief, her spirits were slowly raised until she was virtually back to her old self again.

The local parish council put up a war memorial in the centre of the village to honour all of the brave men who had died in both of the wars. They never asked the villagers where we wanted it, so over the following weekend, the men from the village all got together and moved it up to our own garden of remembrance. When the man from the council came to inspect it some time later on in the year, he stood by the original site looking at his order sheet, scratching his head. Funnily enough, we never saw anyone come back to inspect it again. A memorial and dedication service was held one bright Sunday morning and a large crowd gathered around the newly erected stone column. It was a moving service and the words spoken by the vicar were just right for a time like this. It felt so very strange to be looking at Phil's name, along with Harry's, John's and Peter's all neatly cut into the polished stone. After so many years had gone by, a shiver ran down my spine and I pointed to Elizabeth the empty line below Phil's. It was never really talked about but there were always fresh flowers on the monument every day. During the service, nearly everyone had tears in their eyes when each one of the mothers who had lost sons stepped forward, placing a small posy of wild flowers on the monument.

Death, marriage and a new future

Chapter 12

I think Sarah was about twelve when, one summer's evening Elizabeth and I were sitting in the garden watching her playing. She stopped and came over and sat in between us.

"Mum, what's the matter with Granny? She's not very well, is she?"

Elizabeth glanced over at me, not really knowing what to say or how to reply.

"What makes you say that, darling?"

"Well, I know she's not a big eater but these last few weeks she's hardly eaten anything, and when she hugs me she's so thin and bony. I've also heard her being sick quite a few times, especially at night. What do you think can be wrong, Dad?"

I'm not sure, darling but I promise you that your Mum and I will look after her, so don't you worry about her.

Now don't go and say anything to her or Grandad about this little chat – it would only upset them, alright?"

We both kept an eye on Mum over the next few weeks and it soon became clear that all was not well with her. It took a lot of gentle persuading by Elizabeth to get her to go to see the doctor and as soon as she did, he was immediately concerned and arranged for her to go into hospital for further tests. It only took a few days before they knew the problem. As I was trying to tell Dad how sick she was, he looked straight through me and just couldn't take it all in. He stood up, falteringly and walked outside in a daze.

Even though Mum knew she hadn't long to live, her spirit was still as strong as ever. I wanted her to come home but as much as she wanted to, she knew it would be too upsetting for Dad and little Sarah. Finally, she died quite peacefully on another bright Sunday morning. The sunlight was streaming in through the windows and we were all there with her. Dad was stroking one hand, whilst I gently held the other. I know she knew we were there as she managed to squeeze my hand just before she eventually passed away. She was buried in the village churchyard by her relatives, adding to the family tradition that went back for generations.

Dad could never come to terms with losing Mum and before the earth had settled on her grave, Dad was buried next to her. In one way, for him it was for the best. He was never the same after Phil had died, and with Mum gone he'd really lost most of what he lived for. Even though it was a terrible time for us left behind, we knew that the love that we had for each other would see us through.

Sarah, as it happened, turned out to be very strong and in the early days when I was feeling low she would always manage to come up with something to snap me out of it. We still used to sit on the rug in the garden in the warm summer evenings until the stars came out and we'd always remember which star was whose. Sarah always tried to jumble them up but we always knew better.

We were soon on our own as Sarah moved away to college and then travelled off to university in London. At first, she would come home at the weekend and sometimes bring friends with her, but as she got older she began working as well and we knew she loved city life. Her visits got less and less, but she would always write every week and when we had a telephone she would ring her Mum often. Elizabeth missed her dreadfully though. You could hear it in her voice every time she rang off. So one day, I decided to arrange a surprise trip to London. I didn't tell Sarah so that it would be a surprise for her, too. Anyway, if she wasn't in, we could always go sightseeing. When I eventually told Elizabeth, she was so excited. As well as seeing Sarah, she had never been to London before. The up and coming trip so lifted her spirits, it gave her the boost she needed.

It was an early start but she was up with the lark and, after what was for us, an eye-opening journey, we soon arrived in London. We both marveled at the sites and decided to have a little look around before going on to see Sarah, so we just wandered around the centre of the city, enjoying the sights and sounds. Around every corner we turned, there was something bigger and better to see.

"You can see why Sarah likes London so much. There's so much to see and do, and look at all the people, the cars and buses. It's so busy."

"It's a bit different from where we live, isn't it?"

"Yes, it is. I wish we'd visited before. I hadn't realised how big it all was. Still, now there's nothing to stop us coming whenever we like."

We found a nice little tea shop and stopped for a bite to eat. When the waitress came, I ordered tea, sandwiches and cake for afters.

"I bet it's not as good as it was at Mum's old place in the market. We used to make the best there was and all fresh food. It wasn't like it is today. I bet you don't remember, do you?"

I held onto my reply whilst the waitress served our food. Elizabeth then poured the tea and we started to eat.

"I do remember, you know. How could I forget? I remember the date, the time and the place where I met the most beautiful girl in the world. The minute I saw you, I loved you and I knew I was going to marry you. Even my brother and our friends knew I loved you from that minute on. They used to tease me all the time about you – even when we were camped out in the trenches. Meeting you has been the best thing to happen to me in my whole life and to me you'll always be as beautiful as the first time we met."

I leaned over the table and gave her a lingering kiss and then sat back down again.

"Ooh, you've always been a bit of a romantic," she said, dabbing her eyes. "I think I knew that from the beginning, too - that we would have a good life together, and despite all the ups and downs, my love for you has only grown stronger as the years have passed by. There's only one thing really where you've ever gone wrong."

"Oh yes, and what would that be?"

"Don't you remember? On our wedding night, you..."

"I thought you said you wouldn't mention that again."

We both laughed aloud, "Still, you've made up for it over the years."

She gave a little giggle just like she used to when she was a young girl. We finished our food and paid the bill and as we walked outside, I commented, "You were right you know, it was nowhere near as good as you used to make with your Mum."

Walking along the busy road hand in hand, looking for the bus, I couldn't help but notice how happy she was, smiling and joking and pointing out this and that. Turning the corner, we came upon a very tall building and she was so amazed by its size, she said, "I'm going to count how many floors it's got."

I smiled to myself and then all I remember was her hand slipping softly out of mine. I heard a strange noise and a thud, then several people started to scream. Looking around for Elizabeth, I started to panic, shouting out her name. I pushed my way through the crowds that were now gathering on the pavement. I overheard people talking about someone having been knocked down by a bus. That's when I felt that cold shiver run through my body. It only ever comes when something terrible has happened, almost an instinct.

The surge of the crowd was so great that it had pushed me well away from where we both had been standing, and it took great effort to push my way through to where the bus now was. Several ladies with their backs to the bus were sobbing and as I tried to move nearer, I was barred by a large man.

"I wouldn't go any nearer mate. Someone's under the front of the bus. They're waiting for the police and an ambulance to come and free her."

I looked him in the eye, "I've lost my wife. Please, let me through. It could be her."

He pushed the crowd aside, making me a passage to the bus. There was quite a clear area between the crowd and the bus now, but lots of people were still trying to get a better view. As I slowly walked towards the bus, there were several men and women on the ground by one of the front wheels. It was her coat that I noticed first. Her best coat, she called it, although she'd had it for years. She wouldn't buy another one, she'd said that she would rather spend her money on Sarah or me. Then I saw one of her shoes and there was no doubt in my mind that it was Elizabeth.

"Hey you, get back. You don't want to come any closer. Go on, get back."

"That's my wife. She's my wife. I must see my wife, please."

One of the ladies got up and came over, "I'm so very, very sorry. I'm a nurse and I saw it happen. She just stepped out into the road. The bus driver never stood a chance. Her death was instant, she wouldn't have known or felt anything. The emergency services are on their way. I'm just sorry we couldn't do anything for her."

"Thank you," I quavered, "I must be with her now."

"I'm so sorry, sir, but can I suggest that you wait until they get her out. She's very badly injured."

"Thank you for your concern but after fighting in the First World War, there's nothing left that'll shock me. Now please, let me pass. I must be with my wife. Thank you."

The other people slowly moved away as I approached her. The extent of her injuries never entered my mind, I could only see my beloved Elizabeth, and I dropped to the ground and crawled under the bus to get close to her beautiful face. There were several cries to come out as it wasn't safe, but at that moment I had more important things to do. Her head, face and neck were untouched by the injuries except for a small trickle of blood on one side of her mouth. Her eyes were open and the sparkle had gone, but she still had that wonderful smile on her face. Nothing would ever take that away. I cradled her head in my arms and oblivious to everything, I just lay there with her, talking to her softly about all the best things we'd shared in our lifetime together.

"Do you remember when Sarah was born after all those years of waiting, and then after giving up hope she just arrived? We used to call her our little miracle, which to us, she was. We used to be so proud pushing her around the village in her pram, and when she grew up it was so much fun watching the two of you play together. What about that summer we taught her to swim in the river? I'll never forget the look on your face when I suggested it. How was I to know you couldn't swim either, but by the end of a glorious summer, you were both better swimmers than me? Do you remember her first day at school and how lovely she looked? You were bursting with pride and joy. There are oh so many good memories. It's hard to recall them all. We used to say we'd have plenty to talk about when we were old. How am I going to go on now you've gone, my darling Elizabeth? I never wanted anything else in my life, only you. I don't know what to do now you've gone. I want to come with you, my love, so we can be together again."

"Sir? Please sir, you have to come out of there, so we can get her out. It won't be safe for you whilst we move her."

"I'm sorry. I cannot leave Elizabeth on her own. She'll be very frightened. I know her, she's my wife, you know."

"Yes, sir, we know that, but we have to get her out. There's an ambulance waiting to take her to hospital. You can go with her. It'll be much better for her in the ambulance. You don't want her lying in the dirty road any longer than is necessary, do you, sir?"

I heard what was being said but my whole body was so traumatized. I knew he was right but I couldn't respond to him. Instead, I did what I thought was best. Struggling to take my coat off, I gently lifted her head and placed it on my folded coat that I'd made into a pillow. Leaning over her, I whispered, "I love you, my darling, more than life itself but I must go for help now. Wait for me, if you can and I'll look for you in the night sky, in our usual place."

Kissing her gently on the lips, I closed her eyes and crawled out from under the bus. I had to be helped into the ambulance and there they gave me an injection to counter the severe shock they said I was in. As I lay there, all I could think of was Elizabeth. It seemed hours before they brought her to me and as we moved away, I reached over to hold her hand. I asked for her face to be uncovered and then I could see and feel that death was slowly taking her away from me. Now the only hope I had to cling to was that we would meet up some time in the future in another place, who knows when or where.

When we arrived at the hospital the time had come to separate us, but I felt that I really couldn't do it. I'd done it before and never seen my loved ones again. I wasn't going to let them do it with Elizabeth. I put my arms around her chest and refused to move. Whatever happened, I couldn't let her go. Several people tried to talk to me but I never heard what they said. I was dancing with Elizabeth at our wedding. I was anywhere but here like this.

"Dad, Dad, it's me, Sarah. Oh my God, Mum, it's Mum. No, please God, not Mum."

I felt the ambulance move as she climbed in. Tears were streaming down her face. She knelt beside me and cradled her Mum's face with her hands, kissing her forehead, her cheeks and finally her lips. Then she stroked her hair, tidying it up for her, putting loose strands back in place. After a short while, she turned to me and we clung to each other and cried.

"Come on, Dad. You've done all you can for her. They're worried about you, after all that's happened. The policeman told me in the car on the way here. We can see her later. It's you who needs looking after now. Come on

Dad. I don't want anything to happen to you, too. I'll have no one then, will I?"

Looking into her tear-filled eyes, I could see her mother looking back at me and I knew she was right. I took hold of Elizabeth's hand again.

"Goodbye, my love. It's only for a short while."

Then I kissed her and slowly made my way out of the ambulance. There were many hands there to help me into a wheelchair and guide me on to the beginning of my lonesome journey into the future.

They kept me in hospital for five days, most of which I was asleep but they did take me to sit with Elizabeth in the chapel of rest a couple of times. Sarah came to see her Mum and I every day. She also arranged the funeral and for my Elizabeth to be taken back to the village. She was so organised, I don't know what would have happened without her.

On the morning I was to leave hospital, the doctor and sister came to see me.

"You've had a terrible shock and it's taken us five days to stabilise you. You're not really fully fit yet and we would have liked to keep you in for another week to be sure, but we know you have to get home. Anyway, there are some tablets here which will help you through the next few days and there's a letter here to give to your doctor."

At that moment, Sarah turned up to take me home. The sister looked at Sarah and gave her a large, sealed, plastic bag.

"It's all right Dad. Just a few of Mum's things."

The sister then handed me a small bag.

"These are all the valuables we found."

I looked through the plastic bag and then at the sister.

"She only ever had four things of value and they're all here."

I passed the bag to Sarah. "Your Mum wanted you to have them for luck."

"Just one last thing. Have you ever had your chest x-rayed? Only, when you first came in they noticed all the old scars on your chest and sent you up for some x-rays and these are what came back."

The doctor held them up to the light and you could clearly see a number of objects dotted about. I glanced at them briefly and then smiled to myself.

"Have you ever heard of the Battle of the Somme, doctor?"

"Of course, First World War, wasn't it? Why?"

"Well, that's my very own souvenir of a German shell, which ironically saved my life."

"You mean, you've been walking around with metal shell fragments since 1916? You should be dead by now, it's amazing."

"Yes, doctor. I know."

"Just like my father," smiled Sarah. "If you knew just a small part of his life, it is truly amazing. Anyway, come on, Dad. Let's get you home. Mum's waiting to start the next part of her journey, too."

The homeward journey seemed to go by very quickly. Sarah had a friend, David, who took us home in his car. Going past the village church and up the hill to the cottage seemed to trigger emotions deep within me and I started to cry like a baby. Sarah helped me up the path and into the kitchen, and after a little while I could hear her busying herself around the sink. A few minutes later, she put a cup of tea in front of me. I looked up at her red, swollen eyes but I just couldn't get the words to come out. She was so beautiful, like her mother, but to see her crying was too much, so I looked away.

"I know, Dad. I know," she whispered.

Then she came and sat beside me. Reaching over, she put her arms around me and hugged me just like her mother used to do when I was going through one of the many bad periods in my life. But somehow, all of those periods put together could never have prepared me for this moment. I'd never noticed, but Sarah had got up and was talking to her friend and, after a few minutes they both went out of the room and left me alone. I could hear Sarah moving about upstairs for a while and in the other downstairs room next door. It reminded me of the time I'd had a bed in the other room when I first came out of hospital after the War. I used to listen to Mum pottering about the place and I'd try to guess what she was doing. Sometimes, I'd shout to her and she'd come running and I'd ask her what she was doing.

"Oh, you're a nuisance! I can't get my work done and keep running up and down after you." Then she would scold me, "Don't call again because I won't come if you do!"

But of course, she always did. Very often, I'd be dozing lightly and would feel her hand running through my hair, as gently as you stroke a baby. I did so wish she was with me now, she would know what to do and help me get through it all.

Getting up stifly, I went into the garden to one precious spot. Even though it was cloudy, I knew they were there and that Elizabeth had journied to meet up with them. This has been the only thing throughout my entire life that I've always been certain of. We will all meet up again and journey on to our next destination. I knew then what I was expected to do. The bond shared with loved ones has to be carried on forever and when our time comes, we will all be together.

Walking back to the cottage, Sarah opened the door for me.

"I thought you might be up there. I was just bringing you a blanket. David's back, he says it's quite chilly out there."

"I'm fine. I just needed to clear my head a little. Your mother wouldn't be too happy if she'd seen me over the last few days. Now, what's happening tomorrow?"

Sarah looked a little surprised as I walked past her and sat down at the kitchen table. I noticed that David had been to get a couple of bottles of spirits, and although I wasn't really a drinker, we all sat together talking about the funeral service and remembering lots of other memories involving Elizabeth.

I was up early, dressed and waiting by the gate for Elizabeth to come home. It was a fine morning and after a while I could see people gathering by the church. The cottage door opened and turning round, I saw Sarah and David step out and walk towards me at the gate.

"Are you alright, Dad? You've had nothing to eat or drink yet."

"I know. I'm fine. I couldn't face anything. Maybe later."

David was hovering tactfully a little way back from us, "How long have you known David for?"

"Dad, what a question to ask at such a time! Actually, we've known each other for fifteen months, two weeks and four days. You like him then?"

"I think your Mum would have said there's something about him. I think he'd be good for you. Anyway, here's your Mum now."

Coming steadily in the distance, you could just make out the funeral cars winding their way along the lanes and tracks, and finally coming to a halt by the gate. The flowers were perfect; a cross from Sarah and a beautiful heart from me. Having helped Sarah and David into the car, I shut the door and stood behind Elizabeth for a minute. Clearly, the drivers didn't know what to do but eventually we set off at a walking pace to the church. Walking down the hill towards the village brought a wealth of memories flooding back into my mind at this tragic time. It wasn't long before we arrived at the church and as they lifted her out of the car, I couldn't help but notice her final resting place was prepared next to her mother's. I knew then that when my time came, there would be space for me between the only two women in my life that I had loved unconditionally.

The service and graveside burial were filled with untold grief for me. Even now, the whole service is still very painful to try to recall. Many of our friends came back to the cottage afterwards where Sarah and some of her Mum's friends had made refreshments for everyone. So they all drank tea and ate sandwiches and offered their sympathy. Afterall, what more could they do? They couldn't turn back the clock, so that I could have Elizabeth here with me, or even let it have been me who was taken first. I just felt that I'd seen so much death, I would have thought I could have coped with it better.

Sarah stayed on with me for two weeks, but finally had to go back to work in London. Oh, how I missed her. Not only the company, but the fact that she was so like her mother. When I was in the log shed she would call me in for something or other and I could have sworn it was Elizabeth calling. I pinched myself many times when she was at home, but even after she'd left she did try to come up as often as she could, and most of the time David was with her.

Nearly a year had gone by when the three of us were sitting in the garden. It was a lovely warm and sunny day and Sarah had cooked a lovely roast dinner, and we were all just letting it settle.

"Dad, we've got something to ask you. I know it's not all that long since Mum died, but..."

"It's about time too. I thought you'd never get round to it. Your Mum would be so excited if she was here."

"But Dad, you don't know what we're going to say."

"Only one thing though, your Mum always dreamt you would marry in our church and she would be so proud if you would wear her wedding dress."

Sarah looked at David and burst out laughing.

"How did you know that's what we wanted to ask?"

"I learnt that trick many years ago from someone who guided me through life for many years."

"And Dad, I wouldn't get married anywhere else and I was hoping that you would let me borrow Mum's dress, if it fits."

We all laughed together and David brought out a bottle of wine to toast the coming wedding.

"Before you go, you can take your Mum's dress with you, just in case it needs altering."

The season's came and went even faster than before, and once again I drew up outside the old church. It was yet again decorated with flowers, as it had been all those years ago, only this time it was my beautiful daughter who was getting married. Stepping from the car, I looked towards the clear blue sky and there was hardly a wisp of a breeze to be felt. The sun was high in the sky and it was lovely and warm. Helping Sarah out of the car, we paused a while as photographs were taken, and then we made our way through the gate and up the path to the church door. As we waited for everyone to get seated, I turned and looked at Sarah.

"Your mother would have been so proud of you today. You look so beautiful. You remind me of her on our wedding day. David's a lucky man, you know."

"I'm lucky too, Dad, to have David as my husband and you as the best Dad ever. My only wish would have been for Mum to be here, but don't you worry about that. She's never far away from us, She'll be looking on from somewhere."

At that moment, the church doors opened and the organ started to play. As we walked up the aisle side by side, I had tears in my eyes. Finally, at the altar, I handed her proudly to David. It was another of the proudest days of my life. The service was unforgettable but we were soon back standing at the doors, waiting for the photographer to start. I saw Sarah whisper in David's ear and then she came towards me. Taking my hand, she led me to the side of the church and to her mother's grave. We both stood in silence for a moment and then she knelt down and placed her bouquet carefully by the headstone. I offered her my hand as she got up and again still holding hands we stood there, deep in our own thoughts. It was only someone calling for the bride that broke our magical spell. As she went back, I knelt down again to wipe the stone a little with my freshly laundered handkerchief.

"She's just like you were, my love. We can both be proud of her. I just wish you could have been here to see her on her special day."

I could hear my name being called, so I stood up and went to the front of the church where the photos had started to be taken. We then all moved over to the inn for a sumptuous wedding breakfast followed by a very lively party which went on until the early hours of the morning.

The bride and groom had long gone on their honeymoon, but plenty of people stayed behind.

"Someone told me you used to be a good darts player, Bill."

Looking up, the local doctor was standing over me.

"Well, it's been a long time. Well before the war."

Someone shouted across the room, "Which one, then?" and somebody else replied, "It might have been the Boer War," which raised a ripple of laughter around the pub.

"Why do you ask, Doctor?"

"Well, some of the men are keen on starting a team. I'm going to have a bash, and then your name was mentioned. What do you think?"

I thought for a few minutes.

"Why not? What night should we have for practice, then?"

That was it. I was hooked. We ended up playing three or four nights a week. We played any pub within a ten mile radius, and as if by fate, it partly took over my life, helping to partially fill the void left by Elizabeth.

The next two years went by before I had even noticed them. Sarah and David came down as often as they could. I started growing vegetables again just to keep my hand in and I was also doing a bit of gardening at the church, which meant I could look after Elizabeth's grave and make sure there were always fresh flowers. What with that and darts at night, I was too busy to notice the time slipping away. It was one Sunday lunchtime in the autumn when Sarah and David had come down and we'd gone for a ride in the car. Sarah suggested that we stopped for lunch. She said, "Dad, why don't you ever come to visit us in London for a change? You could stay as long as you like and it would be really good to show you the sights. You could meet all our friends and see David's Mum and Dad again. Besides, you've never really had a holiday and it would do you good to get away. What do you think?"

"I don't need to think. It was my idea to go to London that led to your mother getting killed. I know you live there but I never want to go near the place ever again."

"But Dad, you..."

"No buts, Sarah. I'll never go back."

"What I was going to say is that there may come a time when you might have to go."

"What? What kind of time are you thinking of then, girl?"

"Well, for instance, I'm expecting a baby and I want you there for the birth."

I was speechless. All I could manage was, "When is it due?"

"Some time at the beginning of May."

"What wonderful news for you both."

David's arm must have been sore the amount of times I shook it, and Sarah and I had not hugged so much since her mother had died. I was so pleased for them both. I could feel tears of joy welling up in my eyes. David must have noticed as he discreetly disappeared to get more drinks to celebrate.

"What can I say? I'm so proud of you. Oh, if only your Mum were here, she would know better than me what to say and do."

"Don't worry, Dad. You're doing just great. Mum would be really proud of you if she were here to see you. By the way, I put fresh flowers on her grave before we came to the cottage and told her about the baby. I'm sure she heard me."

That afternoon, we drank a toast to mother and expected baby, and Sarah made me promise that I would go to London for the birth. After that, life went on pretty much as normal. Sarah gave me a calendar with babies on it with a big X on the expected date. She said it was so I wouldn't forget the date, but I knew it was just an excuse to buy something with babies on.

Emotionally drained

Chapter 13

The first cup of tea in the morning always tastes the best. Don't ask me why but it's a fact. It was 7.30 and I was just about to sit down and drink my first brew. Looking up at Sarah's calendar, I noticed that there were just over three weeks to go, but I wasn't looking forward to going to London in the slightest. However, I had promised Sarah, so I couldn't let her down. Just then the phone rang, and getting up I wondered who could be ringing so early.

"Hello. Bill Stokes here."

"Bill, it's David. Sarah's been rushed into hospital. There's a problem with her and the baby. They won't really tell me much, only that it would be best if her parents were here. I've rung my Mum and Dad and they are on their way. Can you get here as soon as you can?"

He gave me the journey and hospital details and then rang off. My heart kept missing a beat and my breathing was going rather strange, too. I sat down for a minute, trying to think what to do. Picking up the phone, I got through to the doctor and briefly told him what was going on.

"First thing is not to get into a state or you'll be no good for anything or anybody. Put some things in a bag for say, three or four days. Don't forget your pills, money and phone numbers; you might need to call. Then make your way to the surgery. In the meantime, I'll sort out how to get you there."

It didn't take long to gather the few things together that I was going to need and soon I was striding as fast as I could down the hill. As I drew level with the inn, the owner, Reg came out to meet me.

"Come on, Bill. Get into my car. If we hurry, you'll catch the next train which is a straight through to London."

As he drove with skill but at breakneck speed, I told him all that David had told me, and when we pulled up at the station, I got out and thanked him. All he said was to give her all their love and let him know how she's getting on.

"I will, I will," I shouted, as I went through the station door.

As I journied into London, my mind was in such a turmoil with a varied mix of thoughts and feelings that I never noticed all the stations go rushing by. Then, just as we were beginning to slow down, the conductor came onto the tannoy, saying that the next stop would be London. I was lucky to get clear of the station and find an empty taxi at the entrance to take me on the final leg of my journey. After about twenty minutes, I arrived at the hospital and after asking several people for directions, I finally got to the ward where Sarah was.

There was no sign of David, but his Mum and Dad were sitting at a table by the window. We exchanged solemn greetings and all sat down. David's Mum spoke first.

"It's not good news, Bill. They rushed Sarah in last night as she was losing a lot of blood. This morning, the baby's heartbeat became erratic, so they tried to deliver it normally but something's not quite right. They've only just taken David away to talk to him. That's all we know up to now."

We all sat there waiting, not really saying much until David came back with the doctor walking alongside him. She told us to follow her and we all went into a small anteroom with a table and a few chairs. I greeted David with a hug. He looked totally shocked and on the brink of crying, his face ashen. As we all sat down, the doctor introduced herself.

"I don't know how much you all know, but I'll try and explain it all to you as best I can. Who are the mother's father and mother?"

"I'm her father, her Mum died a few years ago. There's only me and Sarah."

"OK. She came in last night very unstable and losing a lot of blood. We got her settled and started giving her fluids and a blood transfusion. We monitored her through the night but then the baby's heartbeat became very irregular and baby was becoming very distressed. So we tried to encourage a natural delivery but there were a few further complications, so we had to do an emergency Caesarean to get the baby out. Now, they are both alive but in a critical condition."

She looked towards me. "Sarah has lost an awful amount of blood and with other problems, she needs a lot of prayers and some good luck over the next forty eight hours to help her through, but the odds aren't in her favour, I'm afraid."

She then looked at all of us.

"I am pleased to tell you though that you have a little granddaughter. She is about four weeks early and she is also very underweight. She has a problem with her heartbeat and she stopped breathing for a short while as they were trying to deliver her. There are also a number of other problems but they aren't so life-threatening. Now, if she gets through the next few days, and I stress if, then she may well live but there is still a long way to go. I have spoken to David about a name for the baby and just in case, you might want to have her christened. You can stay here as long as you like. You won't be disturbed. I don't recommend visiting Sarah yet though, but my staff and I will keep you informed. There's a small chapel down the corridor and you can get food and drink two floors down from here. Is there anything else you would like to know?"

There was a loud silence. All I wanted to do was to scream at her, "Yes! Why my Sarah? Haven't I paid enough in my life? Take me and let them live."

However, these were questions that would never be answered.

"Well, perhaps not yet," she said. "You have enough to think about as it is, I expect."

As she left the room, David's Mum started to cry quietly at first, then louder until her husband put his arms around her and soothed her.

As we all talked about what we knew, a kind-hearted nurse brought us a tray with tea and coffee, but no news. As time rolled by, I think we talked about everything, over and over. I was looking out of the window, watching the sun go down, when David's Mum brought up the one thing that some of us had tried to avoid.

"David, there is one thing we haven't talked about. I mean, the doctor did say it needed to be discussed."

"There won't be any need for that. My daughter and your son will name her when they are cuddling her together as a family."

The room went deathly quiet, so I took the opportunity to leave and find the men's room.

I found myself freshening up and looking into a huge mirror, the biggest I had ever seen. You're looking old now, I thought, it won't be much longer before I go to join the others. I suppose I've had a good run. Lasted longer than all of the others. Who'd have thought it and what a life it's been but I know I won't see my daughter and granddaughter go off before me. I'll go first and break things in, ready for them, as my brother and our friends did when they wouldn't let me go with them on the battlefield. My place hadn't been ready. I understood that now. They knew it was not my time. I still had a life to live and Sarah and her baby do, too.

As I moved towards the men's room door ready to leave, David came in.

"Thanks for that, Bill. I didn't want to say anything or upset Mum any more than she already is. We have a name but..."

"Just leave it until all three of you are together. Now, I'm going for some fresh air. These country folk don't like being boxed in for too long."

I found myself a seat by a little garden, close by the hospital, which I plonked myself down on with relief. Fresh air, you can't better it. Born and bred in it and apart from my wounds, I've never been sick in my life. I'm glad I don't live in the city. There are too many people all rushing around for my liking. It's dirty and smelly and not a healthy place at all. I sat there a long time giving myself a good going-over and finally decided that it wasn't my fault how my life had unfolded. It had done so because that's the way my life had been plotted before I was born. My life may nearly be over but I know Sarah and her baby still have a long way to go yet.

Finding my way back to the ward, I discovered that David and his Mum and Dad were sleeping. So as not to disturb them, I quietly closed the door and wandered along the corridor. On my wanderings, I only saw one nurse having a nap in her office. I was trying to find the chapel but got lost. It took a few seconds to sink in but I was looking through a window in a door, staring at Sarah, or what I thought was her. She was covered in wires and tubes and the likes of things that I had never seen before. I opened the door as quietly as I could, and then shut it gently behind me. I moved closer towards the bed and then I knew it was my Sarah. Moving a chair to the side of her bed, I sat down and gently stroked her hand. Her beautiful hair was matted and all over the place, so I carefully tidied it.

"Must look your best when you meet your daughter."

I thought back to when I had tidied Elizabeth's hair as she lay under the bus.

"Not this time. You will live and both me and Mum will live in you and your daughter."

I stayed with her for the rest of the night, just talking and willing her to live. As dawn broke and the sun's rays filled the room, I laid my head close by her arm. Closing my eyes for a moment, I felt as though I was drifting away from her bedside. If this was the price to pay, I would gladly pay it, my life for theirs but within the darkness of my mind something or someone was telling me again that it was not yet time.

As I started to wake, I felt something touching my hair. As I opened my eyes, Sarah was smiling at me and stroking my wiry hair. Smiling back, I got up and kissed her forehead. She had a long way to go but I knew she would recover. The news raised everyone's spirits and after another two days, they also took the baby off the critical list.

The next eight weeks for me were like being on a merry-go-round. Up to London for a few days, then back home and then back up again, and so on. I was pleased though that amid all the chaos, I did manage to keep Elizabeth's grave tidy and tell her all the news.

Finally, mother and baby came home and Sarah telephoned me every day to tell me how they were getting on. I started to go and see them every few weeks but my health was not what it had been and the journey started to become very tiring and get me down. It usually took me three or four days to get over it once I'd returned from my London visits.

David and Sarah decided to have their baby christened in their local church so that more of their friends could attend. It was a damp weekend but the service was marvellous. Both Mum and daughter looked stunning and we finally found out her full name. They called her Molly Elizabeth. I added a 'little' to it as she had been so tiny when she was born. So Little Molly it was.

Sarah passed her driving test and David bought her a little car so that she could get about better, which also meant that she could come and see me more often. It was a sight to see, the first time she came with Molly. As she pushed the pushchair down into the village, she looked so proud as all her old friends and village ladies crowded round her and she showed off Molly to our little world. I think with the arrival of Molly, life in general seemed to improve and some of the ghosts from the past had, for the moment, been laid to rest. David had a very demanding job but when he had time off he loved to come to the village. There was plenty of room for them all to stay at the cottage and we would often go for picnics over the meadows, or Sarah would cook a meal whilst we pushed Molly to the inn and had a couple of drinks. We would then push her back up the hill, much to the amusement of the regulars who used to catcall and whistle us on our way.

David had started playing football with some old school pals and his friends had won their way through to the final of the local league, so we were all standing on the touch line supporting. Even his Mum and Dad were there, cheering and shouting and Molly was jumping up and down on my shoulders. David came over at half-time to tell us why there was no score, then off he went again to rejoin the team. About twenty five minutes into the second half, David suddenly collapsed. There was no one near him but the referee hastily ran over and knelt beside him. The other players soon gathered round and a stretcher was brought on. We all stood there, totally stunned, not knowing what was going on or what to do. As they carried him off, I noticed that they had covered him completely with a blanket. I gave Molly to Sarah and told them both to stay where they were with David's parents.

"I'll go over and find out what's going on. Now, don't worry, it can't be much. He's probably just fainted."

As myself and David's father made our way to the stationary ambulance that was always parked by the side of the pitch, another ambulance with flashing lights pulled up alongside. It looked like a doctor dashed from one ambulance to the other and then quickly shut the door. We got as close as we could and just waited patiently, not knowing quite what was going on inside behind those closed doors. After about ten minutes, the doors opened again and the doctor climbed out. He spoke to the team's captain first who then started to ask if any of David's family were here. Beginning to fear the worst, the two of us made ourselves known. The crowd parted to let us through and the captain took us over to where the doctor and ambulance crew were standing. We told them who we were and also about his mother, wife and little girl who were also waiting further down the pitch. It was the doctor who spoke first.

"There's never an easy way at times like these and it's particularly worse as he was a fit young man, but I am so sorry to have to tell you that David has died. I am not sure why but according to the first people to reach him, it looks as if he died instantly. A post mortem will have to be held, of course, to discover the exact cause of his death but we're going to transfer him into our ambulance so we can take him to hospital where you'll be able to spend some time with him. Now, I think we should go and see the others and break the news to them. Where did you say they were standing?"

We grasped each other around the shoulders for support as we slowly made our way across the field, flanked by the doctor and the team captain. Being in a daze and totally shocked, I was fighting to find the words, any words that were fitting to tell his beloved family what had happened. As we moved closer to them, I knew I was losing the fight. I think they knew long before we got close, or at least I know Sarah knew. David's Dad gently took his wife in his arms and they both started to sob. Picking up Molly, I wrapped my arms around both my daughter and my granddaughter. Sarah was trying not to cry for Molly's sake, so I broke away with Molly and Sarah went to join David's Mum and Dad. Moving away a little, we sat on a bench and Molly scrabbled to sit on my lap.

"Grandad, why is everyone crying and where's Dad? Is the game over? Is he getting dressed?"

"Well, my little one, do you remember when we sit in the garden at Grandad's cottage until it goes really, really dark? Then what do we do?"

"I know. We lie on our backs and count all of the stars and I always win because you always forget your glasses."

"That's right, sweetheart. Anyway, do you remember what the stars are?"

"Everyone knows that. They are God's angels."

"And do you remember how you can become an angel?"

"You have to be good and love your Mum and Dad and never hurt anyone."

"Well, when God needs a new angel, he looks all over the world until he finds the best there is. Then he takes them up to heaven and makes them an angel."

"Grandad, is that where Dad's gone? Up to meet God?"

"Yes darling. I'm afraid so."

"But I won't be able to see him or touch him again then, will I?

"No darling, you won't, but he'll always be looking down on you and you'll find his star shining just for you."

A few tears trickled down her pale little cheeks, "And for Mum, Grandad. Don't forget Mum."

"No darling, we must never forget your Mum."

David's funeral was delayed a little as they tried to find the cause of his death. Eventually, they discovered a defect in the main blood supply to his brain. They thought that he may well have lived with it all of his life and then, for no reason, it just burst. He wouldn't have felt anything as he was dead before he fell down to the ground.

His funeral was naturally a very solemn occasion. He had lots of friends but it was the speed and shock of the whole thing that hadn't properly sunk in with everybody. Sarah was doing her utmost to cope but was slowly falling to pieces. Molly was a little star when her Mum wasn't coping well. She was there to see her through all the bad times. Still, they are here staying with me now and both of them are blooming again like God's little flowers.

David's Mum and Dad come down quite a lot. I think they've taken a fancy to our village. Molly stays with them during school holidays, so it works out all right, and I'm anything for the easy life now; a little drink and a game of darts. That suits me down to the ground. Molly wearing me out is my contentment these days and being with the two people I love the most of all, of course.

Stars

Chapter 14

I had better rouse myself now as they'll be back any-time. Trying to lift myself from the chair, I slid back as I felt the pains shoot across my chest.

"Damn those German gunners. Here it goes again. Must remember to go and see the doctor again in the week. I'll just lie here a little longer till it goes away. It's such a lovely day, another five..."

"Bill, Bill, over here. Bill, we're over here."

I lifted myself up but couldn't see anyone around about me.

"Bill, Bill. Come on, we're all waiting for you. Come on."

Damn it, I could swear that was Peter's voice.

"Who's that? Where are you? I can't see you."

I felt a gentle touch on my shoulder.

"We're here for you, Bill."

I couldn't believe it, as I turned Phil was there, large as life itself.

"Come on, big brother. You've waited a long time for this moment. We're all here. Follow me but don't look back. We're all going on a journey together."

As I got up out of my chair, all the aches and pains had gone, and I followed him out of the garden, down the path and through the gate. Hesitating, I turned to look at the village, which had been my home all of my life.

"Bill, don't forget, no looking back. Hurry now, the others are waiting."

So my final journey began. No one knows the destination as none have ever returned to tell us.

As we walked down through the meadow, Peter joined us, then a little further on Harry and John tagged on to the rear. As we approached a couple standing facing away from us, I could sense they were Mum and Dad. They came to my side as we passed by. We carried on a little further to the river and there she was, sitting on the riverbank, waiting. As we got closer, she stood up and came towards me. She was as beautiful as ever with that same loving smile, just as I had remembered her, all these long, lonely years. Now we were complete at last and ready to begin our endless journey, destination unknown.

"Coming, ready or not," shouted Sarah, and she turned around and opened her eyes. She scanned the edge of the forest and the clearing, and then she spotted what she was looking for.

"I can see you," she shouted, "you're hiding next to the fallen tree. I saw your head sticking out. Come on," she said. "Play fair."

Slowly, Molly appeared with a frown on her face.

"You always spot me. Why can't I ever find you though, Mum?"

"Arrghh, that's because when I was your age, I played the same game with Grandad and over the years I found all the best hiding places, with Grandad's help, of course. Come on then, we'd better get home. We've stayed much longer than we should have done really, and besides, Grandad will be wondering where his ice-cream has got to."

"Oh Mum. Can't we play just one more game? Pleeeease?"

"No darling," she said firmly, "but I'll race you back to the car. Last one there makes the tea. Ready? 3, 2, 1, go," she shouted, and they both ran along the path, shouting and laughing all the way back to the car.

As they approached the car, Sarah dropped back a little and let Molly get their first.

"I won, I won," she shrieked.

"Only just," her Mum said. "I must be getting old."

"No you're not," said Molly. "You'll never ever grow old. You'll stay with me and Grandad forever and ever." ·

As they both got into the car and drove back to the village, Sarah said, "Darling, that was a lovely thing to say. I really wish that it were true. You see, as you already know, all animals are born, they live their lives in their environment with their families or sometimes without them, and then when their time comes they die and go to heaven. And the same thing happens with people. Except we live longer than most animals."

Molly sat there very quietly for a few minutes and then said, "Mum? You know when the animals go to heaven, do they become stars in the sky, too?"

"What do you mean, darling?"

"Well, Grandad says that when we pass away and go up to God in heaven, we then become stars that come out at night."

"Well," said Sarah, "if Grandad says that's what happens, he must be right as he's a lot older and wiser than us.

Right," she said, "here's the shop. You stay here and I'll nip in and get the ice-cream."

A few minutes later, they drove up the hill, past the monument and turned into the driveway.

"Molly, can you please shut the gate whilst I take the ice-cream over to Grandad?"

"OK, Mum. Then I'll come over. Maybe Grandad might let me have some, too."

As Sarah walked over the grass to where her father was sitting, she spoke in a slightly raised voice.

"Sorry we're late, Dad but Molly and I went walking in the wood and then played a few games of hide and seek. You know, like we used to play when I was her age."

As she got closer to him, for a split second she thought there was something wrong but quickly dismissed the thought from her mind.

"Anyway," she said, "we didn't forget your ice-cream and it's not even started melting yet."

She reached out and touched his shoulder, gently giving it a loving squeeze to wake him. It was then that she knew all was not right. She moved around to face him and then she realised. All kinds of thoughts and memories started to fill her head and she could feel herself going dizzy and faint, with tears welling up in her eyes. She dropped to her knees and gently took hold of her father's hands, which still felt slightly warm and meant that he couldn't have died long ago. Or was it the warmth of the sun?

At that moment, Molly started to cross the lawn towards them.

"Mum, did you tell Grandad why we were late?"

It was this sound that jolted Sarah back to reality. She stood up quickly.

"Molly, darling," she said, "could you please go back to the cottage and see if you can find the big picnic blanket? Grandad's a little chilly now the sun has gone in."

"Alright Mum, but don't forget to tell Grandad to save me some of his ice-cream."

As Molly disappeared into the house, Sarah knelt down again and carefully laid her head on her Dad's lap. She started weeping and then an uncontrollable flood of tears ran down her face and on to her Dad's hands. She stayed like this for a few minutes, mindful that Molly would soon find the rug and be coming back, "And you wouldn't want that, would you Dad?" she said. "I think you had a good idea what was going to happen and you wanted to be in your favourite place on your own when it happened, didn't you?"

"Mum, Mum, is this the blanket? It's the only one I can find."

Sarah looked up to see Molly standing in the doorway, holding up a checked woolen blanket.

"Stay there, Molly. I'll come and have a look."

As she got up, she leaned forward and kissed her Dad on the lips, which by now were turning blue with cold. With loving hands, she closed his eyes and straightened his hair, just as he had hers after she had had Molly.

As she was carrying out these rituals, she whispered, "Please God, take him into your care. He was a good man and father. Let him find peace with his beloved Elizabeth, so that they can be reunited and together forever."

"Mum, Mum are you coming?"

"Yes, yes," she said, raising herself up tall. She strode across the lawn with only one thought on her mind. How would she tell Molly? How do you tell a young girl that one of only two of the most precious and irreplaceable people in her life will no longer be there for her? She hadn't even had the chance to get over the death of her father properly and now she would have to face this new and even more devastating blow in her ever so young life.

As she approached Molly, who had already started to cross the lawn, she managed to reach out and grasp her tiny hand and say, "Come back inside, darling. I have something to tell you."

"But Mum, what about Grandad's blanket? He'll be catching a cold if we're not careful."

"Don't worry, darling. We'll take it over in a few minutes."

As mother and daughter went into the cottage, the sun was dipping down behind the distant hills and all was still and calm. An uncanny silence hung over the cottage and garden, but after a few minutes, that silence was broken by the unmistakable crying, sobbing and weeping of both young girl and older woman, and it carried on and on into the early evening. Eventually, very slowly the tears of pain and loss began to subside and it was during this time that Sarah made several telephone calls which she knew would put into motion the unavoidable process that sudden death brings.

When she went back to look for Molly, she found her standing in the garden, holding the blanket that she'd been to fetch.

"Mum," she said, "do you think Grandad would mind if we covered him up? He looks so lonely out there and it is cold."

Sarah looked over to her Dad and she could just make him out in a fast-fading light.

"No, darling. I think he would love you to cover him up. Come on, we'll both go over together."

As they walked over the lawn, there seemed to be a calm and soothing atmosphere around Grandad and the tears that had been clearly trickling down both their faces seemed to dry up.

Standing back from the scene, there appeared to be an aura of light and if there had been anyone looking on, they would clearly have seen the young girl arrange the blanket over the old man and tuck it well in, as she had done so many times in the past. The words that were spoken were only to be heard by the mourners, but just as the girl leaned forward and gave her Grandad a last kiss and hug, the blue light and bell of the ambulance could be heard in the distance.

Suddenly, Molly shivered from head to toe.

"I am sorry, darling. Let's go in if you're cold."

"It's not that, Mum. I was looking up at the stars and just as I was thinking about Grandad, I saw a tiny flicker in the sky, just there, next to that big star."

She pointed, and where they were both looking, it suddenly became brighter until there was a really bright star.

"Do you think Grandad has got a star already?"

After gazing at the star for a few seconds, Sarah said, "Do you know, darling, I think you're right and now he's watching over us. We know where he is, so we must be strong and look after each other over the next few days especially, and then for the rest of our lives."

With that said, they both turned around and went inside and in their own ways prepared themselves for what was to come.

As they were relaxing after three days of visitors, the doorbell rang once again.

"Not more visitors?" Molly said, with a big sigh. "I thought we'd seen everyone by now?"

"I'll get it," said Sarah, and disappeared through to the door.

"Hello, Doctor. Come in. We thought you were more villagers come to pay their respects."

"No such luck," he said. "I've got some news for you, though."

He followed Sarah through to the back room and sat at the table.

He then reached into his case and took out an envelope.

"This is for you to keep with your other copies. You may need it in the future. It's the autopsy report. Now, there is a lot of medical mumbo-jumbo but the gist of it is that they found quite a number of metal shards in his chest. They've confirmed that they were shrapnel, which must have been left in his body when he was operated on after being wounded during the First World War. What happened was that one of these pieces of shrapnel shifted across his chest over a period of time and came into contact with his heart. So the end would have come very quickly and if he were asleep he wouldn't have felt anything. They also said that even if we had known about it sooner, it was in such a position that it couldn't have been operated on. It would have been too dangerous."

After a few minutes, Sarah said, "So the pains he could feel in his chest over the last few years were caused by the shrapnel, which by this time had moved close to his heart?"

She hesitated once more, in which time a gentle, wry smile crept across her face.

"After all this time, it was the First World War that ended his life. He would have appreciated that, and I also know that he would certainly have appreciated the military honours that he'll now be entitled to."

The Doctor looked her straight in the eyes.

"Yes," he said. "And at least we can thank God that he went with relatively no pain and peacefully in his sleep. Look, I'm dreadfully sorry but I'm afraid I've got some more calls to make, so I'll have to be off now, but I'll speak to the undertaker and he can finalise his arrangements now. Be strong and I'll see you on the day of the funeral, but if there is anything else you need beforehand, give me a ring."

The funeral cars arrived at the cottage just after three. There was only one car as there weren't many people going from home. There was a beautiful cross of flowers on top of the coffin, with the rest of the flowers placed all around and on top of the car. Molly had been out into the meadow that morning and had picked a large bunch of wild flowers, which she'd spent some time making into a bouquet shaped like a heart. It had been good to see her occupying herself as it had taken her mind off the day ahead.

As they walked down the path to the cars, Molly was squeezing Sarah's hands so tightly that it brought tears to her eyes, or that's what she was telling herself. They reached the car and the kind-faced undertaker opened the door for them.

"Can I take your flowers for you, young lady?" he said to Molly. For a brief moment, Sarah thought she was going to give them to him but then she smiled at him, saying politely, "No, thank you, I would rather carry them myself."

The number of times Sarah had been up and down the hill from the cottage to the village and back were countless, both as a child and then as a grown woman and mother. At that moment, as they slowly made their way down the hill, images came rushing back through her thoughts; when she used to ride on her Dad's shoulders when she was tiny, then on his back when she was getting bigger; the times they used to slide down in the snow. Oh so many memories. They passed the memorial on the way down, but she never even noticed it this time. The time she brought David home to meet Dad. On her wedding day, it was such a glorious day, they'd all walked most of the way to the church, which made them late but Dad said if David really loved her he wouldn't mind waiting. They went slowly past the inn and shop, and she noticed a number of people with their heads bowed, standing on the footpath, who then followed behind as they headed for the church.

The last few years had been difficult for them all. Sarah remembered Mum's funeral in the same church. Up and down the same road. The tears of joy on her Dad's face when Molly was born and how proud he was carrying her into the church for the christening. Then, as they'd followed David's coffin to the church all the happiness had again turned to grief and sorrow, but as Molly grew, she'd brought the laughter and smiles back to both of their faces. They used to go up and down that hill together; so many times it had happened without anyone really noticing. It was a great part of their lives and deaths, just as it was today.

Locked in her thoughts, Sarah hadn't noticed the cars had stopped until the door opened and a softly spoken voice said, "We're here now. Would you like to step this way, please?"

Her father's coffin was in front of them as they got out of the car. It was being carried by six of his friends from the village inn, who he'd played darts with so many times in the past few years. she glanced around briefly and noticed that if not all, then nearly all, of the people from the village were there. Some looked on and then bowed their heads, not knowing what else to do. Others that didn't know what to do just looked away. As they slowly walked towards the church, the vicar took hold of her hand for guidance, just as his predecessor had done with her father a few days before he'd set off to war with his pals.

She was surprised that the church was already half full of people, most of whom, at first glance, she couldn't even recognise. As they were ushered into the front pew, she watched her Dad's coffin being lowered onto a stand. The flowers were lifted up and an elderly man with medals on his chest draped the Union Jack flag over the coffin and then put the flowers back on top. She must have given the man a strange look as he came over and explained, "Our sincere and deepest sympathy for the loss of your father. He was a very brave man. It's a tradition for the country's flag to be draped over an ex-serviceman's coffin, just as your father was. We who are left hope this is acceptable to you?"

She thought for a while and then said falteringly, "Thank you to you and your friends. It's very kind of you."

She'd never thought of her father as a soldier really, or of the time he'd spent in the army. It was something he'd never really talked about much, and as for being brave, yes, she could picture that if it was called for.

She could still hear people coming into the church when Molly said, "Was that man in the same war as Grandad? Did he get all his medals for fighting? Did Grandad get any medals? I've never seen them."

Sarah turned and spoke quietly to her.

"Yes, he did get his medals in the same war but your Grandad's were buried with your Grandmother because she was so proud of them."

The service was more of a celebration of her Dad's life than of his death. There were Bible readings that he would have acknowledged and hymns to raise a smile to his face. Several of his old friends got up and spoke about him. It was all very moving but to Molly and Sarah, no matter what was said, it wouldn't bring him back. No sooner had the service started than it was over and once again they were following Bill outside the church over to the plot next to Elizabeth. Through her tear-filled eyes, she could make out a freshly dug hole and next to it a dirt pile that was discreetly camouflaged with green coverings. When all of the congregation had gathered around, a short prayer was said and then they started to lower the coffin into the ground. When Molly took Sarah's hand, she looked down and Molly was holding her flowers up and looking her in the eye. Sarah knew what she wanted. She said softly to the bearers, "Could you please hold on as my daughter has one last thing to do?"

Molly stepped forward and knelt down beside the coffin and placed her flowers lovingly next to the name-plate and said, "Good night, Grandad. I'll always love you and I know where you are if I need you."

She then got up and came back to Sarah's side as they then finished lowering the coffin into the ground. They both turned and hugged each other and cried unashamedly in front of all of the village.

As each of the people passed the grave, they all stopped and tossed in a handful of earth. When they reached Sarah and Molly, they received a hug, a kiss, or a handshake and some kind words. It seemed to go on forever. Sarah was so surprised at the number of people her Dad had known. She knew she felt it and she was sure that Molly, young though she was, also felt it. They had an immense sense of pride that the man they were all talking about had been her Dad and Molly's Grandad.

Finally, all the people had gone. Sarah could see the Doctor and the vicar waiting discreetly by the church gate. She knelt down and scooped up a handful of soil. Molly came and knelt beside her and sharing her soil, they sprinkled it onto the top of the coffin. All the words had been said and many tears had been shed too, so they just knelt there for a few minutes, alone with their private thoughts.

As they approached the gate, Sarah said to the vicar, "Thank you for such a good send off. I'm sure Dad would have said the same had he been here."

"It was a privilege for me but it's not quite all over yet."

She looked at him with a blank expression.

"Didn't you wonder where all our friends have gone?"

"Well," she said, "I thought they'd gone home a bit quick."

"No," he said, "they're all waiting in the inn to give your Dad the send off he definitely wouldn't have missed. So come on, let's go and join them."

As they approached the inn, they could hear the usual noises you would expect to hear. That was until the Doctor opened the door. The change from noisy conversation to complete silence was utterly remarkable. As they were gently ushered to an empty table close by the fire, which was also the table her father and his friends had sat at frequently, the people they passed on the way all offered kind words and their condolences. Some of the people there Sarah had known all of her life and they were coming to them and hugging both Sarah and Molly with genuine affection and tears in their eyes.

They finally got seated around the table, and drinks and sandwiches appeared from the back of the inn. Sarah turned to the Doctor and asked who had organised all of this for her Dad.

"Oh, don't worry about it. We all knew you had a tremendous burden to start coping with, so the whole village got together and with the landlord's help, they organised this little send-off. After all, your Dad was born, lived and died here, so it's the least they felt they could do for him."

At that moment, Sarah suddenly felt so emotional and overwhelmed. The tears just kept running down her cheeks and now she understood why her Dad wouldn't move out of the village to them when they'd lived in London. She was so glad he'd brought Molly and herself back when David had died. It was at times like these when you need as much support as you can get. Living in such a tight-knit community is a tremendous advantage, and also enhances everyone's life when they are down and facing hardships.

After a while, all the sadness was starting to lift and one or two old friends of Dad's told them a few of the stunts they'd got up to in the past, which raised the sound of polite laughter. The landlord, who'd only known her Dad for about twenty odd years, rang the bell behind the bar and called everyone to order.

"Now," he said, "as you know, I hate speeches and never make any, so when it was decided that a speech was to be made, I agreed wholeheartedly but when I was voted to be the speaker, I started packing my bags. Anyway, I'll try my best. Short but sweet, as they say. We all knew Bill, some a lot longer than others. He was a hard-working, devoted family man and a good friend to many of you when the times were not so good. If he could afford it, he would stand anyone a pint. If they hit hard times, he never thought twice about helping them out. All the children knew and loved him, and he always had time for them. When his wife Elizabeth died, we all thought he wouldn't be able to carry on, but he turned out to be much stronger than we all thought. Then, when tragedy struck again by taking his son-in-law, David, we all wondered how much more he could take but in another way this turned out for the better for him as his daughter Sarah and granddaughter Molly came back to live with him. It was as if overnight, the changes in him were amazing. It was as if he had a new lease of life, and as we all know, he stayed like that until the end. Well, that turned out longer than expected, too! So, I would like you all to raise your glasses and we'll drink a toast, not only to Bill, but also his daughter Sarah and granddaughter Molly, who we hope will stay in our village and carry on the way of life that Bill would want them to."

There was a shuffling of chairs and feet as everyone stood up and raised their glasses.

"Goodbye and God bless you, Bill. Cheers," said the landlord.

Everyone in the pub said the same.

"Bill, cheers," they all shouted.

Then he turned to Sarah and Molly.

"Cheers," he shouted, and so did all the other people in the bar.

Sarah turned to Molly and wiped away the tears running down her face, and Molly reached over and did the same for her Mum. Sarah then stood up and faced everyone.

"I don't know what to say. I can understand more and more each day why Dad didn't want to leave the village when he had everything he needed right here. The warmth of feelings, friendship and helpfulness that you've all shown us over the last week has also been tremendous. What more can I say? Both Molly and I thank you all from the bottom of our hearts. Thank you."

Everyone in the room began to sit down again and the queue at the bar gradually grew longer.

"Mum, how much longer shall we stay? I'm feeling quite tired."

"I know darling. It's been a long day. We should just stay a little while longer and then make our excuses. Do you want to walk home or should I ask someone to give us a lift?"

Molly thought for a while and then said, "No, I think we'll walk. It looks like a clear night and we can go past the monument. If we feel tired, we can always have a rest sitting on Grandad's bench."

After about three-quarters of an hour, Sarah spoke to the Doctor, saying that Molly was very tired and it looked like the send-off would go on for much longer, so they would leave quietly now.

"Yes, that's fine. Do you want a lift?"

"No thanks. Molly wants to walk and it's not a bad night."

After a few minutes, they both got up and headed for the door. The landlord and a number of villagers noticed they were going but no big fuss was made. They all seemed to understand that discretion was needed, so there was only the odd wave, smile and nod of a head from those who understood, but they weren't noticed by the majority.

The cool night air soon surrounded them and they both shivered as they made their way up the hill towards home. Nothing was said by either of them as they were fully immersed in their own memories and thoughts. It was a beautifully dark and clear night with the moon full and unusually bright. As they approached the monument, Molly said, "Mum, can we sit down for a while and look at the sky? We might see Grandad's star if we look hard enough."

"Of course we can darling, but not for too long, it's getting colder and we don't want either of us to catch a chill."

Just as they sat on the bench, a wisp of a cloud started to pass the moon and took away part of the light that was shed on the monument, so they both gazed into the sky searching for that special star.

"Do you know, Molly, when I was your age, Grandad and I used to come here and stand staring at the sky trying to spot our special stars. We often saw shooting stars as well. Even when my Mum died, we still came here, not so often but as much as possible. Grandad would say he had special stars for all his lost loved ones.

"Look, Mum," said Molly, pointing her fingers high into the sky. "Those two are very close together. I'm sure that's Grandad's and Nanny's stars. That's where Grandad told me Nanny was, and to look there for him, too.

"Where are you looking, Molly?"

"Just there," she pointed excitedly, "next to that big one."

"Oh yes, I see it. You know, you could be right."

They both stood for a few minutes, fixing the position in their minds forever.

"You know, Molly, when Grandad couldn't find his brother's star or his friends' stars, he said he would always look at the monument and be reminded of those who went off to War with him."

They turned to look at the names.

"You can't see them, Mum. That cloud is in the way of the moonlight."

"Don't worry, we'll come back another night when the moonlight is better."

At that moment, a light breeze picked up which just managed to disturb their hair but what it also managed to do was to gently nudge the cloud shielding the moon. And as they looked up slowly, the names of all his friends became legible. One by one they appeared and then the last one, his, had become visible. Where there had been a space, Bill's name and dates had been freshly chiseled into the stone to match the others; the date he was wounded and the date he had died. They knew he would have been so proud to finally be reunited with his beloved friends. Gently hugging each other, they stood staring at the monument but neither of them noticed the two stars that were twinkling at them, high up in the heavens.

293

THE END

ISBN 141202939-2

9 781412 029391